MY BESTIE'S EX

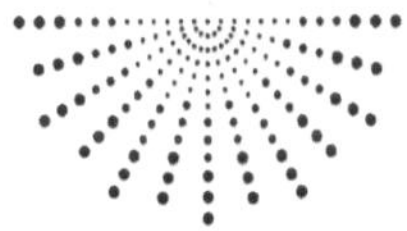

PIPER RAYNE

Cover Photo: Wander Aguiar Photography

Cover Design: By Hang Le

Line Editor: My Brother's Editor

Proofreader: Shawna Gavas, Behind The Writer

My Bestie's Ex

I can't borrow him.
He's not a sweater or a skirt.
He's not even her favorite dress—the lucky one she wears on
first dates. The one she probably wore on her first date
with *him*.

In my defense, I didn't know who he was. To me, he was a
cool, calm, confident stranger. He was perfection for the
entire hour and a half train ride while the concrete jungle
turned into a rolling green landscape.

To an outsider, we probably appeared more friends than
hopeful lovers. But my blush came quickly, and his dimples
indented with every smile. We definitely shared a spark of
what could be.

Too bad I didn't know who he was before I fell for him,
because he can't be mine.

MY BESTIE'S EX

PROLOGUE

Blanca

You know the saying... when one door closes another door opens?

I'm assuming that applies even if you choose to close the door yourself, right? Don't answer that. I'm gonna go with it because I prefer to live in fantasyland. Especially lately.

After quitting my finance job—the one I spent four years in college earning a degree in—I kyboshed my future in banking.

I wasn't all that stellar at it anyway. I wasn't horrible, but I wasn't the shiny new graduate who followed my boss's loafers like he was my master either. News flash, numbers are boring. Sure, my brother Dom gets a hard-on for them and so did most of my co-workers which should've been my first sign that I was the round peg forcing myself into a square hole.

That's all why I thought that the day I reconnected with

Sierra could be a sign even though I don't usually believe in them.

I hadn't seen Sierra Sanders for years. Sure, we were friends on Instagram and Snapchat. A heart here and a comment there. 'You haven't changed at all!' Promises of future get-togethers that never happened.

But after my two weeks' notice was up I headed out the doors of the building in the financial district of Manhattan with my big box of personal items. I'm Italian and I like to be homey at the office, don't judge. And BAM. There's Sierra Sanders, my childhood best friend from the neighborhood just sitting there under a tree with the sun shining down on her like she was waiting for me.

Okay, disclaimer. She wasn't waiting for me. She was actually talking with someone and she wasn't exactly sitting under the tree, she was standing by it with a camera aimed at her. I should mention, she's a reporter for a small station outside the city.

I hovered and waited for her to finish talking to the arborist about the trees while the same picketers from last month corral behind him, fighting to fit their faces in the small camera frame to show their opposition to removing the original trees that had succumbed to some beetle invasion or another.

I thought maybe we could catch up over a cup of coffee or dinner. Or if she was heading to her dads, I could tag along with her on the train. Mama's never upset over a surprise visit.

"Sierra!" I waved from the top of the stairs once she finished.

She looked around, finding me standing there and squinted. Yeah, that's how long it'd been for us. We were the usual story of separate colleges tearing us apart after we swore they never would.

"Blanca?" She handed the mic to the camera guy and headed into my direction.

We met at the bottom of the concrete steps and she went in for a hug, but my box made it awkward, so she stopped trying after five attempts at different angles. Her eyes dipped to the contents of the box and her shoulders slumped.

"I'm sorry." She ran a hand along my arm.

"Don't be. I quit."

Her eyes lit up and her back straightened. "Where are you off to next?"

I waved her off. "I don't know yet, but that place was sucking the life out of me."

"Then we need to celebrate. Come on."

Before I could process what was happening, she told the camera guy to hop on the next train, and they'd go over the tape tomorrow. We walked over to a corner restaurant who was preparing for their dinner rush of traders and wannabe high rollers on Wall Street.

By the end of the conversation that was mostly about me, Sierra had opened the proverbial door for me.

"Move to Cliffton Heights. It's so beautiful and you're only an hour and a half train ride out of the city. You'll be close to those heartthrob brothers and your parents. It's perfect really because we just had a roommate leave." The more she talked, the more excited we both became about the idea of us rekindling our friendship. "Oh my God, it'd be like what we always planned before you decided to switch colleges at the last minute."

Oh shit, that's why we kind of fell out of touch. I had forgotten. We had been all set to room together right before we graduated, and I switched course. That pissed her off because she had to room with a stranger. Can't say I blame her.

"My other roommate, Rian, is awesome. Bakes all the

time. She writes math textbooks for a living so it's not like we party all the time. But we have fun too and oh, come on. I've missed you so much!"

She begged and pleaded. I'd always considered myself a New York City girl. But at that point in my life, watching my brothers' fairy tales grow sweeter while I had no one and nothing, a fresh start sounded perfect. A change of scenery. A place to reinvent myself. And I missed her too.

"I'd love to," I said without even having a job to pay the rent. I knew some people commuted to the city, but I wasn't sure I wanted to ride the train for three hours a day. But that was a problem for another day. The first of many.

Let me tell you, hindsight really is twenty-twenty and it comes back to bite you in the ass, because now, months later, I wish I would've pried her for more information. I should've asked more questions because it wasn't just Sierra and a new beginning on the other side of that proverbial door—he was standing there too. And he was already a part of Sierra's life. Sure, her past life, but hers all the same.

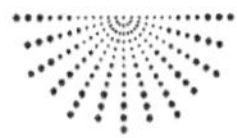

CHAPTER ONE

Blanca

I trudge up the steps of the train, smile at the conductor and walk through the doors to the seating area. With an 'oomph' I fall into the last seat of the last car on the last train from New York City. Destination: my new home, Cliffton Heights.

With me is a container of meatballs from my family's Sunday night dinner and I place my jacket over the container to try and stop the smell from leaking throughout the train car—an impossible feat.

My phone dings so I pull it out of my bag. Of course it's from my oldest brother in the thread we share with our other two brothers.

Dom: *You on the train?*

Me: *Yeah.*

Carm: *Don't talk to strangers.*

Me: *Okay. *eye roll emoji**

Enzo: *Text us as soon as you get into your apartment.*

Me: *Sure thing. *military salute emoji**

You'd think they'd trust me more than they do, what with me being twenty-eight and all. To them, I'll always be the baby sister.

Enzo: *I have no idea why you wouldn't let us just pay for an Uber.*

Enzo is the second born and probably the most paranoid about safety. I'm out of the big city now, but moving an hour and a half train ride away is apparently more nerve-wracking than when I was smack dab in the middle of New York City. I even gave them the stats on crime in Cliffton Heights compared to New York. But to them, Cliffton Heights is a foreign land and until they come and see how beautiful it is, and most importantly how safe, I should expect nothing less from them.

Me: *Because I'm an adult and I enjoy the train.*

Carm: *Don't pick anyone up.*

Me: *Oh, and here I was unbuttoning my blouse to entice the slumped over gentleman three rows in front of me.*

Carm is the youngest of my brothers but still older than me. He's probably laughing right now, but that doesn't mean he doesn't share the same form of overprotectiveness as the other two.

My only saving grace lately is they all have women in their lives now who they need to worry about more than me.

Me: *I'm going to rest. Dinner was great. Catch you guys next week. Love you.*

Dom: *Don't shut your eyes on a train full of strangers!*

I shake my head, looking at the only other man riding in the car with me. He's either passed out or dead. Not much of a threat.

Me: *I won't. Someone might steal Mama's meatballs.*

Enzo: *Those are hot commodities.*

Carm: *I'm snacking on them right now.*

Dom: *We just ate.*

Carm: *Like an hour ago.*

Me: *I'm putting my phone in my purse, so no one tries to steal it.*

Enzo: *Good idea but keep it within reach just in case.*

Me: *Bye guys.*

Carm: *See you.*

Dom: *Love you, sis.*

Enzo: *Remember to text us when you're in your apartment.*

Me: *Aye, aye captain.*

I click the button on my screen and toss my phone into my purse.

The conductor comes on the speaker to announce the name of the train line and route we're on before the train jolts to a start. I close my eyes and lean my head against the vinyl seat. Even with the ladies in my brothers' lives helping me in the kitchen on Sundays, I'm still tired. My hands are dry from the dish soap like they always are. Doesn't seem to matter how thick I lather the lotion on afterward. My stomach is bloated from all the salt in Mama's food.

My family is the typical Italian family. Big dinners, big personalities—big everything. Mama is over the moon about my brothers finding the love of their lives. Dom and his wife, Valentina, are expecting the first grandchild. Annie and Enzo are planning their wedding. And I'd bet Carm has a ring for Bella already hidden, ready for an impromptu proposal.

All three of my brothers are successful. We're talking advertising executive, high-end real estate broker, and a Wall Street trader. They have more money in their bank accounts than I'll probably ever see in my lifetime.

"HOLD UP!" I hear someone yell and my eyes pop open. There's a man running alongside the train like in one of those romance movies where the guy has to get on the train to declare his love for the woman of his dreams.

He has a backpack secured on and carrying a plastic bag similar to mine filled with Tupperware. Inching toward the glass, I watch him grab the metal handle of the train, running along like he's trying to rev up more energy to make the final jump. Oh shit, he's going to hit the steel beam. His feet move faster and just before, he jumps on the step and the train breezes by the steel beam.

I mentally hope he decides to come on this car instead of

the one in front of me. I'd like to see the type of guy who can pull off that stunt like he's filming a movie.

Sliding to the edge of my bench seat, I tip my head to see him and the conductor talking through the residue covered glass window. He hands him a plastic container and the two do some type of handshake before he mindlessly presses the button for the doors of my car to open.

He steps into the car that only holds me, a passed out guy and the smell of my mama's Italian sauce. All the air rushes out of my lungs. He's drop-dead sexy. I have no idea how to describe him. He's gorgeous. Light brown hair that sticks straight up on top and trimmed on the sides. Enough scruff to make my thighs shake with want. Ripped jeans, a dark button-down and a pair of sneakers. So casual and so mouth-watering at the same time.

Just when I'm about to slide over and beg him to sit with me, his lips tip, his mouth opens in the most beautiful smile I've ever seen on a man. Perfect straight white teeth. Damn, I'm not sure I've ever been this attracted to someone before. It's not even just him. It's how he's looking at me. Like he's been searching all over the world for me and he just found me.

"You're new?" He opens up the plastic bag and places a Tupperware container next to the man passed out.

"Do you know everyone who rides the train?" I ask and he keeps walking toward me and I find myself holding my breath the nearer he comes because with every step, my heart beats a touch faster.

"I know everyone who rides the last train on Sunday night. Yes." He slides his backpack off, sitting in the seat right in front of me. He leans his back against the train window and extends his feet along the bench of the seat. "That's Gil." He nods toward the sleeping man. "He'll be getting off at Peekskill."

I lean forward. "Is he okay?"

He laughs like I'm not crazy for asking. "Yeah. Watch. He'll get up at Peekskill without anyone waking him up." He bends forward and I hear the plastic of the bag rustling. "You hungry?" He holds up a third Tupperware container.

"No, thanks."

He nods. "Good idea not to take food from a guy on a train that you don't know. Someone taught you well." His smile deepens and a dimple forms in his right cheek. Seriously, who sent this man my way, the train fairy?

"I have my own anyway." I lift my jacket and he peeks over the seat.

"What is it?"

I open my container of meatballs. "Italian."

He sighs and his hand moves across the seat, grabbing a meatball with his finger and thumb, the sauce is about to drip right before his head falls back and he drops it into his mouth like a cherry. Please tell me he gets off early because my libido is revving in overdrive and it's going to stall out soon.

"Aren't you afraid of taking food from a stranger on a train?"

"Nah. You look sweet. Something tells me you didn't bring food on the train to poison a random stranger."

He's funny. And so at ease and free-spirited.

"It's my mama's and if she knew I was sharing with you, she'd want me to tell you that there's something off in her meatballs tonight. Unfortunately, she'll figure it out at midnight and feel the need to text me."

He retrieves a bottle of water. "Nothing wrong that I can tell."

"Too much garlic. It's overpowering the meat. My brother miscalculated."

He stares at me for a moment and I cross my legs,

becoming uncomfortable under his scrutiny. "If you knew, why didn't you say anything?"

I shrug. "I like garlic?"

His eyes narrow, but in a teasing you-intrigue-me way. "Sibling rivalry. I get it." He sips his water as I admire his Adam's apple bobbing up and down and secures the cap on the bottle.

His eyes fall back on me and I straighten my back like I wasn't just ogling him. "I don't have sibling rivalry."

"Okay." He lifts a Tupperware container up over the seat. "Try one of these."

I raise my hand. "I'm okay, but thank you."

"Come on. I promise they aren't poisoned. I tried the staple of your culture. Try mine?"

"Shrimp?"

"Garlic prawns." He moves it closer and though my stomach says no more food, my eyes say damn that looks good. When my nose joins in on the debate, I raise my hand to grab one.

If my brothers saw me, they'd knock it out of my hand saying I'm crazy and what am I thinking. I laugh imagining the whole scenario.

"What's so funny?" He picks up a shrimp himself and eats it, closing up the container afterward.

"Nothing."

"That's the way you're going to play it, huh?" He looks around. "We're all by ourselves and I'm the last stop. Humor me until you get off."

He's getting off at Cliffton Heights too? That shouldn't make my stomach feel like it's filled with helium and it might float away, but it does.

I bite into the shrimp. It isn't rubbery and it's still warm. The butter drips down my chin as I take another bite. I've had garlic shrimp before but never this good.

"Told you it was good." His cockiness draws me into him further. Maybe it's growing up with three overly confident brothers, but the more sure a man is of himself, the more I seem to want him.

"It's excellent." I finish the shrimp off and he holds up a napkin for me to dispose of the tail in. "You're so prepared."

He nods. "Don't worry, in ten minutes you won't feel a thing. You'll just pass out."

I stare blankly at him and then he laughs.

"I'm kidding. Seriously. Kidding." He extends his hand. "Ethan."

I place my hand in his, ignoring the way the heat from his large hand travels up my arm. "Blanca."

"Beautiful name for a beautiful girl."

Heat rises to my cheeks. "Thanks."

He wiggles in his seat, spreading his legs out a bit more and getting comfortable. "So tell me what was so funny."

"I was just thinking about my brothers."

"Clearly you have more than one?"

"Three," I answer.

"Older or younger?"

"All older."

His eyes widen and he nods. "Must be some sibling rivalry going on."

"There isn't any sibling rivalry."

His smile only grows. "Italian family. Three older brothers. They all successful?"

I shake my head.

"No?"

I frown. "Okay, yeah."

He smirks. "Married?"

I roll my eyes in a playful way. "One is."

"The other two?"

"Seriously? Engaged and committed."

He raises those perfect eyebrows like I should just admit he's right.

"I'm telling you. I'm the baby sister. The *only* daughter in an Italian family. I'm not starved for attention."

"And yet you know your brother put too much garlic in the meatballs and haven't told your mom yet because a small part of you wants her to figure it out and blame your brother."

"NO!" I screech and then lower my voice. "No," I whisper-shout. "I would have said something if I knew when they were being made, I could just tell when I tasted them."

He nods a few times like, 'okay continue to lie to yourself.'

"You're not right."

"I am." He winks and those balloons in my stomach take flight. Damn traitor.

The conductor announces Peekskill and Gil stands up, swooping up the Tupperware container. He looks around and when he spots Ethan, he nods in appreciation.

"Have a great night, Gil," Ethan says.

Gil doesn't respond and I watch him stumble down the stairs and out onto the platform. When I look back to Ethan, he's smirking.

"I'm almost always right," he says, but his facial expression tells me he doesn't necessarily believe it.

"You know nothing about me or my relationship with my brothers."

He taps his index finger on his chin like he's thinking. "I bet they're protective?"

"That's not rocket science. Three Italian brothers being overprotective of their baby sister is somewhat expected."

"But I bet it bothers you."

I shrug. "It would bother anyone."

He shakes his head. "There are some people who like

protectiveness from other people. Makes them feel cared for. Loved."

I look around the train car. It's only the two of us. "Am I on the psychoanalyze me train?"

He laughs. "This is the most fun I've had on a Sunday night in months."

"That's not something to be proud of," I deadpan.

I'm not going to admit that it's the same for me because he's a stranger and I know nothing about him. He could be buttering me up to kidnap me later.

He says nothing and since I hate awkward silence, I finally succumb.

"Fine. You're right, it bothers me."

"Because you want to prove to them you're an equal?"

I shake my head. "Okay… next topic."

To my surprise, he does let it go, taking out a container of cookies. Chocolate chip at that. So classically American.

"What culture are you from?" I ask.

"Spanish. Not the cookies though." He holds the container out toward me. "Peace offering. I tend to interrogate people because I love digging and dissecting what makes them tick. My apologies."

I pick up a cookie hoping I'm not about to drop unconscious before we hit Cliffton Heights. "Thanks. Apology accepted." I bite the cookie and an explosion of sugary goodness fills my mouth.

"Which one is your stop?" he asks.

"Cliffton Heights."

He gifts me with a deep smile that draws his dimple out. My ego soars at being the one to pull it out of him.

I'm in so much trouble.

CHAPTER TWO

Ethan

Todd smiles at me with a silent question of 'who did you pick up tonight' in his eyes as I allow Blanca to walk in front of me down the aisle of the train. She's carrying a multitude of bags and I purposely didn't offer to take one because I'm not the savior a girl like her is looking for and I don't want her to think I am.

"Where do you live?" I ask after we say goodbye to Todd and climb down the stairs to the train platform.

"I'm not telling you that." She walks over to a bench. It's dark outside. If we weren't in Cliffton Heights, I'd follow her just to make sure she was safe.

"You ate my food and look, you're still alive."

"It could be twenty-four hours before I feel something. Sorry." She bats her long eyelashes.

She's so cute in her skinny jeans, her Vans and a T-shirt that says, 'I hate being sexy, but I'm a teller so I can't help it'. She looks down noticing me reading her shirt and her cheeks redden. "It's from my aunt. She's kind of obsessed with giving people T-shirts about their jobs."

"You're a fortune teller?" My forehead wrinkles.

Blanca smiles and I try to think of some other obscure profession to guess again, just to see her face light up like that.

"I *was* a bank teller. A long time ago but…" She touches the shirt with her forefinger and thumb, rubbing the fabric in between fondly.

"It's one of those T-shirts? One of the ones you can't bear to part with but should've given up long ago." I finish her sentence and her foot slams on the ground.

"Should your shirt read, 'Psychologist: Warning I will be psychoanalyzing everything about you. #sorrynotsorry?'"

"Well, I'd hope it would say something more about being sexy, like yours does."

She giggles and her head dips down as she shuffles her feet. "I need to get home."

Just as she says it, her phone rings and she blows out a deep breath, retrieving it from her purse.

"Brothers?"

Her eyes widen. "I'm starting to get creeped out."

It's really just my journalistic tendencies of trying to decipher everything someone says or does. To figure them out with what little information they give you. I always felt like I was born with the instinct to read people. Over the years, I've been fooled more than once though.

Like my dad's boss when I was seven. I thought he was a real life Santa Claus. At the company picnic, he brought in ponies and carnival games, even sat in the dunk tank himself. He gave me some cotton candy, ruffled the hair on top of my head, and said he'd see me next year. That Monday he fired my dad and there was no company picnic the next year. There wasn't a lot of anything exciting that next year.

Blanca's almost transparent though. Even now with her head buried in her phone, her fingers typing as small huffs leak out of her, I can see that she's jutted out her hip and blown a loose curl from blocking her vision at least five times. Whoever is on the other side of that text exchange is annoying her.

I have a younger sister myself, so I get it. I'd have her text me too. I'd also be pissed if she took food from a stranger on the train.

She finally tucks her phone back into her purse. "Sorry."

"No need to apologize."

"I gotta go. Thanks for the food. Bill me for the therapy."

Oh, she's got jokes. Nothing is sexier than a woman who can make me laugh. My ex took everything so seriously.

"Maybe I'll see you next Sunday."

She shrugs. "Maybe. Bye." She turns around and I watch her until she disappears around the corner.

My mind tells me to go after her because although Cliffton Heights isn't huge, it is big enough that I might never run into her again.

My own phone rings and I pull it out, turning to go the opposite direction as Blanca went.

"Hey, Mom."

"You make it home okay?" she asks.

I smile at the fact that she still checks up on me.

"Yeah, I sent you a text." Which I did as soon as I got off the train, but I should know better. The woman hates texting.

"That could be anyone sending that message. I need to hear your voice to know that you're okay."

She sounds so tired. I wish she would've just gone to sleep when I left.

"Well, I'm fine. Go to bed. I'll call you tomorrow."

"Thank you for today, hun." There's a pause and I know

before she says anything who she's going to bring up. "Your dad looked good, right? Healthy?"

"Mom," I sigh.

"He's getting stronger."

"Yeah, he is. You're right." My mouth dries when the lie rolls off my tongue.

"I know." Her voice goes up an octave and I realize I'd lie to her all day to hear that.

"You working tomorrow?"

"Yeah." I arrive at my apartment and insert my key into the door of the building.

"Love you. Thanks for today."

"You don't have to thank me for visiting," I say, annoyed after an entire day of thank yous. She acts like I don't love my dad. I do, there's just a lot of baggage there.

"I thought maybe I'd come out and see you one of these Sundays."

When I moved out of New York City for my old job, my mom guilt tripped me for months straight, she still does. I think it hurt her so much because she thinks I wanted to be away from *them*, not just *him*.

"Sure, we could do that, but it's easier for me to come to you."

I open up my apartment door and step into the solitude and peace I've been searching for all day. Other than the train ride. I would've gone round trip with Blanca if it hadn't have meant I'd end up stuck in New York City.

Her smile comes to mind and it makes me grin to myself. I hope I run into her again.

"I gotta go, Mom. Love you."

"Love you so, so much," she says.

"Bye." I click the phone off before she has the chance to keep me on for another half an hour.

Shrugging off my backpack, I put it on the hook by the

door and place the food in the fridge. Continuing with my usual Sunday night ritual, I strip off my clothes on the way to the shower and spend the rest of the night figuring out this week's article.

The only deviation from my regular routine is the thoughts of Blanca I can't help but find myself distracted by. I can only hope that fate is smiling down on me and that I'll see her again.

CHAPTER THREE

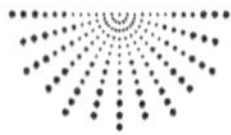

Blanca

*O*nce I've walked up the stairs to my new apartment, I open the door to find out that our place is tonight's hangout. All three guys from across the hall are over which seems to be a common occurrence.

"What's up, Blanca?" Dylan looks over his shoulder at me from where his head is in the fridge.

"Are you hungry?" I set the leftovers on the kitchen table.

"How was the city?" Sierra gets up from the couch and walks over, taking the container out of the bag. But as soon as she places them in the fridge, Dylan picks them up and uncovers them.

"Tiring. The train ride was long, but…" I want to tell Sierra about the guy I met, but there are four other people in the room. People who are virtual strangers to me.

"What?" Sierra takes the container out of Dylan's hands and he sighs.

"Do you want some?" I ask Dylan when I grab the container with cake inside.

His eyes pop open with excitement, only for his shoulders to fall when Sierra snags the last container off the table.

He looks at me like I'm holding a juicy steak in front of him. "Please. I won't eat it all."

Sierra peeks inside the container. "Cute. I love Mama Mancini."

I set the cake on the table and take off my jacket and hang it up on the hook by the door. "Actually, Annie ordered it."

Sierra's eyes are wide, and her mouth is hanging open when I turn back around. She knows that Mama has always baked the cakes for our family. A princess cake for my fifth birthday, a rainbow one for my eighth birthday, and a four-layer cake for my sweet sixteen.

But Annie said she wanted to try this new bakery that opened up, so it's fine. Really.

"I have to meet these women who plucked your brothers off Manhattan's most eligible bachelor lists."

Of course Sierra was one of my many friends who had crushes on my brothers. Something I've lived with my entire life but still manages to gross me out.

"I'm sure they'll all visit at some point."

Sierra has relinquished her hold on the food and placed the containers back on the table, so Dylan grabs a fork and stabs a meatball, shoving it into his mouth. A loud moan falls from his lips. "Mama Mancini is welcome anytime." He sinks down into a chair at the table. "Seth, you gotta have some," he calls over to Seth, who is sitting on the couch, then stabs another and pushes the container away.

Seth stands, peeling his eyes away from *Blue Bloods*. I reach into the cabinet and hand him a fork before he sits down beside Dylan.

"Just one more." Dylan stabs one right after Seth and the two of them moan like they're receiving the best blow jobs of their life.

"Shit, Mancini. You've been holding out. Yesterday you were making the instant mac and cheese. And not even the boxed kind, the individual one." Seth's blue eyes twinkle in delight as he opens up another container. "Lasagna." His fork goes in right away and Dylan's follows.

"Just because my mama can cook doesn't mean I can," I say.

Sierra and I exchange a smile. She knows how culinary challenged I am.

"I thought it was every Italian daughter's quest to learn how to cook in order to land a husband?" Seth stares at me like he's serious. "Isn't that the reason you're born? To breed?"

Sierra slaps him on the back of the head and I raise my hand for a high five.

"It was a joke, people."

Dylan shakes his head at him like he's an idiot.

"Knox. Rian. You hungry?" I ask.

"Shh… Donnie Wahlberg's on." Rian holds her hand up in the air at me, eyes not leaving the screen. She's wearing a pair of leggings and a plain T-shirt, her blonde hair pulled back in a simple ponytail. "Can you believe he's like fifty? Do you think you'll look that good at fifty?" she asks Knox.

If I had to guess, I'd say he will. The man takes care of himself. Not that Dylan and Seth don't. But I haven't seen Knox eat one unhealthy thing since I met him. Which I should mention was only last week. But Sierra told me he's a police officer so maybe he does it to keep fit for his job.

"Um… yeah." Knox responds as if it's obvious.

Seth chuckles over his mouth full of lasagna.

"If you haven't figured it out by now, Knox is the one with the ego here," Sierra says in a good natured way.

"So is this a Sunday ritual?" I sit down at the table and put my feet on the empty chair next to me, stretching out. "You all watch *Blue Bloods* like middle-aged empty nesters?"

Dylan mocks offense, but I'm telling you, if anyone asked the guy who owns the Ink Envy Tattoo Shop across the street, whose arms are covered in tattoos, what he does for fun, the last thing they'd think he'd say is watch *Blue Bloods*.

"It's a good show. Don't knock it," he says.

Rian shushes everyone and Seth shakes his head. "You do know he's bald now."

"He's still sexy. Don't be jealous." She waves him off.

"Do you think she even pays attention to the plot?" Sierra asks, standing beside the table.

"No. She's waiting for him to get naked or some shit." Seth's fork wavers between the meatballs and lasagna.

Dylan forks the cake with gusto. "I don't get the appeal."

"His ego's probably so inflated from all these young women loving him," Seth whispers because Rian has quieted the room again.

"No one has an ego quite like Sigmund did." Sierra digs into a piece of the cake.

The mood at the table shifts and I catch Seth eye Dylan and Dylan eye Seth.

"Who's Sigmund?" I ask.

Seth glances at Sierra with wide eyes. "Her ex."

Sierra forks a bigger piece of cake but doesn't say anything.

"I'm sorry. Was it recent?" I put my hand on her arm and her face softens.

"We broke up six months or so ago. Dated for a little over a year."

I mentally catalog this information in the back of my brain so I can ask her more about it when we're not surrounded by other people.

"He's a cool guy," Dylan says, still deciding what he's

going to eat. He doesn't notice Seth and Sierra's eyes on him. When he glances up and shrugs. "Come on, he is. You two just weren't right together."

"And why is that?" Sierra asks, her fork clattering onto the table before she crosses her arms over her chest.

"This is Blanca's first Sunday with us. She brought this great food to share with us. Do we really have to do this?" Seth asks, widening his arms around the table like he's ready to hold hands and sing Kumbaya. I'm guessing he's not a fan of confrontation.

"You went from a date to datttinngg," Dylan stretches out the word. "I mean, who does that?" He looks at me and I hold my hands up, not about to get in the middle of this.

"People who like each other do. Normal people, Dylan." Sierra's gaze ventures over to Rian and back to him. I think I'm the only one who notices.

Seth looks like he wants to crawl under the table and tell Mom and Dad to stop fighting while Dylan lays his fork down calmly and crosses his arms, causing the muscles in his arms to bulge out from under his tattoos.

"Dylan introduced them," Seth whispers over the table to me.

I nod.

"You always took his side on everything. This is why..." Sierra's face matches her vibrant red hair now.

"Why what?"

"Why we didn't work out. Maybe if one of you would've told him that the way he was acting was wrong—"

"SHHH!!!" Rian says and instead of breaking the tension, it does the opposite. Both Sierra and Dylan lean over the table in each other's direction.

"I'm not gonna get into this," Dylan says.

"Thank you." Seth picks up his fork, his posture relaxing a bit.

"You're just blaming me because I'm the woman. You're such a womanizer and commitment-phobe you don't know what a real relationship is supposed to look like."

Seth places his fork down. "I guess they're not finished."

"Me?" Dylan points to himself, eyebrows raised.

His outer appearance says he would be. I mean, he screams bad boy from any angle you look at him. The black jeans, the white T-shirt, the tattoos. Even the natural edge he gives off.

"We all know Sigmund's name has been banned from the apartment, so why are we even discussing this?" Seth says, but they both ignore him.

Dylan leans back, grabs a twenty from his pocket and hands it to Seth. Seth takes it and stares at it like it's foreign currency. Standing, Dylan tucks in his chair and leans over the table again. "Sigmund, Sigmund, Sigmund, Sigmund…"

Sierra narrows her eyes into small slits. She stands and tucks her chair in, mimicking Dylan's moves, leaning so she's right in front of his face. "Whore, Whore, Whore, Whore…"

Dylan's jaw grows rigid and it's obvious he's holding back. When his gaze moves to me, I widen my eyes. "Thanks for the food, Blanca."

"Um… you're… welcome," I stutter out.

He turns to leave and seconds later, the apartment door slams behind him.

"He drives me crazy!" Sierra stomps into the family room.

"Excuse me," Rian says, swaying her hand in the air to tell Sierra to move along. She's completely oblivious to what just happened because she starts a conversation with Knox about what's going on in the show.

I wonder how many seasons I'll need to catch up on in order to join in with them.

Sierra huffs and stomps down the hall to her bedroom.

"So that's a touchy subject." Seth picks his fork up and slides the cake closer to him.

"I can see that Dylan was friends with him, but why's it such a big deal?" I ask. Sierra hasn't mentioned anything about a bad break-up since we've rekindled our friendship.

Seth stares over at me. "Dylan took Sigmund's side when they broke up. I think that's why she was so quick to find a roommate because Dylan moved in here just so Sigmund could move in with Knox and me. Their promise to be friends didn't pan out, so he moved out a month ago."

I hate that I'm getting all this information from Seth, when it should be coming from Sierra.

I drop my feet from the chair beside then stand and push in my chair. "I'm going to go check on her."

"It's a touchy subject. It sucked for everyone when they split. We were all friends." Seth looks like tears could fall from his eyes as he continues to pile the cake into his mouth. Amazing how much I've found out about him from this one interaction—he hates confrontation and eats when he's upset.

I head down the hallway and knock softly on Sierra's door. After she says a quiet 'come in,' I enter, shutting the door behind me.

"Hey," I say.

"Hey." She's sitting cross-legged on her bed with a pillow across her middle, bent over flipping through her phone.

"Want to talk?" I ask.

She clicks off the screen. "It's fine. I'm over him. I really am. It's just still a little raw."

I sit next to her and put my arm around her shoulders, drawing her in closer to me. "You can tell me anything. I know we've been separated for a few years, but I'm still a great secret keeper." I do the whole locking my lips and throwing away the key like I used to when we were younger.

"Honestly, there's not much to tell. We just argued all the time. But that doesn't mean I didn't love him. God, he was so aggravating though." She sits straighter and shifts to face me. "You know that he punched Ben in the nose?"

I can feel my jaw slacken. "He punched your brother?"

She nods. "He was so ultra-competitive. Like a game of football on Thanksgiving morning was that important." She rolls her eyes.

I refrain from mentioning that I've witnessed those Thanksgiving family football games and how heated they can become. My brothers have returned with someone needing an ice pack on more than one occasion. But punching someone in the nose seems a little over the top.

"I'm sorry," I say with a frown.

She nods. "If only one of your brothers were still available." A smile tips her lips.

"So gross," I mutter.

"Or Prince Adrian from Sandsal. I'd take him in a heartbeat."

"Who?" My forehead wrinkles.

She looks at me with her mouth hanging open. "Seriously, Blanc?" She swipes her phone off the mattress and opens up some royal gossip site on Sandsal to show me picture after picture of Prince Adrian Marx from Sandsal. I feign interest because it's clear talking about this is making her much happier than when she was talking about her ex. By the time I leave, she's much happier, as am I because I feel like I've fulfilled my duty as a friend. Talking shit about an ex and ogling the guy you're using to distract yourself from said ex, is practically in the handbook.

I shut her door to find only Rian, cleaning up all the takeout and leftovers I returned with. The boys are gone, and the television is off.

"You go to bed. I got this," Rian says. "You have a big day tomorrow at your new job."

"Are you sure?"

She laughs. "One thing you'll figure out about me is that I like everything just so. I'm more than happy to do this. Go."

"Thanks so much." What a sweetheart she is. I could use a really good night's sleep before I start at my new job tomorrow.

Twenty minutes after my bedtime routine of washing my face and brushing my teeth, I lay down in my bed, the nerves about tomorrow already flaring to life. As my eyes close, a face pops into my head—Ethan. Not a bad vision to fall asleep to at all.

Sweet dreams to me.

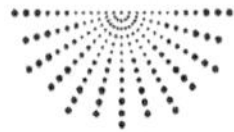

CHAPTER FOUR

Ethan

I stop in at Andrews Bagel Co. on my way to work and Mrs. Andrews' smile grows when she spots me.

"Good morning, Ethan." She reaches into the display case, grabbing my Asiago bagel and handing it to one of the employees, telling her sliced, cream cheese, not toasted. Then she pulls an empty coffee cup out. I bypass the line to meet her at the cash register. I'm here often and Mrs. Andrews gives me preferential treatment since I used to live across the hall from her son, Seth, back when Sierra and I were still a thing.

"Good morning, Mrs. Andrews." I pull out my wallet, handing her over a twenty. "How are you?"

"Monday is a good day. Busy day. All you kids don't want to cook for yourselves." She hands me my change and I glimpse behind me to the line. Sure enough, mostly everyone waiting are young professionals probably trying to work their way up the corporate ladder. Most are dressed similar to me in business casual attire, computer messenger bags swung over their shoulders. "So what are you up to these days? Still freelancing?"

I tuck my change in my pocket, picking up my bag and cup. "Yep, writing here and there."

Once I stopped in here after Mr. Andrews read my article about sex toys and Mrs. Andrews pulled me aside and asked where she could find some. She even pulled out the folded sheet from the magazine and everything. It was mortifying. Now I try not to let her know where I'm writing by keeping it vague. It helps avoid those awkward conversations.

"I have to ask." She leans forward and we both glance to the line forming behind me. "Do you know of any publications that have a woman to write about more womanly things?"

I smile. "As luck would have it, I heard a rumor that someone is starting at that Mars And Venus magazine this week."

"Really?" Her eyes light up.

My eyes lit up on Friday when I found out that they were going to bring a woman on to write articles as counterpoints to mine. The difference is, my eyes lit up with anger. The last thing I need is someone coming in and trying to overshadow what I'm doing. To offer suggestions on something I've already perfected. Someone to win over my readers and potentially pull them away. I worked hard to gain the following I have in the short time I've been at Mars And Venus.

"Yep, really. Maybe see if she's in the next edition."

Mars And Venus is a bi-monthly magazine that's a little like Maxim, Men's Health, and Cosmopolitan all rolled into one and is geared toward men. Another reason I don't understand the benefit of adding a woman's perspective to the writing team.

And no, that's not me being a misogynist, it's me being a realist. Would Working Woman have included men's articles in their spreads?

"Oh, I can't wait!" Her shoulders wiggle side to side like I just promised her a Ferrari or something.

"Well, have a good day." I hold up my bagel and still empty cup. "Thanks."

"You too, Ethan." She waves and starts to ring up the next customer.

I fill up my coffee, secure the lid, and head out of the shop, walking the five blocks to my office.

Something already feels different the minute I walk into the small reception area of Mars And Venus.

"Hey, Mandy," I say, breezing by the receptionist toward my cubicle.

"Hey, Ethan. Nine o'clock office meeting," she hollers down the hallway at me. I raise my coffee in the air.

When I arrive at my cubicle, a feminine scent wafts over from the normally empty cubicle next to me. I glance over the cubicle wall and there's no one seated in the chair, but there's a bunch of personal artifacts overfilling the small space.

I abandon my bagel and coffee on my desk, intrigued by who the new addition to the Mars And Venus crew might be. The minute I step into the small space, it feels like I'm in a foreign land. Decorative pink and purple paper cover the interior and a sign has been hung up that says 'Welcome to my cubicle' in a girly script. A collage picture frame sits on the desk and the standard pen holder has been replaced with a metal one covered in painted flowers. I pick up a candle sitting on the desktop and turn it over to figure out what the scent is I keep smelling.

"Jasmine," a woman says from behind me. "Anything else I can help you with?"

The voice sounds familiar. When I turn around, I try to keep my jaw from hitting the floor. "Blanca?"

She takes the candle from me and places it back down on her desk, completely unfazed to see me. "Hello, Ethan."

Blanca positions a few things just so while I pick up her picture frame. The top photo is of an older couple, her parents I assume. The three pictures below are each of a man and a woman. "These are your brothers?"

She takes it out of my hands and puts it back on the desk. "That's them."

"Big guys."

Intimidating would be a better descriptor.

"Yep." She pops the P at the end.

I lean on her desk. "So tell me why you're not surprised to see me."

"I was when I showed up this morning and checked out your cubicle."

I tilt my head. "I have no pictures in there."

"Why is that? Maybe it's time I analyze you."

I laugh. Maybe I should be more upset that she's the woman I'll be working next to since I'd already built it up in my head not to like this woman. "Seriously though? How did you know I worked here?"

She sits in her chair and crosses her legs. I can't help but study her movements. Her chair twirls and she taps a pen to her lips. "You seem so worried about how I found out."

I inhale through my nose, trying not to show my frustration.

"Oh my gosh, relax. Your picture is on the board. Though I was surprised because the byline on the pieces in the magazine are always attributed to a Grant Sheffield." She quirks a brow and motions with her hand to the large board on the wall behind us that has all the employee photos.

Right.

I blow out a breath. "Yeah, I use a pseudonym here."

"How come?" She tilts her head to the side.

Because I don't want anyone to know I work here. "I like to keep my privacy and I'm hoping this isn't the high point of my career. I'd rather save my real name for when I'm where I really want to be. What's the big deal?"

"Are you this high-strung all the time?" she asks.

"No," I say maybe a little too defensively.

"Ethan, I see you met Blanca." I turn to see Phil Copeland, our boss, standing at the opening of her cubicle. "Show her around and we'll do the company introduction at nine." He smiles wide at Blanca.

Who wouldn't? She's so sweet looking she's probably never been told no.

She hops up from her chair when Phil leaves.

"What are you doing?" I ask.

"You were told to show me around."

Right. I nod, needing to get my crap together. This lovesick puppy act isn't going to be good for my career. I'm still redeeming myself from my second article here four months ago when I wrote about break-ups and a lot of our female readership didn't take kindly to my remarks.

"Come on."

I allow Blanca to walk in front of me, which is a bad idea. Her ass fits snug in her grey pants and her blouse shows off her olive-colored skin and toned arms. The heels make her taller than that night on the train. Not that she's near my height at all. I still have more than a few inches on her.

"This is the art department." I motion to the door on my right as we pass, but don't slow down.

"This is—" I look back and find her stopped at the door

and talking with Clara. The two of them are carrying on about what Clara does here at the magazine.

Taking a few steps back, I wait off to the side. Clara glances at me and back to Blanca. "I love your name," she says.

I did too until I found out it was going to be printed opposite mine in the magazine.

"Thanks. Clara is great too."

I roll my eyes.

"We'll have to do lunch sometime," Clara says.

I wave my hand in the air in a wrap it up motion. I do have a bagel to get to before the nine o'clock meeting.

"Definitely." Blanca smiles at her and I try to ignore how beautiful it makes her look.

"Okay, see you at nine." Clara looks my way. "Good morning, Ethan."

"Clara." I nod.

She laughs and I swivel on my heel to continue our tour through the office.

"Why didn't you stop to introduce me?" Blanca asks.

"You seem to be doing great all on your own."

"I make friends easily. I'm thinking that's not the case with you though?"

"I'm friendly." I shrug.

"But friends?" She looks to her side at me, but I continue staring straight ahead as I walk down the hall.

"I have friends." I signal to the next batch of cubicles. "This is the accounting department. No need to introduce yourself, you probably won't ever talk to them."

Two seconds after I tell her that she's over beside the cubicles and I hear, "Hi, I'm Blanca Mancini. I'm new here."

Mancini? That sounds familiar?

"Carl." He stands from his chair, towering over Blanca's small frame. He could be the proverbial company water cooler because he's tall enough to see into everyone's cubicle and know what everyone is up to. "Welcome to the team."

She makes polite chitchat for a minute but doesn't linger or suggest that they do lunch sometime. Relief shouldn't be the first thing to hit me, but it is.

"See you around." She waves.

"Ethan." Carl nods in my direction.

"Carl."

Blanca and I fall in line again. "Hmm. You were friendly last night."

I look to my side at her. "I told you, I'm friendly."

She shrugs her shoulders and a sound falls from her mouth to suggest that, no I am not. I'm friendly… enough. I don't need to be best friends with everyone I work with.

I lead us into the kitchen area. There's two small tables, a fridge, and two microwaves because Carl complained that Clara took over the microwave every lunch hour. Opening the fridge, I point to the five shelves. "Each department has their own shelf."

"Great. I'll probably start bringing my lunch." She nudges me out of the way and peers in.

"It goes without saying that you don't take someone else's stuff."

She squints her chocolate-colored eyes at me. "I'm not an asshole." She walks out of the kitchen.

"Fuck. What am I doing?" I mumble to myself.

"Being a jerk as usual," Bill from production says as I follow Blanca.

When I return back to our cubicle area, she's seated at her desk writing something down.

I lean on the wall, taking in her space again now that I know it's hers. Somehow, I love that she's taken something so bare and made it her own. But I probably acted like the opposite. Time to man up.

"I'm sorry, okay?" I start. "It just threw me, finding you here. I really liked you last night."

She circles around in her chair. "And today you decide to treat me like a new step-sibling?"

I chuckle. "I don't like to mix my personal life with my work life, and I'd hoped you might turn personal."

Her face softens. "Oh."

"I'd hoped to see you on the train again this Sunday and I had intentions of asking you out."

A smile quickly forms before she has a chance to stop herself. "You were?"

I step closer, leaning on her two-drawer filing cabinet, my hands on either side of my hips. "What would you have said?"

Again, her smile. Seriously, it's heartbreakingly beautiful. "You'll have to ask me to find out."

I shake my head and stand up straight. "I won't." Her smile falls. "I don't date people I work with. It's my rule."

It's a good rule, one I need to enforce. Even now when something inside of me says she's different.

"Oh. Okay then." She circles her chair back around to face her desk.

I spin the chair around so she's facing me again.

"Tell me what you would've said."

"Nope." She giggles.

"Why?"

The nine o'clock meeting gets announced through the speaker in the phone and she stands up. "Because like I said, you have to ask me to find out."

"I just told you my rule."

She stops at the opening of her cubicle and turns one more time to face me. Crossing her arms over her chest, her eyes lock with mine. "Some rules are meant to be broken. Surely you know that."

Before I can respond, she's out of her cubicle and halfway down the hallway to the conference room.

Picking up my coffee and leaving my bagel for later, I follow knowing I'm screwed because she's right. There's an exception to every rule, and she just might be it.

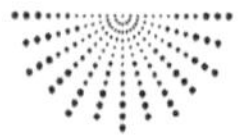

CHAPTER FIVE

Blanca

When I'm at the outdoor entrance of my apartment building after work, someone screams my name from across the street.

I turn to find Dylan halfway out the doors of Ink Envy, waving me over.

Looking both ways like my mama taught me, I jog across the street. "What's up?"

"Come on in," he says. "I'll be right back."

I walk in and find Seth there, sitting down on a couch in the front of the tattoo shop with a giant Slurpee in his hands. He pats the seat next to him.

"Nice. What flavor?" I ask.

"Blue raspberry mixed with cherry and a squirt of Coke."

I nod my approval. "So, why am I over here?"

"This is where we hang. Well, here or the rooftop." He props his feet up on the table in front of him.

I glance around. The shop has soaring ceilings and the walls are covered in large picture frames filled with various tattoo designs the different artists have drawn. There're a few artists at their stations, fewer clients.

"It's early. Knox will be here shortly. So how was your first day of work?"

"Okay." I shrug. "What do you do?"

He's dressed in dark jeans and a Henley so I'm thinking he doesn't work in an office of any sort.

"I'm a photographer."

"Oh, that's awesome. Like family portraits, weddings, landscapes? Have you been published?" I can't stop the questions coming out of my mouth because I've always been intrigued by photography, but I never had the knack. My selfies still look horrible. Me and photography are similar to someone who wants to be organized but can't get a handle on their clutter.

"Try boudoir." Dylan comes over and sits down on the couch.

I take a seat on the couch opposite them. "Really? Like naked women."

"No." Seth looks offended, so I try to decrease my judgment. Not that I'm judging. I wish I had the guts to do it. Sadly, I know no one to give the pictures to. "Lingerie. And it's just for experience and money until I can do what I really want to do."

"He's really good at it," Dylan says.

He sips his Slurpee giving Dylan a pissed-off look like he was making fun of what he does for a living.

"Hey, Blanc." I look over at Dylan surprised that he's already shortened my name. "I wanted to apologize for last night. Sierra and I just don't see eye-to-eye on the situation with her and her ex. You must've been really uncomfortable. Sorry."

I shake my head. "It's okay. I get it. After last night I think as long as you don't talk badly about Prince Adrian Marx, you'll be fine."

"She told you about her crush, huh?" Dylan laughs. "That girl. God help her if she ever saw him face to face."

"You mean God help the prince," Seth adds, and we all laugh.

The doorbell rings and Sierra and Rian walk in. Dylan stands and holds his arms wide open. Rian looks to Sierra and joins me on the couch.

"You're an asshole," Sierra says, but she walks right into his arms. "You're lucky I love you."

He exaggerates the hug by keeping her in his arms longer and rocking them side to side.

"Okay you two," Rian says, and I glance over at her. It's then I notice that there's a longing in her eyes. Not a jealousy per se, but almost as if she wishes she was in Sierra's position.

Dylan releases his hold on Sierra and no one other than me seems to notice Rian's comment or reaction.

Sierra takes a seat, and everyone rehashes their day. I'm quiet because they all know each other so well. Their conversations weave seamlessly from one to another. I sit back and become the observer instead of an active participant.

Sierra had to report a story about a thirty-year-old being evicted from his parents' home by a judge. Rian wrote an entire chapter of math problems for the fifth grade textbook she's working on right now. I always wondered what kind of people wrote those math problems. Seth had two clients, housewives who wanted to bring the fun back into their marriage. Dylan sits quietly and listens along with me.

My phone buzzes inside my purse and when I pull it out 'Unknown Caller' is on the screen, so I click deny and let it go to voicemail.

A second later, a text pops up.

Unknown Caller: *How about dinner?*

I smile already knowing who it is but wondering how he got my phone number.

Me: *I thought there were rules?*

Unknown Caller: *I'm asking for professional advice. So technically it's a business dinner.*

Me: *Oh well, that might change my answer.*

Unknown Caller: *To?*

Me: *Sure.*

Unknown Caller: *I feel as though you'd be disappointed if we did Italian because it wouldn't live up to your mom's cooking. How about Mexican?*

Me: *Okay. When and where?*

Unknown Caller: *Las Tacos 6:30?*

Me: *See you then.*

Unknown Caller: *Wait? What would you have said if it wasn't business?*

I laugh, my two thumbs already typing out my response.

Me: *You have to ask to find out.*

Three dots appear and then disappear.

"Who's making you smile like that?" Sierra asks. Everyone's head turns my way.

I tuck my phone back into my purse. "No one."

"Liar."

It vibrates inside my purse again, but I ignore it. "Just a guy from work."

"Oh. Day one and he already has your phone number," Dylan says. "I like the guy already."

"It's not like that, it's work related. He wants to talk over an article."

Seth straightens in his seat. "What do you do again?"

"I went to school for business, but I started this blog in college that did pretty well. Worked in finance for a bit and now I'm trying to get into journalism. It's hard, so I'm stuck writing fluff pieces until I prove myself."

Seth opens his mouth to say something and Dylan kicks his foot, causing his slushy to almost spill into his lap.

"Smooth," Rian mumbles from next to me.

I look around hoping someone fills in the missing piece for me.

Sierra sighs. "Sigmund was a journalism major. That's what Seth was going to say."

"Oh."

"But he works for some tech magazine," Sierra says. "I doubt that interests you."

I laugh. "Beats having to write about how to keep the sex alive in a long marriage."

"Don't get married," Dylan says. "Problem solved."

I'm pretty sure Rian whimpered next to me.

"My parents have been married for almost thirty years," Seth chimes in. "It works for some people." Seems the guy with the all-American looks comes from the all-American family.

"Do you really want to bring this topic up?" Dylan cocks an eyebrow.

Knox walks in and waves to someone at the back of the shop, taking the chair across from Dylan. "What'd I miss?"

"We're just talking about how happily married Seth's parents are," Dylan says with mirth, though I don't know why.

The other girls sigh.

"Someone has to fill me in," I say.

Knox's chuckle is deep as is his voice when he says, "Seth's mom asked..." He glances across to Sierra. "A mutual... someone for a vibrator recommendation."

Dylan bursts into laughter. Seth rolls his eyes, slurping up his drink. "You guys are assholes."

I give him an exaggerated frown. "If it makes you feel any better, my mom asked me about masturbation once. Imagine that conversation."

"At least she asked you and not your friend," Seth grumbles.

"Oh, come on." Dylan knocks him with his shoulder. "Your parents are happy, it just means exactly what I thought."

"And what's that?" Sierra asks, though I think she's asking more for Rian than any of us.

"That your sex life dies with those two little words."

"What two words?" Rian asks.

"I do." Dylan leans back into the couch with smug satisfaction.

"My parents had four kids. Three boys and they still had me. Their sex life was healthy," I argue. I'm not sure about the family dynamics of anyone else here except for Sierra and since her mom died so young, it might be a topic she's uncomfortable talking about.

"You said yourself your mom was asking about clicking her kitty," Dylan says. I ignore the visual that brings to mind.

"Masturbation has nothing to do with not having a healthy sex life," I counter and the girls all nod in agreement.

Dylan's feet fall to the floor and he leans forward, resting his forearms on his thighs. "How do you figure?"

"Well, even if I'm in a serious relationship, I continue to masturbate."

"Why would a girl do that?" Seth looks me dead in the eye like he can't wrap his head around what I'm saying.

"Easy. She's not getting it the right way," Dylan says, a cocky smirk on his lips.

Sierra laughs and touches his arm and makes a loud buzzing sound. "Wrong answer."

I lean forward and high five her.

The three guys look at us and then each other as though we're full of it.

"It must be the same for you guys? Sometimes you just need to release some tension and five minutes or less is all you need," I say.

Dylan winks. "Call me next time, I'll get you off in three minutes."

Almost everyone laughs, but the one person not joining in is sitting to the right of me. Now I'm sure Rian has a crush on Dylan.

"You can't tell me that you guys don't ever just play with your joystick for a minute and voila." Sierra takes her time to look at each one of them. "I'm sure you prefer that over fore-play anyway."

"First of all, not a joystick," Knox says, his voice rumbling deep.

"If you're gonna describe the manhood, at least make it a side stick like in the fighter planes," Seth says.

"I like foreplay." Dylan crosses his arms with a smugness on his face.

"No guys like foreplay," Sierra argues.

"I do." He shrugs.

"I thought those two words together weren't in your vocabulary," I say with a cocked eyebrow.

"Don't you have a date?" Dylan asks.

I pull my phone from my purse to see it's already six.

"Shit, I have to get ready." I stand up and swing my computer bag and purse over my shoulder. "And it's a work meeting, *not* a date."

"I don't get a smile like that on my face when I have to meet with Sargent Joe." Knox raises his eyebrows up to his hairline.

Forgetting them, I push the doors of Ink Envy open and run across the street to our apartment building.

There's no harm in me looking good for a work meeting. I mean, I can't show up in yoga pants and a sweatshirt. What kind of message would that send?

CHAPTER SIX

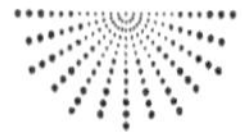

Ethan

The Modelo beer rests between my hands and my eyes are glued to the television, but I have no idea what soccer teams are playing.

This is a bad idea.

I've repeated that same mantra minutes after I sent Blanca the text while I was in the shower, again when I picked out jeans and a T-shirt that make it look like I'm not trying too hard, and just for good measure again when I perfected my hair with gel.

It repeated in my mind like a bad commercial jingle while I swiped the keys off the counter and pocketed my cell phone on the way out the door.

Still, here I am at Las Tacos, waiting for Blanca to arrive.

At least I didn't suggest picking her up from her apartment. I deserve points for that.

Tossing back another sip, my foot taps on the rail of my bar stool.

After Sierra, the last thing I wanted was to get involved in a relationship. Things went from cloud nine to the depths of Hell in a week's time with us. We rushed things by moving in together so we tried to make it work, probably longer than we should have.

If only this pull on my heart that says Blanca's different would stop tugging and demanding attention. Then maybe I wouldn't be at a restaurant with the lame excuse about our articles wanting to share my new fascination with her— Mexican food. Sierra hates Mexican, so after we broke up, I only ate Mexican for a while. Less of a chance I'd run into her.

"Are we eating at the bar?"

Blanca's soft voice pulls me away from the memories of my nightmare of a last relationship.

I swivel on the bar stool. "Nah, we can grab a table."

But she's already sliding onto the stool next to me. "There's a line."

I look back. When I got here, the hostess station was clear. But she's right, there's a line formed now.

"This is fine and I'm hungry, so I say we stay." She takes off her jacket and hangs it off the bar stool along with her purse.

"Sure."

In my mind, I tell myself not to compare her anymore to Sierra, but I can't help it. Sierra always wanted to eat without any televisions around. Said I always got too distracted and didn't listen to her.

She grabs the drink menu from the holder and flips it over, perusing it.

While she's not watching, I allow myself permission to soak her in. She's curled her hair from earlier and she's wearing a cute blouse and jeans with flats along with some gold bracelets, and a gold necklace. She looks over and I shift my vision away but not before noticing that she's got fresh makeup on.

Maybe I'm not the only one who has something tugging on their heart, saying there's something different between us. Something good here.

"Just a beer?" she asks. "You'd fit right in with my brothers." A small laugh falls from her lips and my eyes zero in on her lip gloss. Usually lip gloss or lipstick annoys me because kissing her isn't an option without coating my own lips, but I don't give a shit with Blanca. Let me look like a drunk clown if it allowed me one taste of her.

"Speaking of. Do they know you're here?" I grin.

She shakes her head with a smile and puts the menu back down. The bartender stops in front of her. "Margarita, rocks, salt on the edge." She turns back to me after the bartender walks away. "The answer to your question is no."

"What would they say about being on a date with a stranger?" The word date was a slip, but I notice that she doesn't correct me.

I swivel my chair in her direction and she crosses her legs, positioning herself my way too.

"You're not a stranger. You're my co-worker."

"True, but you just met me." I flick my wrist to check my watch. "Not even twenty-four hours ago."

She grabs my wrist like she needs to see the time for herself. Her fingertips on my skin bring a rush of heat right to my groin. "I feel like I've known you my entire life."

She's right. Somehow it feels like we've known each other all our lives. There's a comfort level between us normally only there after time and proximity. I'm a lucky guy for finding her on that train.

The bartender breaks up our conversation, placing Blanca's margarita down in front of her. "Menus?" he asks.

"Please," she says. Not one glance my way to see if I'm on board. Her confidence is sexy as hell.

Maybe it's because my mom always catered to my dad. Nothing was final until he ruled on the decision. Ever since I can remember, a woman who knows what she wants and isn't looking to me for permission is an aphrodisiac for me.

As though already prepared, the bartender hands us two menus and heads down the bar to serve other patrons.

"Have you been here before?" she asks, her eyes never leaving the menu.

"Yeah, the carne asada is fantastic." I place my menu down.

She eyes the movement and flicks her gaze to me. "That's what you're getting?"

I sense judgment in her tone. "Um… yeah?"

"This place is called Las Tacos, right?"

"And?"

"Have you had the tacos?" She flips through the menu, gaze darting from one side of it to the other.

"I'm not a taco kind of guy."

She gasps like I said I don't like cake or something. "If they think highly enough of their tacos to name the entire restaurant after them, I say you should try some."

I pick up the menu to peruse it some more but think better of it and place it back down. "Okay, how about you order for me?"

Her eyebrows crinkle and she shakes her head. "No."

"I'm not a hard guy to please, don't worry." I wink and she smiles for a second.

"You already said you aren't a taco guy."

I shrug and grab my beer from the bar top. "I'm willing to try anything once."

"You're serious?"

I nod and tip my beer back for a sip. Once I place it back down, I set my gaze on her. "Very. Order for me something I'll dream about tonight. Something no other meal in my life will ever compare to." I grin.

Her attention moves to the menu and all I can think of is how cute she looks when she's thinking really hard. I caught her earlier today at her desk when I made the lame joke from *Office Space* about Mondays and she had a pen wedged between her teeth while her hand was on her mouse scrolling and clicking.

She can't be as great as she seems. I mean, no one is this perfect.

She lays the menu down on the bar top with a smack. "Okay. I've decided."

"What am I having?"

We lock eyes and there's silence for a moment as sexual tension swirls between us rising to an almost catastrophic level until she clears her throat. "You're having three different tacos, beans and rice. And we're having nachos as an appetizer."

I nod. "Cool."

Her pink lips cover the edge of the margarita glass and she sips it, leaving the residue of her lip gloss on the glass. "You're very easy," she says. "My brothers would have been like, 'screw you.'"

"I'm not your brothers."

"I'm well aware." She chuckles.

Again, silence falls between us and my fingers itch to touch her thigh that's resting only millimeters away. I clench my hand. She's my co-worker and I can't cross that line.

"What are you writing about this week?" I ask just to give us something to talk about and occupy my brain from thoughts of what she might look like naked.

She side glances me while taking another sip of her margarita. "And have you steal my idea?"

"How can I steal your idea when I write for the opposite sex?"

She looks me over like she's trying to do an honesty test with just her eyes acting as judge and jury. I kind of like the way they stop at waist level and then slowly draw up my chest until our eyes meet once again. From the pink on her cheeks, I'd say she likes what she sees.

"You could spin it to work for you." She shrugs.

"Fine. I'll tell you first. I'm doing the ten best hoodies for fall."

"Hoodies? In July?"

"Yes, hoodies for the fall."

She haws and tilts her head like okay, but clearly doesn't think it's a good idea. Costco is already selling snowsuits, so it's not like I'm getting ahead of myself.

"This is the part where you tell me what you're doing…"

She smiles and sips her drink again, twirls the glass in her hand, the ice clinking together. "I'm doing five ways to be a better friend."

"This coming from experience? You have close friends?"

She seems like the type. The kind of girl that has a group of lifelong best friends. I only have Dylan and lately it's felt like Sierra won him when we broke up. I don't blame the guy, he tried to keep the peace but knowing Sierra she doesn't make it easy.

"I've grown apart from some, but most of them are in the city."

"But yet you live in Cliffton Heights now?"

She giggles, shaking her drink which I figure out is a distraction technique. "I reconnected with a friend a month or so ago and it was like old times. It all seemed to fit, you know?"

"You miss the city?"

She shrugs. "Sometimes, but I do like the small-town feel."

"Cliffton Heights is small town?"

She pushes me in the shoulder, and I tip a bit on my stool but recover quickly. "Compare it to New York City and yes, it's small town."

"So violent." I rub my shoulder like she hurt me.

"Sorry, reflex from having three brothers. It was a way to get them to pay attention to me."

I pick up my beer. "How do you like the magazine so far?"

She nods. "No complaints except for the guy next to my cubicle." She rolls her eyes in dramatic fashion and I just know the smile on my face looks cheesy as hell.

"Yeah? I bet he's like the hottest guy you've ever seen."

She shrugs. "He's all right."

I shake my head and take a pull of my beer. "Just all right?"

"I haven't quite figured him out yet."

"I bet he's a great guy you should spend more time with. You know, to get to know him better."

The waiter finally comes back and takes our order, which I'm thankful for. I could use the breather to remind me not to flirt too much with her.

He walks away and we start a conversation about our families. She tells me all about her three brothers and their significant others. How there's a baby coming from her oldest brother and she's sure to be shoved out of the picture. The love and affection she holds for her family is obvious throughout the conversation. The jealousy that's always present whenever I hear about someone with a normal childhood strikes but it's not as jarring as usual. I'm happy she never had to grow up the way I did.

"What about you?" she asks.

"What about me?"

"What's your family like?" She tilts her head to the side, waiting for my answer.

This is where it always goes south with the woman I'm interested in. Because she doesn't want to hear the stories of my mom using food stamps to buy groceries. The sighs from people behind us when we had to have the cashier take products off because we didn't have enough money. She wants to hear stories about sibling arguments and Christmas traditions. I'm not sure receiving a gift from a rich family who thought they were doing good out in the suburbs is what she's expecting.

"I have a younger sister. She just graduated from NYU."

Her eyes widen. "That's awesome. What was her major?"

"Education."

"Great profession."

Except it makes no money. Not that being a writer is filling my bank account right now, but I wanted her to pick something more secure financially.

"Her first job is at a small catholic school. Pay is horrible."

"Happiness isn't about money." She tsks with her finger like she's my mother.

Except my mom never told me that.

"You can't survive without money. A big heart doesn't put food on your table or a roof over your head." I sip my beer knowing I need to leave the bitterness from my childhood buried, at least for our first time out together.

"That's extreme, but I did leave my job in finance to write and I did it because I was unhappy."

Shit, I knew she was different. But to throw away a life where you might never have to worry about money for one that is unstable in today's market is a big gamble. No one wants print anymore. Newspapers, magazines, they're all becoming obsolete. "I'm not sure if that's stupid or brave."

"You sound like two of my brothers."

"Not all three?"

A big smile warms her face. "Dom, the married one with the baby on the way, he had a big revelation this past year. He pushed me to make the change and so far I'm happy I did."

I knock her shoulder with mine. "It's only day one."

She holds my gaze and shivers scatter along the back of my neck. "I know."

Yeah, I need to listen to my gut more often. I think staying at the tech magazine would've been *much* easier.

CHAPTER SEVEN

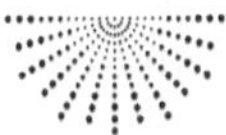

Blanca

*E*than is either a serial dater or he's taken classes on how to charm a woman because I've never felt more listened to, more understood, more wanted—and he hasn't even laid a single finger on me. I think he's trying to mask it but the desire in his eyes makes my skin burn. The way his gaze holds mine while I'm talking. His eyes soften when I talk about my family, roll when I talk about my evil ex-boss, and light up when I make a corny joke. He'd win me over with all of that, but it's his eyes when I'm *not* speaking that have me ready to pull him into an alley and kiss him senseless.

"Have you been to Scrumtuals yet?" he asks.

"Scrumtuals?" I scrunch my forehead. What a weird name.

He chuckles. "It's not sexual. Well, unless chocolate makes you…" His words trail off and a light blush hits the center of his cheeks. Needless to say it's adorable. "It's a dessert place. Only serves dessert and they're small portions so you can try a bunch."

"Oh. For a second I thought this… work meeting was going in a different direction."

His hands are shoved into his pockets as we walk side-by-side toward the downtown portion of Cliffton Heights. Other than coming and going from the train last Sunday, I haven't had much of a chance to explore.

"How long have you lived here?" I ask to break up the awkwardness when he doesn't respond to my last statement.

He thinks about it for a second. "Two years? Shit, it doesn't feel that long."

"And you like it?"

He glances at me and smiles. "I do. I almost moved back to the city a few months ago, but then I found the job at Mars And Venus."

"Is that your end game? To work and Mars And Venus?"

He laughs and opens the door to a cute bakery with a black and white striped awning adorning the outside. When I step inside I see that it's decorated in pale pink, light green, and white.

How did I miss this place?

A sweet sugary scent wraps me up in a blanket and instantly, I'm in love.

"This might be the best work meeting I've ever been on." I elbow him and he bites his lower lip, his eyes absorbing my excitement.

"Yeah. Tacos and a dessert bar. Great combo."

He takes out a tray and heads down the line of cupcakes, brownies, cakes, pies, and cookies. Everything is mini and it all looks like a small piece of heaven.

"Come to daddy." He places a plate of mini chocolate covered pretzels on the tray.

I raise my eyebrows. "Seriously?"

"What?"

"Chocolate covered pretzels when you have all this gooey cakey goodness right here in front of you?"

He shrugs. "I like chocolate covered pretzels."

I nod, grabbing a whoopie pie and a brownie.

"Don't hold back," he says, allowing me to handle the tray which I happily take charge of.

"I don't intend to. You're just my co-worker, so you can sit there and watch me consume thousands of calories in desserts. Not like this isn't just about business, right?"

I can do this all night. I will *not* slip up and call this a date —again.

He chuckles and his tongue slides out of his mouth, licking his bottom lip. I can't stop myself from wondering what he tastes like.

"I like a woman with a healthy appetite. Especially if I can feed it to her."

"TMI for a work meeting, Ethan," I say, grabbing some truffles.

He leans in closer to me and whispers, "Nah, TMI would've been if I told you I like to feed them to her naked after I've already fucked her brains out."

Ethan steps away and walks down the counter to where coffees, hot chocolate, and tea are served while I stand there, thighs clenched together inhaling a deep breath in an attempt to bring my body temperature down.

He starts to converse with the woman behind the counter and I remain where I am—in shock, motionless, and wishing he'd call mercy.

"Excuse me, miss."

I look down to a cute kid waiting expectantly, pick up my tray and let him pass by. "Thank you," he says and his mom smiles at me as they pass.

"You're welcome. You have a very polite son," I say to her.

She smiles like I made her day and they continue on their way.

Ethan returns with nothing in his hands and doesn't mention his previous comment. The one that makes me want to take these desserts to go and have him fuck my brains out and feed them to me post orgasm. How can he look so calm and collected?

He walks along the winding tiers of desserts without rushing me or mentioning how there's no possible way I can eat them all. But hey, isn't that what takeout boxes are for?

"Ice cream!" I say a little too loud and he chuckles next to me. He's not annoyed because I just announced it to the entire restaurant, but his laugh seems more like, 'she's awesome am I right?'

Why does he have to be my co-worker?

I open up the freezer and sure enough it's filled with small containers in a variety of flavors.

"Did you kill me and we're in heaven?" I ask.

"No. But I kind of feel like we should've skipped the tacos and came straight here."

"I'd agree with you, but then you wouldn't have experienced the best tacos ever." I hit him in the stomach, which I realize is as rock hard as I thought it would be, and then grab a container of chocolate ice cream.

"You sure do like to hit a lot."

Crap. "Sorry, did I hurt you?" I forget how used to hitting my brothers I am. Seems I'm *way* too comfortable with Ethan.

"Are you crazy?" He holds up his arms and flexes. "You're a little thing."

I narrow my eyes. "Rule number one if we're going to be work BFFs is that I don't like words that have anything to do with little. No squirt or pint or mini."

"Work BFFs?"

A smile wraps around my lips. "Sure. Day one and we've already gone out for drinks and dessert. You clearly love what I love—Mexican food and sugar. The bagel you brought in this morning looked awesome. Wouldn't mind one of those myself. We're a match. You know how people have work husbands and wives? You can be my work husband." I rest my head on his arm. "You know, because you don't date people you work with."

I pick up the tray and the woman wearing a cute fifties-inspired outfit rings us up. Ethan pays and grabs the tray to find a table.

The woman hands me a to-go box. Little does she know what this body can consume. I take it in order to not be rude and follow Ethan to the table.

He sets the tray on the table. "I'm going to grab our hot chocolates."

I watch him cross the room. There's a group of women at another table slyly checking him out. He smiles and thanks the employee behind the counter, then says something else I can't make out. She laughs, handing him two chocolate covered plastic spoons.

I've seen women lose their footing around my brothers. Confident, successful women who somehow can't find their words because they find them intimidatingly handsome. I thought I was immune to that sort of thing. I've never been at a loss for words around a guy, but Ethan is different.

Somehow this thing between us feels like it could be big, but the co-worker thing is definitely a problem. A problem big enough that he's put the brakes on anything developing between us.

I should listen to him, he's obviously smarter than my sex drive.

"Courtesy of Betty." He hands me one of the plastic spoons and places the hot chocolates on the table.

"Betty, huh?" I look past him. "Betty looks younger than me."

He chuckles, sliding into his chair. "I don't think Betty is her real name unless it's a family name."

"Or we've warped back to the nineteen fifties and Kenickie is picking her up after her shift."

"Hell, I bet Kenickie is the cook."

My eyes search the restaurant. I don't see one male employee. "Oh, do they dare date, being co-workers and all?"

Ethan watches me steadily until I fidget under his scrutiny. "Let me ask you a question?" He slides his chair closer, his hot chocolate and dessert untouched. Meanwhile, I'm already deep into my whoopie pie and ice cream. "Do you want to explore this?" He waggles his finger between us.

I shrug. "I didn't say that. I said that you had to ask me to find out."

He releases a breath. "I like you, Blanca."

"Well, thank you. I do think I'm very likable," I joke but he doesn't laugh.

"But you said you needed the job and I do as well."

I put my spoon down. "Okay, so we'll just be friendly co-workers then." I shrug, pretending that disappointment doesn't press heavy against my sternum. "It's just funny to razz you about it because you've basically taken me out on a date but keep referring to it as a work meeting."

"It could be a getting to know you work meeting. I mean if we're going to write articles opposite one another then I should know you."

"Ahh…" I lick my spoon clean and his gaze zeros in on my mouth. "Nicely played."

"I thought so." He grins.

I cross my legs and look him over, leaning back in my chair. "What's your article about this week?"

He mimics my stance but grabs his hot chocolate and takes a sip. "How not to date your co-worker."

I laugh and shake my head. His cocky smirk says he's messing with me.

"Great. Let me know how that goes."

"And yours?"

I shrug. "I was going to do healthy habits for women in their twenties, but now I'm thinking I need to write an opposing piece to yours. Maybe the benefits of dating your co-worker."

He chokes and almost spits his hot chocolate at me but ends up swallowing it down. It's the first time he doesn't appear to have it all together since I met him. "I don't think there are any."

"Mr. Ryland, are you questioning my journalistic abilities?"

"I'd never dream of it, Miss Mancini." His words are serious, but his eyes flirt with me.

Am I necessarily pro co-workers dating? No. But as with everything in my life, you tell me no and I want to prove you wrong.

Like when Carm said I couldn't run a 5K because I never exercise. I trained for months and ended up beating his time. The look on his face was worth the months of torture. Or Mama when she dared me to cook an entire meal on my own. It might not have been the best meal my family ever had, but no one got sick.

"Do you feel like putting a wager down?"

His eyebrows crinkle in the most adorable way. "Wager?"

"Yeah."

"How is the winner determined?"

Huh, I hadn't thought about that. "Whoever gets the most comments online agreeing with their side of the argument?"

He narrows his eyes like he's not sure I'm serious. What can I say? This is how I solve things. Competition and bets.

"What does the winner get?"

"Hmm…" I tear off part of my brownie and pop it into my mouth while I think.

"We do a platonic getting to know each other like tonight? Loser pays?"

I suppose we're still pretending this isn't a date, which is absurd.

"Nah. That's like a tease."

"Loser has to buy lunch for the week."

That was disappointing. I'd thought he'd come up with something better. Something sexual would've been nice. I stretch my hand out over the table between us. "Deal."

He shakes my hand and I feel the contrast of calluses and soft skin. "Deal."

CHAPTER EIGHT

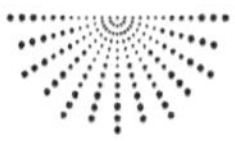

Blanca

I walk into my apartment and Rian is sprawled out on the couch with the remote pointed at the television. Sierra has her legs propped up on the coffee table with a magazine on her lap.

"Oh look who finally returned from her *work* meeting," Sierra teases, flipping the page of her magazine.

"Damn, I just lost the bet. I had you doing the walk of shame tomorrow morning." Rian peeks over the edge of the couch.

"Sorry to disappoint you." I drop my purse on the kitchen table and slip off my shoes, throwing myself into the chair across from Sierra. I glance at the television. "Do you watch any shows from our generation?" I ask over the audience laughter of something quirky Sophia has said onscreen.

"Hey now, *Golden Girls* is a classic," Rian says, and I nod.

"You're right. But *Blue Bloods* I'll never understand."

"Don't knock it until you try it."

"Speaking of knocking it?" Sierra interjects and I glance over to see her smiling wide, tossing her magazine on the table.

"I told you it was work."

"And then you came in looking like you just fell in love." She raises an eyebrow.

I sigh and my head falls back to the chair. "Have you ever had that feeling like…?"

"Yeah," Rian says and sighs, her own head falling to the pillow on the couch.

"Not really, but then again I've never met Prince Adrian," Sierra says.

All three of us laugh.

"What about Sigmund?" I ask.

Rian glances over to Sierra as though she doesn't know the answer. I'm desperate to figure out why this guy made such a lasting impression on her, but yet they broke up.

"Not really? I mean there was an instant attraction and I want to sleep with you factor but I'm not sure I ever looked the way you do right now."

Rian raises her hand. "I can attest to that. They went from googly eyes to dating one another to hating one another to despising one another."

"Hey!" Sierra throws a pillow at Rian.

"What? It was toxic."

"You're just agreeing with Dylan because you're in love with him," Sierra says.

And there it is. One of the many questions I've had about my new set of friends. All those looks from Rian at Dylan weren't my imagination. The good girl always loves the bad boy.

Rian sits up straight, panic in her eyes. "I am not."

"Oh please, it's Blanca, she's not gonna tell him."

Rian sets her questioning gaze on me.

I hold up one hand in the air and one like it's on a Bible. "Your secret is safe with me. Can I ask a question though? Why don't you tell him?"

Sierra stands from the chair and heads into the kitchen, returning seconds later with three glasses and a bottle of rosé wine. "I've asked the same thing." She pours three glasses, handing one to each of us and sitting down next to Rian. "Maybe the two of us can refute her insecurities together."

Rian slumps back into the pillow and whimpers. "I thought we were talking about Blanca's magic connection?"

"Nope. We're on to you." I point, sipping my wine and crossing my legs to get comfy on the chair.

For the next twenty minutes Rian describes how she had that feeling I was describing in the pit of her stomach the first time she met Dylan. And how she purposely makes her heart-shaped cookies every Valentine's Day just for him, although he doesn't know it. That she's tried to get him out of her mind by dating other people, but no one compares.

Sierra and I are interrupted from telling her how lucky Dylan would be to have someone like her when my phone dings in my purse. If only I wasn't as transparent as Rian because the smile that transfixes to my face the minute my phone dings is just as blaring as her whimpers. I get up to grab it and then sit back down.

Ethan: *As an older brother myself, I feel like it's my obligation to make sure you got home okay.*

I down the last drop of my wine.

Me: *Brotherly love?*

Ethan: *Just plain old stalking.*

Me: *If you were stalking, you'd already know I'm home.*

The three dots appear and my stomach fills with flutters waiting for what he'll come back with. Just as my phone vibrates, it's snatched out of my hands.

Sierra waves it back and forth in her hands. "What kind of lines does this guy have to make you smile that way?" She sits down on the couch and Rian slides closer preparing to have a glimpse at my phone too.

I'm usually an open book. Not that I'd share personal intel on Ethan, but checking out his flirtatious lines would be something I would share with my friends. Just not yet.

"It's nothing." I hold out my hand.

It's still so new and fresh and awesome that I'm not ready for anyone to say otherwise. And girls *always* have their opinions.

Sierra sighs and shakes her head, putting the phone back into my hands. "I can't wait to meet this guy."

I ignore her and look at the text.

Ethan: *It's my way to stay undercover. Look like I'm the good guy.*

My thumb poised to fire back a response, but I look up to find two women on the couch sulking.

"What?"

Sierra cocks her head to the side. "Have you been out of a girl gang that long?"

I put my phone down on the armrest. "What does that mean?"

"Rian just poured her heart out to you about Dylan. You know all about my obsession with my prince. And here you are all lovesick over a guy and yet we know nothing about him."

Sierra's right. She just entered my life again and it's been a long time since I've had true girlfriends I felt like I could be close to.

Me: *Well good guy, I'll see you tomorrow. I have to go gossip about you with my girlfriends.*

Ethan: *Are you having a pillow fight in your underwear after?*

Me: *I guess you'll have to use your spy gear and find out. ;)*

I place my phone on the table and refill my glass of rosé, filling up Sierra's as well. Rian's half full one still sits on the coffee table.

"It's crazy. I've only known him for twenty-four hours, yet I didn't want to leave him tonight. He says he can't date people he works with, but tonight felt like a date from start to finish."

"You kissed him?" Rian asks, her eyes wide as saucers.

"Or did you sleep with him?" Sierra looks at the clock like she's trying to do the math.

"No and no, but I would've done both if the opportunity presented itself. What does that say about me? I've never been someone who sleeps with a guy right away."

Sierra laughs hysterically. "Um, it says you're a woman with a sex drive. That you know what you want and it's your sexy co-worker. Do not let that Italian good girl guilt eat you up inside. Let him eat you up instead."

"Sierra," Rian gasps.

I can't help but laugh. "It's not that."

"Are you sure? Your brothers were always warning you about guy's intentions." Sierra has a point. My brothers have not only lectured me most of my life about boys who use girls for sex, but I witnessed it firsthand when they did the same. None of them had settled down until recently.

But I've had relationships before and I'm not that thirteen-year-old girl who needs advice from anyone.

I pick up the pillow next to me and scream into it.

"What?" Sierra still knows me well. "What did you do?"

I peek over top of it. "Nothing."

"How do you know she did something?" Rian asks, truly curious. She probably never heard my name until Sierra said I was moving in.

"She's beating herself up and she only does that when she thinks she's made a fool of herself."

I drop the pillow. "Not a fool of myself, but I did make a bet."

Sierra laughs because she's her. She's the same person who found it funny when I bet Tony DeLuca I'd eat a cricket for every touchdown he threw that Friday night. In my defense, he was saying my brothers weren't worthy of their legendary status at our high school and he hadn't even thrown a touchdown yet that year. Family sticks up for family and I ate four crickets for the Mancini family that year.

"What was the bet?" Sierra leans forward.

"We're writing opposing articles and whoever gets the most comments on their side has to buy the other lunch for a week."

They both stare at me like I just admitted to owning six cats.

"What?"

Sierra covers her mouth with her hand as she exaggerates a yawn. "Boring. It's not even sexual."

"I don't think I'm his type."

Rian quirks an eyebrow. "You're everyone's type."

"I've tried everything I can think of to get him to admit we were on a date tonight and he wouldn't budge. And shouldn't I play hard to get anyway?" Maybe I do need some advice.

The plus side of having three brothers should be that I understand men, but they're as confusing as ever. Then again, once I was in adult relationships, none of them let me come to them for any real advice on the opposite sex. They'd rather imagine me saying the rosary in a head to toe flannel nightgown every night.

"Write the articles and see who wins the bet." Rian finally sips her wine.

"Then you can make another bet with sexual favors involved." Sierra waggles her eyebrows.

I roll my eyes in return. I love Sierra and she pulls a side of me out which I adore, but we're different on some levels. Not good or bad, just different. Then again, I bet she wouldn't have thrown little hints out there like I did with Ethan. Sierra would've thrown herself at him and gotten what she wanted. Just like she did when we were fourteen and at the mall to buy Justin Timberlake's new CD. She flirted with a guy in the store and I ended up waiting on a bench with his friend while she did whatever she did in the photo booth behind the curtain. She's always had the self-confidence to go after what she wants, and I've always been more reserved. Is that what made our friendship work so well?

"Let me figure out this article first. A little scary with it being the first one I'm writing for the magazine."

Sierra shakes her head and glances at Rian. "She's a self-doubter. You two are almost replicas of one another." She laughs, finishing off her wine and setting the glass down before grabbing the remote. "Let's watch some You Tube videos of Prince Adrian."

Rian groans like this is something she's forced to do regularly.

Sierra clicks on a video and for the next half hour my thoughts drift back to Ethan. How am I going to nail this article *and* squash my attraction to him? Leaving for another magazine can't happen until I gain enough experience at this one. So I have to train myself to ignore those dimples.

Damn, like magic his face comes into my mind.

Whack.

I pick up the pillow from where it fell onto my lap and look over at a smiling Sierra. "Daydreaming about Romeo over there? Stop the moaning, it's making me horny."

Rian giggles and lays her head on the pillow.

I snuggle the pillow into my chest. When did my life get so complicated?

CHAPTER NINE

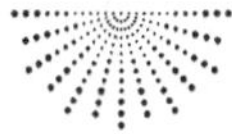

Ethan

For being a type A personality, I really lack skills in time management. Arriving late to work isn't a new thing for me, but this morning I'm an extra ten minutes late because Mrs. Andrews decided to chat with me about her concerns over Seth. I mentioned that Dylan was probably a better candidate to have that conversation with since he still lives with him. Then her questions about why I wanted two bagels instead of one today started and I couldn't get out of there fast enough. Lying to her didn't feel great.

Dropping off a French toast bagel with plain cream cheese on Blanca's desk was something I envisioned from the moment I decided I'd do so last night.

In my head she'd be all flirty smiles and hopefully forgot to button her blouse all the way up. Okay, yeah, I knew that last one was a long shot. But I didn't think she wouldn't be there when I arrived, and I sure didn't think I'd be the second person to leave a bagel on her desk.

My eyes bore into the sesame bagel with chive cream cheese and a bite mark out of it sitting on her desk. I scan the immediate area for which dog is pissing around my tree. Was it Carl from accounting or Bill from marketing? Who else has their eyes on Blanca in this office?

Shit. I run a hand through my hair.

Cool down. You're not trying to win Blanca Mancini over, remember douche?

"What's with the face?" Blanca slides by me and all I smell is her perfume. She's purposely upping the enticement. I just know it.

She sits down and crosses her legs, her skirt riding up her thighs.

Can I please gouge my eyes out right now?

"What face?"

"The murderous one." She points at me like I know what I look like. I smack on my smile and her frown forms a crease between her eyebrows. "No need to fake it on my account."

She picks up her bagel and it's then that I notice the wet spot on her blouse. She must see me check it out because she shakes her head. "Cream cheese fell off."

"Very convenient place." I shift my gaze, but it immediately floats back since the wet spot is literally right above her right breast.

Someone up there finds this funny, right? I take a quick glance upward.

"Oh, you already got a bagel?" she asks, her shoulders sagging a bit as she stares at the one in my hand.

I look down like I didn't know it was there and hand it over to her. "No, it's for you, but I see someone else..."

"Go check your desk." She giggles, taking the bagel from me.

I peer around the thin partition between our desks and sure enough a bagel sits there from The Bagel Place. "You got me a bagel?" I ask.

"You sound surprised. Then again, the things I've heard about you already… I can see why maybe no one would bring you a bagel."

I step over to my desk, quickly typing in my password so my computer can start the painful process of booting up. "What did you hear?" I step back over to the partition so I can see her.

"Nope. I'm not going to be the water cooler of the office." She falls back into her seat.

I unwrap the bagel she got me. The Bagel Place isn't even comparable to Andrews Bagel Co. but she's new in town so she wouldn't know that. "I'm impressed." I change the subject because I can imagine the stories she's heard. I'm not a well-liked guy around here because I don't do their Friday night drinks and I didn't contribute to the potluck last month. Nor do I join the weekly lottery pool. I guess it holds no weight that I chipped in for Carl's birthday cake or gave a gift to Mandy when I didn't even attend her wedding. People probably don't see me as a team player.

"I impressed you?" She spins her chair around.

I can't help the smile on my face when I see that she's ditched her bagel for mine.

"You guessed right." I hold up the Asiago bagel with plain cream cheese in my hand.

"Oh good. I wasn't sure about the flavor of cream cheese, but I spotted the Asiago yesterday. I'm not a mind reader or anything."

I prop myself up on her desktop, opening up my bagel. "You could've just said 'yeah, I'm pretty cool like that.'"

"I am cool, but I don't take credit for things I didn't do."

She tears off a piece of her original bagel, setting the French toast one down.

"So I guessed wrong, huh?" I nod toward the discarded bagel.

She laughs. "I'm a savory over sweet kinda girl but I see why you thought sweet, what with dessert last night."

"Then why would you take a bite?"

"It's called being polite, which I hear you have a hard time being." Another giggle falls out of her lips and I want to swallow it down. Preferably with my tongue. Then she eyes the bagel in my hands. "You'll come to find out that Andrews Bagels are the best."

"Then I guess you'll be picking me up one next week after I win?"

"I thought we were doing lunch?"

"Do they not serve sandwiches on bagels?" Both her eyebrows raise.

I jump down from her desk. "You'll be buying mine."

"We'll see about that."

Just as I'm about to leave her alone because I'm probably really looking needy right now, Mr. Copeland stops in front of her cubicle with his morning cup of coffee in hand.

"Glad to see you guys are getting along."

I'm sure he means that more like, 'I'm glad to see you get along with someone, *anyone*, Ethan.' He's the biggest "rah-rah co-workers are second family" in the office.

"Good morning, Mr. Copeland."

"Please Blanca, call me Phil."

She smiles but doesn't repeat it.

"I got both your proposals for the mid-month issue and I have to ask, did you plan it together?" Neither of us have a chance to respond before he speaks again. "Post lunch meeting in the conference room. Say one o'clock?"

"I'll be there," I say.

"Sounds good," Blanca says.

"Great. You're both so amenable this morning." His stare lingers on me. I tend to swim against the current, but I'm behind this opposing-articles idea Blanca came up with. He steps away but doesn't leave, sipping his coffee for a moment. "Get a rough sketch of your article together. I want to see where they're going."

"Sure thing." Blanca's face is all smiles. I wonder if she ever goes against the grain.

Phil walks down the hall, stopping at a cubicle farther down to wish them a good morning.

"You should get to work," Blanca says, swiveling her chair to face her computer.

"Yeah, I'm going to make a list of my favorite lunch places."

I tear myself away because I'm fairly sure I could stay and watch her the entire day. Sitting at my desk, I put in my AirPods so I can concentrate on something other than the fact that she's right next to me.

I MAY HAVE BEEN late today, but I use my time wisely, researching stories of co-workers who dated and digging to find real life people who had a horrible experience after dating a co-worker.

After scanning article after article and one Reddit story after another, I've determined that most work romances are all about secret sex in the copy room or inappropriate touches under the conference table. It's then that I nail down the direction I'm going with my article. Work romances are a taboo thing that people get a high on just like a drug. It's the thrill of possibly being caught.

By the time one o'clock arrives, and I pass Blanca in the

hall talking to Tina from proofreading, I know I'm gonna be the winner.

"Hey Ethan," Blanca says, waving to me.

"Blanca." I nod. "Tina."

"Ethan," Tina says with zero excitement in her tone.

I sit in the chair next to where Phil will sit. He's a creature of habit and believes his chair is the one at the head of the table. Blanca arrives minutes later and slides into the chair across from me.

"Tina's nice."

I nod.

"What is with you? Why are you so against socialization at work?"

"I get paid to work, not find out that one of Tina's lizards is constipated again."

Blanca laughs, one of her curls falling in front of her face. She's so beautiful that it's almost a physical ache that I can't have her. Especially after the dreams of her under me, riding me, stripping for me. I'm almost scared to close my eyes. "How on Earth did you…"

"I might not speak but I have ears."

She steadies her gaze on me like she's searching for something. "You are one mysterious man, Ethan Ryland."

"Why do you say that?"

I'll be damned if I give her any personal information but at the same time I fear she has the capability of getting it out of me without me even knowing.

"Because you don't want to get close to anyone here, yet you listen to their woes…"

"Since I have functioning ear drums I can't stop from hearing their complaining." I raise an eyebrow in challenge.

"You're not closed off with me. You even got me a bagel this morning."

The reason I became a writer is because I need time to

think about what I want to say. I'm not good on the spot, so I take a brief moment to consider my response. But before I can say anything, Phil and Cassie walk in. I'm saved.

Blanca gives me a challenging smirk that says she's thinking the same thing as I am.

"Okay you two. Blanca, this is my assistant, my niece, Cassie." He holds out his hand toward the young woman at the end of the table who's pulling out her phone.

"Hi, Cassie," Blanca says with a genuine smile.

Cassie returns the smile and pops a bubble from her gum, positioning her phone in her hands with both thumbs armed to take notes. I roll my eyes and see Phil release a breath.

"Ladies first," Phil says, leaning back and swiveling his chair to face Blanca.

It's the first time I've seen her ill at ease. She's smiling, but it's not the casual one that suggests she's in control. Her teeth are biting down on one side of her lip and then she clears her throat. "I took the position of co-worker relationships being a positive thing."

Phil nods and waits silently.

"I have a list of five reasons why dating a co-worker is healthy." Her gaze flicks to me.

"Okay, I'm not sure I want you to list them yet." He swivels his chair my way like he's Dr. Phil. "Ethan?"

"I've got six reasons why you should never date a co-worker with a great final argument." I glance at Blanca who's back straightens.

"More doesn't necessarily mean better," she says.

I swear my dick perks up when she fights back.

"Maybe not, but it's more of an argument than your five."

"How do you figure? Your reasons might not hold as much weight as mine."

"Oh, they do."

"How can you be so sure?"

"Okay you two." Phil stutters out a laugh holding his hands up in the air. "I never would've predicted this dynamic between you two when I hired Blanca." He concentrates his attention on her. "I thought you were a school fish."

"School fish?" she asks, eyeing me like I can fill her in.

I have no idea what the hell he's talking about.

"That you'd swim with everyone—but I like this shark attitude. Ethan needs someone to keep him on his toes." He stands up and signals to Cassie that he's done here. She blows another bubble and has to take the gum out of her mouth to get the residue off her lips.

We all watch her until she's done, Phil's eyes closing briefly.

"I just wanted to see the dynamic of the two of you talking about the articles. I can't wait to see what I get. Articles are due Friday."

He leaves the room and Blanca stands.

"School fish?" she says more to herself I think. Her disappointment of being classified that way bothers her, I can tell.

"You do have a goody two-shoes vibe."

She scoffs.

I laugh at her pouty lip.

"But after today I'm thinking you might have a big bite when you get cornered."

She smiles wider. "Just ask my brothers."

Yeah, Phil definitely underestimated this girl who grew up with three older brothers. I guess I did it too, which only turns me on more.

I wish that was a good thing.

CHAPTER TEN

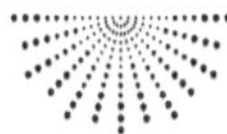

Blanca

Friday afternoon at three o'clock, I click send an email to Mr. Copeland, which contains my very first article that will be published in a magazine. Exhilaration spreads through my veins. I finally accomplished what I wanted. I am going to have something published in print.

Sliding out of my chair, I peek over the partition to find Ethan wearing his AirPods, his back to me, typing away. I use the moment to savor the glimpse of his back muscles flexing as he raises his shoulders up and down for relief. If we were girlfriend and boyfriend, I'd be able to give him a massage and relieve some of that tension.

Breezing by him, I head to the break room to celebrate by myself, wishing there was a bottle of champagne around. Instead of popping the bubbly, I pull out my phone and message Sierra that I've submitted my article and how excited I am.

Sierra: *Party on the rooftop tonight!*
Me: *Rooftop?*

Sierra: *It's been too hot out to show you, but tonight we're gonna show you what's so great about our building.*

A second later, a group text comes through with a bunch of numbers I don't have in my phone.

Group Message: *Blanca finished her article. Party tonight on the rooftop.*

Seconds later a stream of messages ping my phone.

Unknown: *I got the beer.*
Rian: *I'll bake a cake.*

Unknown: *Chocolate?*

Rian: *Yes, Dylan, I can do chocolate.*

Unknown: *I'll put in an order for wings.*

Unknown: *Blanca, do you like wings? Are you a spicy girl?*

Unknown: *Or a sweet girl?*

Unknown: *Or a combination of both?*

Sierra: *Slow down there Seth. Let her answer you.*

Me: *Um... whatever is fine. Maybe medium? And thanks Rian for the cake idea but it's not necessary.*

Dylan: *Blanca, don't speak for all of us.*

Unknown: *I'll grab champagne too.*

As the messages keep vibrating my phone in my pocket, I crack open the Diet Coke I brought back from lunch yesterday. Ethan walks in and leans his shoulder against the doorframe.

"Celebrating?" His arms are crossed, and I really like the way it makes his biceps bunch. So much so that I have to clench my thighs a little tighter to relieve the ache between my legs.

I raise my Diet Coke in the air. "Yep."

"It feels good, right?"

I sit down at the table and a long stream of air flows out of me. "It feels amazing."

"I see you're the type who gets the high." He grins and gestures to me.

"I do feel like I could conquer just about anything right now."

He chuckles, grabbing a water he had marked with his name on it. His forearms constrict while he loosens the cap and I watch his Adam's apple bob like I did that night on the train.

"Are you going to your parents this weekend?" The question falls out of me before I can take it back. I probably look really needy right now.

He smiles over the rim of his bottle. Maybe he likes where my mind is headed. After he gulps down another sip, he secures the cap. "Every Sunday. You?"

I nod.

"Maybe we'll catch each other." He shrugs.

Disappointment jabs at me like a stick when it shouldn't.

He owes me nothing. I guess I just thought he might say we can head into the city together and catch the last train back.

I shake my head. What am I thinking? He doesn't want a work relationship. He may flirt a bit here and there and yeah, he brought me a bagel, but that doesn't mean he wants to pursue anything. He's been clear on that.

"Yeah. Maybe."

Mr. Copeland walks by and stops at the break room door. "Got 'em guys, take the rest of the afternoon off."

Ethan pushes off the counter and walks toward the door. "Great. Thanks."

"I'll send edits back this weekend. Get me the final on Monday before noon. We go to print Tuesday and I heard Tina saying something about her cat having to go to the vet."

"Sounds great. Have a great weekend, Phil." Ethan nods and leaves the room without so much as a goodbye or backward glance.

"Come on Blanca, I just told you to leave early on a Friday. Get out of here." Mr. Copeland smiles, his coffee mug nestled in the palm of his hand. I have no idea how he drinks so much coffee and doesn't seem wired for sound. Maybe it's decaf.

"Thanks, Mr. Copeland."

I leave the break room and ignore the pull that wants me to ask Mr. Copeland if he's looked over my article yet. Did he see anything glaring that needs to be changed? Dom told me not to let my insecurity shine. "Have a great weekend." I smile and wave, turning down the hall.

"You too, Blanca."

I duck into my cubicle, shutting down my computer and packing up all my stuff. When I'm ready to leave I look over the partition to say goodbye to Ethan, but his cubicle is empty. My shoulders slump and I hate the disappointment I feel.

Walking down the hall, I pull my phone out to read the texts in the group chat that's now turned into Dylan and Knox arguing about some game that's going to be on while Sierra tells them that there is no way they are bringing an iPad up on the roof to watch the game. Rian is asking Dylan what type of frosting he'd like, and I want to mention that it's supposed to be my cake, so stop catering to the guy. But it's none of my business.

I reach the reception area to find Ethan there, standing at Mandy's desk, chatting with her. She laughs at something he said.

"Have a great weekend, Blanca," Mandy says over her infectious laughter and waves at me.

"You too. Bye." I wave to both of them.

Ethan glances at me briefly but continues his conversation with Mandy. Walking out of our glass doors, I press the elevator button, my gaze flickering to the two of them. Of course he's all smiles and Mr. personality with Mandy—she's twenty-three with an incredible rack.

Shit. I can't do that. It's not her fault he has an interest in her.

The elevator doors open and thankfully there's no one else in there.

I press the number one on the elevator panel and lean back on the metal wall, eyes closed while the doors close.

I hear something and when I open my eyes, the doors are parting, and Ethan joins me in the elevator.

"Hey," he says all casual and suave like he hasn't been giving me whiplash with his attitude toward me all day.

"Hi."

The doors shut and all I hear is a thud as his bag hits the floor right before my back is pressed harder to the cool metal and Ethan's hands cup my cheeks. He presses his lips to mine and his tongue slides into my mouth. I make a sound of surprise and easily give into the kiss as his body presses to mine and the feel of his hard length hits my stomach. Too soon he pulls away.

"I'm sorry. I just… I was trying so hard to not do this," he murmurs before his lips capture mine again in a frenzy. He slows his rhythm, his tongue now sliding effortlessly along mine, his fingers sliding into my hair. My nipples pebble in my bra and I push my chest into his, demanding more friction.

I feel him pulling away before he fully steps back, his lips the last part of him to leave my body. He runs a hand through his hair and adjusts his length while I catch my breath.

"Sorry. I shouldn't have done that. It's the high."

"High?" I'm still flustered, and I can't make sense of his words.

"The high from turning in an article." He steps backward until he's on the opposite side of the elevator from me. "Shit. I should've asked you first."

I shake my head. "No. I liked it."

The elevator reaches the first floor with a bounce and I can feel the energy shift in the small space before he even opens his mouth to speak. The doors open with a ding.

"I'm sorry, Blanca. I never should've done that. You know my rule," he mumbles and bolts from the elevator without another word.

By the time I'm in the lobby of our building there's no sign of him anywhere. I put on my sunglasses with the hope that they disguise how upset I am.

Why does he have to be such a good kisser? If he'd been bad, at least I wouldn't still want him.

∾

Sierra leads me up the stairway that will take us to the roof while Rian carries the cake behind us.

We push through the door that says 'Roof Access' and there sits Dylan and Seth on a set of lawn chairs with a table between them. Sierra plugs a cord into the wall and a string of lights come to life around us. A view of Cliffton Heights at twilight spreads out around us and the sunset in the far distance that paints the sky in shades of orange, yellow, and amber steals my breath.

Despite a confusing end to my workday, a feeling of bliss and rightness wraps around me. I'm where I'm supposed to be.

"Congratulations!" Seth and Dylan say in unison, standing from their chairs and deserting their beers on the table.

They each come and give me a tight hug. I'm grateful that they've enveloped me in their friends group so easily. I needed this with the crossroads I'm at in my life right now. Good friends, new job, and new town.

"Thank you all so much," I say.

Rian puts the cake down and Dylan swipes his finger along the frosting.

"Dylan," Rian says without any fight in her voice. She really needs to stop putting him up on some pedestal like he's too good for her.

Seth sits down and kicks a chair out. "Take a load off."

I sit down and Seth puts a wine glass in front of me, pouring a glass of rosé that he got from the cooler at his feet.

"Do you guys always hang out up here?" I ask.

"When the weather's nice. Fall and spring nights are the best," Seth says.

"It can get really hot up here in the summer during the afternoon, but this time of day is nice," Sierra says, holding her glass out for Seth. He finishes pouring mine and then pours hers.

"Always with the glass half empty." Seth rolls his eyes at her.

"Whatever, bagel boy." Sierra takes the seat across from me, leaving the one next to me open for Rian to take since it's the closest to Dylan. Seth can say what he wants, but Sierra's always been a good friend.

"Bagel boy?" I ask, not understanding the reference.

"Seth's parents own Andrews Bagel Co." Dylan nods at his friend.

"Shut up!" I hit Seth square in the arm. He sits back, rubbing the spot I hit. "Oh… sorry. Three brothers."

"Did they make you lift weights with them? I'm embarrassed to say it kind of hurt." He continues to rub at his arm.

Dylan laughs. "He's a wimp."

"Have her hit you." Seth nudges me.

"Don't worry, eventually she will." Sierra smiles over the rim of her wine glass.

"Why the excitement about Andrews Bagel Co.?" Rian changes the topic.

"Oh." I set my wine down. "The guy from work… he brought me a bagel today from Andrews Bagel Co. and it's funny because I'd brought him one from The Bagel Place."

Seth's hand slams down on the table. "I'm sorry, you did what? You went to The Bagel Place?"

"Bad move, Blanca," Dylan says, humor lighting in his eyes.

"Why?" I look between the two of them, confused.

"They're his arch nemesis." Sierra laughs and Seth shoots her a glare that would cause a younger person to whither.

"The families have an on-going feud," Dylan explains. "The only bagels around here are Andrews Bagel Co. bagels."

Seth clears his throat. "Because ours are ten times better than The Bagel Place."

"Okay, so only Andrews Bagel Co. from today on." I put my hands up in front of me in a placating gesture.

"Glad we've come to an understanding." Seth leans back in his chair and sips his beer. "Your work crush sounds like he's a winner though." He winks.

"Because he eats your family's bagels?" Sierra asks.

Seth sets his gaze on her. "Yes. That's enough in my book."

"I'm not sure your opinion matters," Sierra says with a smirk.

Dylan's phone rings and he pulls it out, silencing it immediately.

"The shop?" Rian asks.

Dylan shakes his head and he gives her a look that says drop the subject. Both of their attention flickers to Sierra for a moment, so I can only assume it must be Sigmund since Dylan and Sierra's ex are still friends.

"PIZZA!" Knox walks out onto the roof with a stack of pizza boxes.

For the rest of the night, I find out a lot more about my new group of friends—Dylan really can consume half a cake all by himself and Rian's eyes fill with hearts watching him do so. Seth is a man's man even with him saying me hitting him hurt, and he and Sierra might bicker, but they're close as evidenced when they team up against Knox and me in a game of beer pong.

By the time the sun is completely set and darkness fills the sky along with stars, I'm exhausted from my first week in a new place.

"We're heading out. Anyone wanna join us?" Dylan asks.

Knox has the empty pizza boxes in his arms.

"Nah, I'm done for tonight." Sierra sits down next to me

in the chair, leaning her head on my shoulder. I swear I see relief on his face after she speaks.

I decide to follow the guys down to get another bottle of rosé, and they stop me outside my apartment door. Dylan places his hand on my back.

"Hey, we're going out with Sigmund. Can you maybe keep Sierra in for tonight? I mean, Cliffton Heights is too small for us not to run in to each other at the few places open at this hour. And I'm not in the mood for a fight."

I nod. "I don't think she wants to go anywhere."

Seth and Knox eye one another. "I thought you guys were friends. Sierra gets a second wind eventually. She's never down for the count," Seth says and Knox nods in agreement.

"Okay, I'll try my best." I open the apartment door.

"One day I'd love for you to meet Sig. I think the two of you would get along great." Dylan leans over and gives me a hug and the other two guys follow suit. They're lucky I'm Italian and used to affection.

"Well, he's already been clearly marked off limits." I chuckle.

Dylan nods. "I'm talking about a friendship."

I shake my head. "Have a great night guys."

"You too."

I enter the apartment, grab the bottle of rosé and I rush back to the rooftop where Sierra's put on a 90s playlist and is now dancing.

Rian looks over at me. "Sierra has her second wind."

I sit down next to Rian, pouring her a glass. "I've been warned to keep her in."

"I figured," Rian says. "I'm glad you moved here." She smiles at me and a warm feeling heats my chest.

I return her smile. "Me too."

We lean back in our chairs and watch Sierra dance around enjoying life. I haven't been this happy in a long time.

CHAPTER ELEVEN

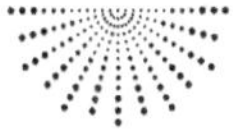

Ethan

$\mathcal{I}$ sit on the last bench of the last train leaving the city toward Cliffton Heights. Gil's five rows up and over from me. With my takeout containers next to me, I wait, knowing this is the worst decision I could've made. But for some reason when it comes to Blanca Mancini, I have no restraint.

My dad was unable to join us today, which left me as the only one my mom could play twenty questions with since my sister Kori said she had a project at work she couldn't get away from.

I check my watch. Just as I close my eyes thinking Blanca must've took an earlier train, the doors open and my eyes spring open. She's like a vision standing there on the far end of the train. Her smile is immediate as is the pink flush to her cheeks. Why do I love to torture myself?

I watch her closely as she walks down and places a

container next to Gil and continues her way to the bench across from me.

"Are you stalking me, Ethan Ryland?"

"I told you I was, so you shouldn't be surprised."

She laughs and it's the best sound I've heard all day. It's all a bad idea. The fact that she's across from me after another shitty Sunday. Every week I leave my mom's with a mix of knotted up emotions I can't unravel. Now two weeks in a row she's like an angel who makes me forget all the shit I'm leaving behind for another seven days.

"It's sick that I hoped I'd find you here. What does that say about me?" she asks.

I get up from my seat, leaving my food and bag, sitting down next to her. "That you can't get that kiss out of your head."

"Ethan," she sighs and stares out the window.

The train jolts and starts moving down the track. More tension leaves my body as the distance grows between my past and my future.

The expression on Blanca's face looks pained when she glances over at me.

"What?"

"This." She waves her finger between us. "The hot and cold."

"I wasn't aware there was any cold."

She raises her eyebrows. "Really? You gave me the cold shoulder Friday afternoon, then kissed me breathless and ran out of the elevator? I'd say that's the definition of hot and cold."

Of course, she's right. But the high of finishing an article is nothing to joke around about. I always want to party and celebrate, but Friday afternoon, I wanted to throw Blanca over my shoulder, drag her to my apartment, and fuck her six ways to Sunday. Because she would be the ultimate celebration.

"I'm sorry. I'm not mature when it comes to my feelings."

She laughs because she gets my humor. Although there's always some truth inside a joke. "Seriously, what's your plan here?"

I shrug. "I like you."

She sighs.

"Do you like me?" I ask.

"Are you sure you don't want to pass me a note where I check off yes or no?"

I reach over to my bench and grab the tortilla espanola I made. "Here."

"You're dodging the question with food?"

"I am."

She breaks off a piece and holds it over her open palm, bringing it to her mouth. "Umm."

"You like it?"

She swallows. "I do." Then her eyes grow wide. "Oh, I'm sorry do those two words make you itch?"

I stare blankly at her and shake my head. "Not at all. If you hadn't shown up Monday morning at my office, I guarantee you I'd be offering to put more in your mouth than my espanola right now."

Her gaze turns heated and I notice the way she pushes her legs together. "I'm wondering how long you can hold out."

I shift in my seat in an attempt to make room for the blood rushing to my dick. My head falls back to the seat and I inhale a deep breath.

Blanca busies herself getting her leftovers out. "I cut the chicken parmesan into small bites and I brought you a fork." She passes me over a plastic fork. "Disclaimer, I had nothing to do with this meal."

"Didn't let your brother ruin it?"

Her jaw ticks. "No."

I fork a piece of chicken and eat it. It's so delicious it makes me want to cook Italian. I've only ever really cooked Spanish or American food. "It's delicious."

"Maybe one Sunday you could come to my parent's house. They live in Carroll Gardens. Where are you from?"

I stall until I realize she's not going to let me not answer. "Mont Haven."

"Bronx." She doesn't have the same tone to her voice most do when I tell them. Not like I tell many people though. The only person who really knows where I'm from is Dylan and that's only because he met me the first day of freshman orientation.

"And your family? You never really mention them."

"My mom loves my caramel chocolate chip bars." I grab the container and open it for her. "Try one."

Her mouth hangs open and she takes one like she's trying to dodge the stickiness of the caramel. I'd lick the remnants off her finger if she were mine. Placing it on her tongue, her mouth closes and her eyes light up as she chews and swallows. "Have you ever thought of being a baker?"

"Nah, I learned because sweets made my mom and sister happy when I was younger."

She lets the topic go and doesn't pry for more information. Blanca's polite and understands my need for privacy and I feel bad that I've left her in limbo like she said. Taking her on a date that I said wasn't a date, then bringing her bagel, flirting with her non-stop, kissing her in the elevator and bolting afterward.

I place my hand on her knee and she twitches at first, then relaxes, staring up at me with those doe eyes. What I have to tell her might not even register because she's lived a happy childhood.

"It's not fair what I've been doing and I'm sorry."

Her lips tip down in the corner. "Maybe we should draw the line now?"

"Like either friends or more?"

"I'm guessing since you have such a problem dating a co-worker, we're going with the friends side of that offer."

Since when did the word friend sound like she should put money in the swear jar after saying it?

"I really like you," I say, like that's going to make this any easier.

"So you've said." Her tone isn't anything like it usually is. Her flirtatiousness has dimmed significantly. She's mad, I think. "It's fine. Honestly."

"PEEKSKIL!" the train conductor announces, and Gil stands up, staring at both the Tupperware containers, confused. He raises them in the air, leaves the train and stumbles down the platform.

Once we're alone, any resolve I had vanishes. "This is a hard decision for me to make. You have no idea the amount of sleep I've lost over it."

She nods, but she's looking anywhere but at me.

"Blanca, please understand," I plead.

Finally, her gaze meets mine. "What exactly do you want from me? To tell you I'm cool with being in limbo? Give you permission to kiss me whenever the mood strikes you and then run away scared?"

"Scared?"

"Yes, you're scared. Over what, I have no idea, but I just wish the back and forth would end. Either you want to pursue this with me, or you don't."

Shit, I wish that fight inside of her didn't do it for me the way it does.

"I didn't want to kiss you," I say.

Her face drops. She moves to grab her stuff and her hip hits mine to slide out, but I dig my feet into the floor.

"I didn't mean it like that." I run my hand over the back of my neck and pull to relieve the blockage that is obviously stopping the oxygen from hitting my brain and allowing me to form a proper thought.

"You're batting a thousand tonight. Let me save you some time. I'll go sit up front and you can stay here. We'll get off at Cliffton Heights and I promise you tomorrow morning I'll only be your co-worker."

Here we go. This is like Sierra all over again.

I slide out of the bench and go to my side. Just like she promised, she takes her bags and leaves. As if she can't even stand to be in my car, she gets up and goes to another car.

When Todd walks through, he raises both eyebrows at me. "What did you do?"

"Nothing."

He sits down and I open up the caramel bars for him. He takes one and leans back in the seat. "Come on. You guys were going to be the story I tell my grandkids. The two strangers who met on a train."

I blow out a breath. It's not like I have anyone else to talk to about this. Dylan says nail her. Seth says don't. If my mom found out, she would get all hopeful.

"Turns out we work together."

"So?"

"I can't date someone I work with."

His eyebrows move together. "Against company policy?"

I don't even know if it is. Knowing Phil, it's not. He'd probably go get ordained online so he could marry us. "I'm not sure but that's not it."

"Then what is it?"

We're almost at Cliffton Heights so I get my bags together. "It'll end in disaster."

"Have you had a work relationship before?"

"No."

"Then how do you know?" He steals another bar and I put the lid back on and pass the container to him. "The kids will love these."

"How many relationships do you know that turn out well? Plus, it'll make me weak."

He chokes on his cookie from laughing. "Weak?"

"Yeah, you know because I'll worry about how I look in her eyes. It'll compromise my craft, change me."

He blinks a few times like he can't process my words. "Are you different at work?"

"A little. I like to keep a distance between me and them."

"Them being your co-workers?"

"Yeah."

"So, your co-workers are the enemy?"

"No." I stop and consider what he's asking. "I just mean… if they see my weakness they might use it against me."

"Like an enemy would." Todd chuckles.

"You're ridiculous. That's not what I'm saying."

"If you view your co-workers as enemies then you view her as an enemy and maybe that's what's really going on here."

"I just said you have it wrong. Quit with the enemy thing."

He laughs and I stand to get off, seeing her through the train windows.

Todd stands right behind me. "It's a shame. From the way you look at her whether you pursue a relationship or not, I'm pretty sure your work relationship is already affected. Even though you might try to, you can't control who you're attracted to." He clasps my shoulder. "And you and that girl are like magnets right now, sooner or later, the draw is going to be too powerful and you'll come together. Work or not."

The doors open and I spot her rush out of the train car ahead. I say goodbye to Todd and walk down the steps.

Todd's words trigger something in me. He's right that

work has already changed because she's there every day and I seem to have no control over my feelings for her. Isn't it best to play your hand before the opponent does? I need to get a handle on this before it spins out of control.

"Blanca!" I call out and she turns to face me. I'm surprised that I didn't have to chase her.

"Yes, Ethan?"

I walk until I'm right in front of her. "Have dinner with me? After the article publishes. We'll celebrate." My hand itches to grab hers, but I refrain from not going too fast.

"Are you asking me out on a date or another *work meeting?*"

My shoulder deflate. "A date to celebrate our work success."

"That's pretty ambiguous."

I blow out a breath and when I look back at her, she's smiling. "A date. Blanca, go on a date with me."

"I'd love to. Thanks for asking." She swivels on her heels and walks away.

I watch her for a few moments before my phone rings in my pocket.

"Hey, Mom," I say.

"You're home?"

"Yeah, I'm home." I walk in the opposite direction as Blanca no matter how bad I want to be walking beside her.

CHAPTER TWELVE

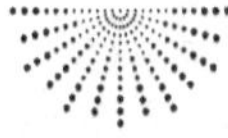

Blanca

I'm sitting at my desk on Friday. The articles go up online at eleven and my heart beats like I just hopped off the bike in the middle of a cycling class.

"D day."

I swivel my chair to find Ethan standing behind me with his cocky stance that gets me hot and bothered on display. "I'm nauseous."

He chuckles and situates himself where he usually does, sliding his ass along the top of my two drawer filing cabinet, his legs hanging in front of him. He tosses an apple from hand to hand before taking one big bite out of it. "Relax," he speaks over a mouthful of apple. "It's your first."

"What does that mean?"

"You'll get used to the nerves." He bites another hunk of apple off, chewing non-stop.

"You sure about that?"

He laughs and follows my vision to the apple in his hand. "Well, I'm not nauseous."

"I'd rather be nauseous than eat my weight in food because I'm anxious." I tap my pen on my desk and lift my cell phone off the table to check the time.

"Comments won't start for a while. We won't know anything until later." The sound of him biting another huge bite of apple rings through my cubicle.

I say nothing in response to his comment. The man hasn't mentioned anything about us going to dinner since Sunday night after we got off the train.

We sit in silence except while he continues to eat his apple. I grow more and more annoyed with his cavalier attitude about dating me. I told myself that when I got involved with someone, I would be that person's number one. It's probably because I witnessed my brothers fall down on the sword of love. They'd do just about anything for the women in their life. This half-assed approach of Ethan's isn't working for me.

The sound of his feet landing on the ground alerts me that he's probably leaving. I refuse to turn around. At this point I'm embarrassing myself by openly throwing myself at him.

His fingers slide into my field of vision, pushing a piece of paper across my desk. I keep my eyes on my computer screen.

"I'll check back in a little bit, but don't sweat it. Everyone gets a pass on their first article."

A strangling sound echoes out of me. He finally leaves my cubicle, allowing me to breathe.

I pick up the piece of paper to find a scrawl of male handwriting on the note.

Come to my house so I can cook a hot meal for you.

Seven o'clock
726 Copperton, Apt 3D

I slowly fold the piece of paper back into a rectangle and tap it on my desk.

Two voices battle inside my head. Or more like my libido and my 'I am woman hear me roar' voice. My libido says this is it—dinner at his apartment means sex will happen. The 'I am woman' voice says that he should be wining and dining me. He should have followed up with me days earlier, not the day of.

My phone dings a second later.

Ethan: *Please.*

Does he know he's doing wrong expecting me to come? Another ding sounds and I quickly silence my phone.

Ethan: *Do you want me to beg? Because I will.*

Then a whole slew of messages come through.

Ethan: *I promise the dessert alone will be worth it.*

Ethan: *That's not some sleazy come on either. By dessert I mean a chocolate ganache pie.*

Ethan: *No expectations. I'll walk you home after dinner.*

Ethan: *I just want some time alone with you. No distractions. Just you and me.*

I finally decide to respond.

Me: *Yes. I'll come, but that ganache better be worth it.*

His chuckle echoes over the partition between our cubicles.

"It will be," he says and I place my phone down.

When I notice the time on the computer screen, I realize that the article went live as we were having our little exchange.

My first line of business is to see how Ethan's article went. Taking the opposing side of mine, I'm not surprised by the fact he's weighing in heavy on the taboo part. But to suggest that it's a high people chase makes me take pause for a second.

Is that what intrigues me about possibly dating Ethan? I realize that I don't even know if I'd be Ethan's first co-worker romance. My eyes scroll, not reading as deep into the article as I should. It's then I spot his admission.

"I've never had a work relationship, nor did I ever think I would. Which leaves the most important question of this article. How important is finding the one? Does it hold more weight than financial security? Because if you cross the line once, you must prepare yourself for the consequences and statistics aren't on your side. One survey noted below said half of all Americans have had a workplace romance when only fourteen percent made it down the aisle. Add on the national divorce rate and do I really need to say more? The workplace is not where you should be looking for your happily ever after."

I lean back in my chair, my limbs heavy with annoyance. Annoyance because of his facts which I'll reluctantly admit have a good point.

His cologne fills my cubicle and a dark shadow falls over my desk.

"Good article," he says, not coming any closer.

I swivel my chair around. "Thanks. You too."

"I think your points hold a lot of weight." He leans his shoulder against the cubicle wall and I half wonder why he's not taking his usual spot on the filing cabinet.

"I don't have nearly the statistics you have."

A cocky grin splashes on his face. "So you agree with me now after a few statistics?"

"Did I say that?"

"Statistics are used to prove theories."

"So let me get this right. You write this article with all these facts..." I put facts in quotation marks with my fingers. "But then I get this on my desk." I hold up the piece of paper with his address.

His grin grows so wide the indent from his dimple could fit a half dollar. "I'm not sure what answer you're looking for."

I shrug and my own smile breaks across my face. "I kinda feel like I won."

"Won?" He almost chokes on his own saliva.

"I'm your co-worker and..." I hold up the paper like it's a trophy.

"What can I say? You're worth the risk."

My entire body heats and my stomach flips and flops like a gymnast doing her final trick for the judges after a perfect routine.

Mr. Copeland appears and stops at the edge of my cubicle, leaving Ethan no choice but to fill the small space. Cassie isn't far behind with her usual wad of gum cracking and popping. I shouldn't love being this close to Ethan, but the crispness of his cologne puts all my lady parts on high alert.

"Love it, you two. The comments are flooding in, shares, mentions. I think we have something here. Meet me in the conference room at two to discuss what direction we need to go. We can't let this go to waste."

He knocks on the top of my cubicle and disappears down the hall without either of us even answering.

Ethan raises his hand and I high five him.

"Way to go with the idea. I say we compare bagel places next issue since you're still going to that awful Bagel Place." His eyes zero in on my coffee cup.

Guilt presses heavy in my chest since I now know they're Seth's family's competitor. "I kind of like the girl there. She's sweet and already has my order memorized."

He tsks. "You're missing out."

I sip my cold coffee just to prove a point. "I dare to be different."

"That you are."

But there is no judgment in his eyes, there's just pure, dare I say it… lust.

LATER IN THE AFTERNOON, we're sitting in the conference room, once again waiting for Mr. Copeland.

"In all seriousness, what are you really thinking for the next issue?" I ask Ethan who's been tapping his pen and swiveling in his chair like a child who can't sit still.

His eyes meet mine like he forgot I was in the room. The guy does nothing for my self-esteem sometimes. His tongue slides out and licks slowly along his bottom lip. "Something controversial. Did you see the comments on our articles?"

"I read a few." I read every single one.

"Did you stop reading once you realized how many people were siding with me?" He smiles and stops tapping his pen.

"You know what they say, people with negative things to say are louder than the positive ones."

"Touché." He bows his head at me. "Still, you owe me lunch next week according to the tally right now."

"I hope you like The Bagel Place." I smack on my biggest smile.

Mr. Copeland and Cassie join us in the boardroom, both taking a seat.

"Great job, you guys. We haven't had this much interaction since you wrote that article about Ethan's ex."

I tilt my head in Ethan's direction and see his jaw clench. Neither of them enlighten me about what article they're speaking of.

"It's a little controversial. You're either for or against. That's why." Ethan picks up his pen and he taps it once on the conference room table.

Mr. Copeland side glances him. "Let's see if you can make magic happen twice in a month. I want your next articles to me by mid-week. And let's continue with topics people will feel strongly about but stay away from politics and religion."

"You should stick with the sex." Cassie pops a bubble.

This is exactly what I was afraid of. I don't want to write heavy topics, but I don't want to write all fluff pieces either. I want to help people with my writing. But I can't argue when Mars And Venus took a chance on me.

"Yes." Mr. Copeland points to his niece. "Everyone loves to talk about the difference between the sexes. So, Ethan you represent the typical male and you the typical female, Blanca. And I'm going to set up a photo shoot for you two. We need a catchy name for your articles too. Think about that this weekend." Mr. Copeland stands, and Cassie joins him. "I'm so excited about this, guys. This might just put our small magazine on the map." He claps once and I jump in my seat.

He leaves and my stomach is a ball of knots.

"Oh relax, it's going to be fine."

"Who said I wasn't fine?" I stand and Ethan slides out his chair from the table.

"You look like you're about to throw up that horrible bagel you ate."

I shake my head.

"So, I say we write about whether you should sleep with someone on the first date?" He raises his eyebrows and slides out of the room before me.

I watch his backside the entire way down the hallway. Who are we kidding? I have a bad feeling Ethan and I are on the same side of that debate which doesn't bode well for tonight.

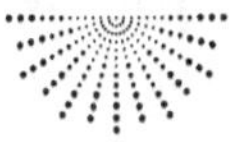

CHAPTER THIRTEEN

Ethan

My phone rings the minute I walk into my apartment with my bags full of groceries.

Clicking on the speaker and placing it on the counter, I unload the bags in my small kitchen.

"Hey Mom."

"Congratulations. Love the article."

"Thanks."

"The girl who writes beside you. Do you like her?"

My mom wouldn't be my mom if she didn't drill me all the time.

"Yeah."

"She's sweet."

"Sweet? You can tell that by the article she wrote?"

My mom laughs and I'll never grow tired of hearing that sound. It so rarely happened when I was younger. "She takes the side of love over anything else. That's sweet. A tad sheltered and naïve, but sweet."

"She really has no qualms on dating at work. It's... interesting." I unpack the groceries on the counter.

"Oh, you *like* her."

I knew I should've dodged this line of questioning well before my mom could hear it in my voice.

"I like her too much, if you know what I mean."

"Oh, mi Tesoro," she coos her usual endearment for me. "All I want is for you to be happy. You know love comes with ups and downs."

"I haven't done anything to pursue it. She's a co-worker, that's all."

"Okay, you bring her over for dinner if that changes. Food is the way to a woman's heart too, you know."

I blow out a breath and grab my frying pan. There's no way I can be honest with my mom now. She'll get invested and it will break her heart when Blanca and I end. She's had enough heartbreak in her life without me adding to her suffering.

"Yes. I will. How's it going?" I ask, looking to change the subject to anything else.

"Your dad was in a good place today. I think this Sunday will be a good visit."

Anything but that.

"Hey, Mom, I gotta go. Work." Guilt tugs at my insides.

"You need to take that girl out and forget work for a night at least." Little does she know. "See you in a few days. Love you."

"Love you, Mom."

I press end on the phone and lean against the counter for a second.

My entire head has been at war over having Blanca here tonight. She'll be in my space and there's no changing that fact. Every time I walk in, I'll have images to recollect about her on my couch, her in my kitchen and if we're both on the same page, in my bed.

The images of that would haunt me.

It'd be pure torture.

I pick up my ingredients and put them in the fridge and tuck the frying pan back under the cabinet.

Protect yourself, my brain screams at me.

Grabbing my phone, I type out a quick text message.

A minute later I get the answer I assumed I would. She's fine with the change of plans. Ignoring my blue balls that say I'm fucking this up, I head to the shower and wash away any doubts.

I sit in the exact same spot I did weeks ago.

"It's like déjà vu," Blanca says, taking her purse off and hanging it off the bar height chair before sliding into it next to me. She's wearing fitted skinny jeans and a loose-fitting shirt tonight and all I can fixate on are the shape of her legs crossing over one another.

"Sorry for the change of plans."

She shrugs. "I'm used to the noncommittal with you."

I swivel on my bar stool, abandoning my beer. "I'm sorry."

She nods but I can tell she doesn't truly believe me. I wouldn't either if I was her.

"Why did you come?" I ask because if I was her, I wouldn't have. I would have told me to fuck off and walked in the opposite direction.

"I like you." She says it simply as if there isn't much else to know.

The bartender comes over, a different one from the other night, but Blanca orders the same drink. This time she orders her dinner immediately and looks at me for me to order mine.

"Tacos," I say, and Blanca shakes her head, laughing to herself.

After the bartender leaves, I grab my beer again. "Did you expect for me to change our plans tonight?"

She shrugs one shoulder, her eyes watching the bartender prepare her margarita. "I think you're a nice guy, Ethan. Confused and unsure of what you want right now. But we're co-workers and Phil Copeland obviously wants us to work closely on this whole opposing views thing, so we have to get along."

"And that's why you're here? To have a cordial work relationship?"

It shouldn't feel like a knife to the gut. I felt we shared something special. Something I've never had with anyone else. But I've been the one trying to cool things off, so I shouldn't care if that's the only reason she's here. Shouldn't, but I do.

She laughs, accepting her margarita from the bartender who has eyed her chest one too many times for my liking. "Not at first. I'll be honest because I'm not a bullshit or play games kind of person. That first night on the train I was..." Her eyes meet mine. "I really liked you. I felt this pull. When I walked into work on my first Monday morning and there you were, I thought it was a sign and I am not a person who believes in fate or kismet or anything. Then you asked me out only for me to find out it was a work thing, not a romantic date because you don't believe in dating your co-workers. Which I understood. Then you ask me out last week but say nothing about it until today. You were going to cook for me but now we're back at the taco place. And to think they say women are confusing. So at this point in our" —she waggles her finger back and forth between us— "whatever we are, I figure work friends will have to do since I don't see either one of us going anywhere soon."

I stare at her blankly. When she lays it all out like that I realized I've been a bigger ass than I thought. I wonder if Sierra was telling the truth when she said I changed my mind too much. When she'd pry into my business to try and find out *what demons I was hiding that caused me to function like an irregular human.* Her words exactly.

"Fuck." I run a hand through my hair. "I've completely fucked this thing up."

She chuckles, sipping her margarita, showing how different she is than any other girl I've ever dated. "We can be great co-workers."

"I can't be your co-worker." The words leave my lips in a rush before I can think better of it and I realize how true they are now that I've spoken them out loud.

She leans toward me like she has to tell me a secret. "Hate to break it to you, but you don't have much choice on that one."

"What I mean is that I think about you naked every time I see you. I imagine having sex with you everywhere in my apartment, on every surface. The whole reason for bringing you here was so that wouldn't happen. Fuck. I don't know what I'm doing. I've royally screwed this up."

Our dinner arrives and she unwraps her silverware calmly. At first glance, I didn't think my words affected her, but then I notice the flush in her cheeks. Her tongue slides out and she licks her bottom lip, right before biting down on it and inhaling a deep breath. Maybe I haven't screwed this up... yet.

"You know how attracted I am to you, right?" I ask.

She side glances me.

"I'm sorry for being an ass these past few weeks, but I do want you. Don't question that. If we didn't work together—"

"Yeah, yeah, we'd already be dating. Heard that line already." She bites into her taco and chews aggressively. "Let's just stop the whole back and forth thing and remain co-workers who are friends."

"We could, but I'll never survive."

She rolls her eyes. "I'm just going to enjoy my tacos once again. Do we get to go to Scrumptuals again too?"

Her sarcastic tone says I haven't lost this round yet. She's pushing me on purpose.

"Blanca?"

She wipes her face and places her napkin on her lap. "So tell me? How do you see this working?" she asks. "Because I can't figure out what you want."

"What working?" I take a bite of my taco, which is delicious.

"This pull between business and pleasure and the fact that you don't mix them."

I wipe my mouth and look to her to decipher her meaning. "I don't."

She huffs. "Do you want to talk articles?"

I shake my head. "Blanca?"

She leans forward. "Ethan," she whispers, a small grin on her face.

"Check please." I raise my hand and Blanca laughs, our gazes never leaving one another's.

I'm probably a moron for allowing my dick to win this war. We both worked too hard for this job.

She slides off of her stool, putting her purse crosswise over her chest so the strap indents right between her tits. Yeah, like her article pointed out so well, co-workers fuck all the time and nothing bad happens, right?

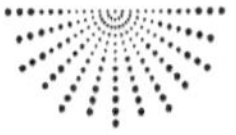

CHAPTER FOURTEEN

Blanca

 've never been a forward girl. Yeah, I know what you're thinking. But I just practically put my hand on a guy's crotch and said let's go back to your place. But truth is, I never do this. Not that I'm against a woman taking what she wants when she wants, but having three older brothers made me nervous of word getting back to them.

This time it won't get back. Because my protective brothers don't know anyone in Cliffton Heights.

Ethan's hand slides into mine when we step out of Las Tacos, clenching to signal for us to start walking together.

There's no conversation during the walk to his apartment, but there's a stirring between us, a silent bomb that ticks the seconds as if we can't reach his place fast enough before it explodes.

He releases my hand to slide his into his pocket,

retrieving a set of keys. When he opens up the building's door, I walk through the double doors first, him behind me.

"Up the stairs. Third floor," he says to my back.

I step first but he matches me step for step and when I reach the top floor, he instructs me again, "To the right. Three-twenty-one."

I turn and his footsteps sound behind mine.

My heart beats fast and my stomach turns as I wait for him to open his apartment door.

A warning flashes in my head once he's unlocked his door. I'm asking for disaster. He's my co-worker. A job I've been wanting forever and I'm chancing it for what might be just one-night?

But he pushes the door open and holds his hand out, a flirty grin on his lips, his right dimple on display. He doesn't seem like a one-night kind of guy. He could be my one and only right? Now I know I'm talking myself into this since I'm not sure how I feel about soul mates.

I accept his hand and step over the threshold into his space, unsure what I just signed up for—one night of good times or something more?

He shuts the door behind me and steps forward, pressing my back to the wall, his hand warm on my neck. "Are you positive, Blanca?" His tongue slides out and tastes my lips like he knows my answer.

Who am I kidding? I know my answer.

"Yes," I whisper and his head dips.

I wait to see stars or to feel dizzy before his lips reach mine. A guy who makes you clench your thighs because he puts everything into his kiss. But there's no explosion because he draws back and his thumb traces my bottom lip.

"I need the job," he whispers.

"Me too."

"Are we crazy?" His thumb continues to slowly run along

my lip and his gaze dips to watch his movements before bouncing back up to my eyes. "I'd do about anything to kiss you right now."

"Except lose your job." I place my hand on his wrist, but his thumb still doesn't stop.

He nods.

"I shouldn't have come onto you so strong." This close I can see his unique hazel eyes, brownish with a hint of green and sparkles of gold.

His thumb stops. "Please don't think that. I love the fact that you're so forward. All I can think about right now is picking you up and tossing you on my bed, if only for a moment to see how perfect it'd feel to have you there. To strip off your dress and see your body. To know if it's how I imagined it. Christ, the idea of the warmth of your skin on mine... but..."

A deep sense of loss claws at my insides. "Ethan," I interrupt his thoughts. "What if this thing never goes away? I can't work if us sleeping together screws it up and I can't work if I'm always thinking about us sleeping together. It's a lose-lose battle."

I hope I'm not coming off like some needy girl. I do want him, and I understand the repercussions of what we're doing.

He stares at me, long and hard. "I guess it's settled." His hand runs along my neck until he sinks his fingers into my dark hair. My eyes drift closed, and he steps forward, pressing into me. "Walk over the cliff with me?"

I pop my eyes open and he's right there, as though he's been waiting for me and he didn't almost cut this off a minute ago.

"I think it's more like jumping, but..."

"Blanca." Will my name always fall of his tongue as though he's tortured? "Time to stop talking."

And then it happens.

His mouth lands on mine, hard like he's taking this moment before he doesn't have the option not to. The low groan from his throat only spurs another round of tension between my thighs.

The kiss is everything I expected. Starbursts fill my vision from behind my closed eyelids and everything in my body says I made the right decision because this will be a night I'll never forget.

His hands are magical and scarily talented as they run along my body, never breaking our kiss. "You're so damn beautiful," he says between kisses. "And a great kisser."

All I have time to do is smile before his lips come down on mine again, his hot wet tongue sliding into my mouth. He kisses like he banters. A little bit of flirting and teasing with a heavy dose of swagger that some might misinterpret as arrogance. Most of all, he kisses like he has us under control. That I shouldn't worry because he knows the terrain and will get us where we need to go safely.

I allow my jumbled thoughts to drift away as quickly as he's gotten my blouse to fall to the floor. My hands search out his hot stomach. Sliding up his button-down shirt, my fingers search his warm rippled abdomen while his finger slides under my bra strap, lowering it off my shoulder.

His eyes trace the movement and he swallows, his Adam's apple bobbing.

The pressure builds and spreads through my limbs watching him admire my body. I help him by sliding my arm out and he works on the other side. The quiet rush of passion surrounds us as he takes his time to commit me to memory.

Once I'm free of the other strap, he steps closer again, his body perfectly molding to mine. Without effort, he undoes my bra and it drops and catches between us as his lips take mine.

"You have too many clothes on," I tell him between kisses.

He freezes, draws back, and puts his arms out. My bra falls to the floor and his gaze fixates on my bare breasts, a scorching heat in his eyes. "I'm all yours."

I lick my bottom lip, stepping forward to reach him again.

He puts up his finger to stop me when I'm only a couple of inches away. "First, you strip for me?"

"I'm already topless."

His eyes travel down to my jeans.

I smile as my fingers linger on the button of my jeans. "What do you say, Mr. Ryland?"

"Please, with sugar on top?"

I laugh and flick open the button of my jeans, turning around to face the door.

"I feel like I should be sitting down for this." His voice is low and husky.

I peek over my shoulder to see him unbuttoning his pants.

"I thought that was my job." I pout and his dimple makes an appearance, boosting my ego.

Hooking my fingers into the waist of my jeans, I shimmy them down my legs. As I continue to study his reaction, his dimple disappears and his jaw tenses when I step out of my pants.

"Happy?"

"I see one more thing that has to go." He nods toward my underwear.

I approach him wearing only my panties. My fingers finding the buttons on his shirt and I make quick work of them. Soon our stomachs are touching, and it feels divine to feel the heat from his skin seep into me.

"You'll have to do some of the work," I say.

He brushes the loose strands of my hair from my face

while I get his jeans unfastened and pooled at his feet in seconds.

"You're a little too skilled at undressing a guy."

I laugh and feel his hard length pressing to my stomach as I rise on my tiptoes and press my lips to his. "Aren't you going to show me your place?"

He grips my ass and hoists me up with his strong hands. "There's only one room you need to see right now."

He wiggles his way out of his jeans and turns toward the hallway. I can't see anything of his apartment because he anchors his mouth to mine without a breath or intake of air until we're in a space that smells just like him. Lowering me down to my feet, his hands slide under my panties to cup my ass cheek and he presses our bodies together, his lips traveling along my jaw and neck.

I haven't had a ton of partners but none of them have ever kissed and explored my body with such passion before. You'd think he's a virgin and I'm his first partner from the way he appears to be hanging on by a thread. His lips are never more than a millimeter away from me and his hands are in search of any inch of my body he's yet to touch.

We fall onto the mattress, which is Ethan's most uncoordinated move tonight. He fixes that by rolling over me with the suaveness of a man who knows how to seduce a woman.

His thigh separates my legs just as his lips find mine again. Our tongues are more frantic as he situates himself between my thighs and grinds his hard length against my core.

"Ethan," I say in between a pant and a beg, my thighs clenching around him, wanting to trap him there forever.

His finger runs down the length of my face. "I know." He thrusts again and my hand reaches between us, palming him over the cotton of his boxer briefs as a way to stop the torture.

He raises his hips and props himself up on his elbows, staring down at me, granting me permission to run the show. Sliding my hand off his package, he groans but I push under the elastic band of his boxer briefs and he's hot and heavy in my hand.

"Jesus… Blanca." Those gold flecks in his eyes light up. "That feels so good."

Turning to his side, I mimic his movement so we're facing one another, and he watches intently while I glide my hand up and down his hard length. Callused fingers sneak under the elastic of my panties, delving into my wetness.

Another exhilarating groan rips out of him. "So wet." His lips press to mine, and I drown in the kiss we're starting to perfect.

He plays me like I'm an instrument, like he's practiced for decades and my hips buck off the mattress. I grip him harder and pump a little faster while he thrusts into my hand. Just as I get a good rhythm down, his hand clamps down on my wrist. "I think we're going to have to call it on that one."

"You don't like?"

"On the contrary, I like it too much."

I giggle but his hand leaves me, and he reaches into his nightstand.

Rolling back over, he kneels in front of me and his fingers dig into each side of my panties, dragging them down my body. He seems to revel in revealing the last part of me to him. Never have I felt more comfortable being naked in front of someone. The heat from his gaze sears my skin.

I return the favor and pull down his boxer briefs. He manages to get them the rest of the way off and drops them behind him.

My mouth waters watching him roll the condom down his length.

"I beat off to this exact scenario the first night we met."

"You mean last night?" I ask, making fun of the short time we've known each other.

His laugh is deep and rumbling. "Yeah. I guess I have no willpower around you."

He rests his weight on his elbows and situates himself between my legs.

"That's okay, me either."

"Good. Because I don't see that changing."

I wrap my arms around his shoulders and spread my knees to make room for him. "Me either."

With a cocky smirk, he pushes into me, inch by inch until I'm completely filled. It's then that I'm certain I'm in real trouble because nothing has ever felt this right.

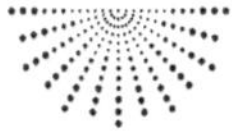

Ethan

I bury my length deep inside her and she clenches around it.

"Ethan," she says as though it takes all her energy to speak.

I get what she means. I have no idea how to explain the feeling that just took over my body. This isn't just a one-time fuck to get each other out of our systems. At least for me, I can't deny what's happening.

I lower my body and lock her head between my forearms, pulling out of her warmth and slowly sliding back in. Her neck cranes back and I take the opportunity to scatter kisses along her jaw.

She's not loud, but she's not quiet either. Every time I shift or explore her body, her moans are scattered like breadcrumbs on an unfamiliar path so that I remember exactly what she likes. I slide my hand up her leg, bringing her ankle up to rest on my shoulder, and a long strangled groan escapes her as I thrust deeper.

"You feel amazing," I say, unable to hold back my thoughts. She could ask me anything right now and I'd be honest because this isn't just sex. Just like that night on the train, this feels different, as cliché as that sounds. And I'm a writer—I hate clichés.

"You too." Her fingernails dig into my shoulder blades and I hammer into her a little harder this time.

For the next ten minutes we vary our positions, all with me on top. When we're both on the brink of ecstasy, I release her legs. She wraps them around my middle, her heels digging into my back.

Brushing away the loose strands of chestnut from her sweaty hairline, I smile down at her right before I capture her lips. She wraps her arms around my neck, anchoring me to her like I'm a life vest.

I'm not going anywhere. If I get anything out of what's happened tonight, it's that work or not, Blanca Mancini is going to be in my life. I'll have to figure it out on my own.

A shudder runs through her and if I'm reading her body correctly, she's about to plunge into ecstasy. The last place I want to be is up in my head about the do's and don'ts of dating a co-worker. I want to commit this to memory.

Our tongues slide together, our hands clench and our bodies tense with the pressure of our impending orgasms. She falls first, her thighs clenching around my middle, her grip firmer and stronger, making sure I go nowhere.

After she whispers incoherent words in my ear, I do the same and lose all control, rutting into her on a groan and holding myself there.

"You're everything," I whisper. "The whole package. Beautiful, funny, sarcastic..." My compliments fall away as my brain grows fuzzy and all I can think of is how great it feels to come inside of her.

Our tense muscles slowly relax, and I roll over beside her.

"I'll be right back." Sliding out of the bed, I head to the bathroom, dispose of my condom in the trash, and wash my hands. "Do you need anything?" I ask while I make my way back to the bed.

She climbs out of bed, grabbing my shirt from off the floor, throwing it over herself. "I can do it."

Of course she can because Blanca might be the most independent woman I've ever dated. I just hope the fact she took my shirt is a sign that she's going to come back to bed because I'm going to want her again in about ten minutes.

Sadly, a few minutes later, she leaves the bathroom and sits down at the foot of the bed.

This is exactly why you shouldn't sleep with someone unless you're both on the same page. I'm guessing we're not.

"Are you hungry?" I ask, using any excuse to keep her here.

She looks at me over her shoulder, her gaze pensive. "Where do we go from here?"

"Well, I thought we'd eat."

Her face grows serious. I knew this about her. I knew she wasn't going to let us explore this without there being some type of classification afterward. Blanca isn't like any other woman I've dated. But that's what's scary about her. She calls me out on my bullshit.

"Then I think I'm going to head out."

"No." I rush to my feet and grab her arm. "Stay."

Our eyes lock and I see it all there. Everything I've been feeling. Blanca is transparent enough for me to see that maybe I'm different to her too.

"Why should I stay?"

"Because I like what we just did, and I want to do it again." I smile but her eyes narrow and her jaw tics.

"Is that what this is? A booty call? Should I call you the next time I'm coming home from the bar at two in the morning so we can fuck?" She strips off my T-shirt and discards it on the bed, grabbing for her underwear and heading out to the living room.

"Blanca," I say, sighing when she shrugs me off.

"No, Ethan. I've given you way too many chances up to this point. I like you but I'm not going to be a fuck buddy or whatever it is you're looking for. I'm a woman who deserves a man to fall on the sword for my love. I deserve to be won over. So I think as great as this was, I should just go before we cause further damage."

I run a hand through my hair, grabbing a pair of track pants out of my drawer, I shrug them on and follow her. She can't be serious. What does she want me to do? Lay it all out there? All my fears. Make myself that vulnerable when we haven't even known one another that long?

"I'm not sure what you want from me?"

She shakes her head as she does up the button to her jeans and then tries to put on one shoe while hopping on the other leg. "Nothing. It's cool if you don't feel what I do. I should've known with the way you've been so hot and cold."

Here we go again with this bullshit. We're co-workers. What does she not get?

"You're seriously just going to walk out of here?"

The hopping method of getting her sandal back on proves difficult so she sits down on the chair to fully unbuckle it. "I've given you way too much of my time and effort at this point. You're playing games and I don't do games. I thought you were just scared. That maybe with time you'd overcome whatever it is that's making you fight this thing between us, but I see now nothing's going to change." She gets one shoe on and tries to slip on the other one.

I steal it away like a fourth grader.

She huffs and holds out her hand. "Give me my shoe."

"No." I hold it tight with both hands.

She stands and I raise it above my head. Am I seriously doing this like we're teenagers flirting or something?

"Fine. I'll go home with one shoe."

My arms fall when her back faces me and her hand is on the doorknob.

"Don't leave," I say.

She slowly turns around, but her hand finds the doorknob once more to tell me that's not enough. That she wants more from me if I really want her to stay here.

"Just…"

I hear the twist of the doorknob in her palm.

Fuck, Ethan, get the words out. Tell her. Don't ruin what might be the one thing you've waited your entire life for.

"Dinner. I owe you a dinner."

Her face falls, all hope disappears from her eyes. She opens the door a crack.

"Blanca."

"It's okay, Ethan. I promise Monday morning will be fine. I won't make it awkward."

I can't imagine not flirting with her. It'd be complete torture to just be her co-worker. I never wanted this, but I can't walk away from it now.

Beelining across the room, I shut the door and cage her back against it. We're chest to chest. "I feel it, okay? I do. And I want you here so I can feed you, fuck you, and cherish you. You're right, I'm terrified because I like you and this thing between us is at a level I've never felt before." I raise my hand to cup her cheek.

Her eyes grow tender and caring after my declaration. "Are you sure?"

I nod. "Just stay. Please."

Her hand comes over mine on her cheek and she nods. "I'll stay."

As a thank you, I bend over and kiss her until we both have no choice but to draw it to a close if we want to breathe. I take her hand and lead her into the kitchen. "I was going to make you Paella. Want to do it together?" I leave her on a stool and open the fridge to grab the ingredients.

"I'd love to."

My time is limited though. I got her to stay, but she wants more from me or at the very least wants me to allow myself to be in this one hundred percent. I know I'm going to have to try harder, I just don't know if I can.

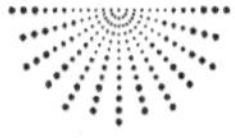

CHAPTER SIXTEEN

Blanca

The fact that I've rarely seen a man in a kitchen is sad, but Mama wasn't always willing to let my dad help us cook. And my brothers are limited as to what they can do. They can roll the meatballs into balls. Mix the seasoning, chop a vegetable. Other than Dom who took it upon himself to learn how to cook after he moved out of our parents' house, but still takes a backseat on Sundays, I've never witnessed a man work his way through the kitchen quite like Ethan.

He opens the fridge and I sit on the stool because I'm not sure I can help him.

He lays out a bunch of ingredients on the counter and pats the spot right next to it. "Actually, come sit here."

"That seems unsanitary." But I don't argue further because it means I'll be closer to him. So I slide up on the counter like he asks and he leans over, kissing me briefly. Good decision on my part.

"I've already done the prepping." He turns to the stove and puts some oil into a big pan, then grabs the plastic container with the marinated chicken.

"Who taught you how to cook? Your mom?"

He glances back as his forearm muscles flex while he uses the tongs to turn the chicken. "A little, but she worked a lot. Being the oldest, it fell into my lap and eventually I couldn't stand the box mac and cheese and frozen dinners anymore."

"Both your parents worked?"

He picks the chicken up off the frying pan and places it in a dish next to the stove, then drops a bunch of spices into the pan. "My dad was unemployed at times but with the stress of finding a job, I took on the responsibility." He shrugs.

"Very cool. My brothers never would've done that."

He places the wooden spoon down on the pan and crosses the short distance in his galley kitchen, leaning in until our lips meet. "Sure they would have. Sometimes it's not a choice."

"Admirable." I lock my legs around his waist.

He laughs. "It'll burn."

"Hmm… I'm not sure what's more important. My stomach being empty or my arms."

"Give me five minutes and then we can have a ten minute break from cooking." He kisses the soft underside of my jaw and slides out of my grasp until he's back at the frying pan. He stirs slowly with one hand while dropping a pile of tomatoes into the pan with the other. I love watching the way he's so attentive and caring with the dish. "Let's talk about those five lunches I won today." He smirks over his shoulder.

My stomach flips and flops. "Oh yes. Just think, if you could've asked for sexual favors."

He drops the rice in and adds some water, putting the lid

on the pot and adjusting the heat before his hands land on my knees. I watch his long fingers graze up my thighs, parting them so he fits between my legs. "We can change it."

"Because it would suit you." I raise an eyebrow.

"You're telling me you'd get no pleasure from sexual favors?"

I move my head side-to-side. "I can't very well hide under your desk and open up your slacks."

He shifts in place. "That's unfair. Now every time I'm at my desk, I'm going to envision you giving me head."

I laugh and his hand moves to the back of my head, his fingers flexing in the strands of my hair. "I'm really happy you're here," he says.

I'm sure my eyes are all dreamy as his mouth lands on mine. Our kiss is slow, relaxed, and easy. We're not fighting for dominance. We're not rushed and it's the most romantic kiss I've experienced in my life.

He backs up and stares at me for a moment. "I'm having a great time."

I bite my lip. "I am too."

"Good. Now wait until you taste my food."

I go to change back into his T-shirt after he says I'm welcome to and for the next twenty minutes or so, I watch Ethan in the kitchen. He brings me a spoon to try the rice before it's all done and from his intent stare, I know how much it means to him that I enjoy his cooking. How could I not? The guy is pretty skilled.

After dinner, he grabs a carton of cookies 'n cream ice cream and two spoons and leads me over to the couch. He positions me so that my ass is right next to him and my legs are draped over his lap.

"Best flavor in the world," I say, digging my spoon into the ice cream.

"One of them."

"What's your favorite? I figured it was this."

"I got this one because it seemed like something you'd like. I'm more of a sorbet guy."

I poke him with my finger. "Sorbet, huh?" His hand falls to his side and he shakes his head. "Sorry. Habit."

"What do you want to watch?" He reaches to the side and grabs the remote.

"Whatever."

He crinkles his eyes. "Gotta love the early stages of a relationship when everyone is so amicable."

"Relationship?" I raise my eyebrows.

He takes my spoon, puts it in the ice cream and I squeal as he gets me on my back. His body weight feels delicious on top of me. His strong legs nudge my thighs to make room for him.

"I told you, I'm all in."

I nod. "I guess you'll have to prove it."

His hands slide up the hem of his shirt that I'm wearing, shivers running up my bare skin. "Oh, I have many ways to prove it." He slides down my body, pushing up the T-shirt as his lips fall to my skin.

My back arches off the sofa and I run my fingers through his hair. The man has a magical mouth and he knows how to use his tongue to drive me crazy.

Peeking up at me right as he gets to the top of my panties, his expression is one of mischief. His finger slides along the top, teasing me and I squirm under his touch.

"I see how you want to play this game. Remember, there's always payback."

He chuckles and hooks his fingers under the sides of my underwear, pulling them down and off, tossing them on the floor.

He glides his hand down my leg and props my knee up on his shoulder. His eyes never leave mine as his lips cast small kisses to the inside of my thigh. "You're beautiful," he says, growing closer to my center.

I hook my other leg over his shoulder then grip the strands of his dark hair, weaving my fingers through just as his tongue twirls around my clit.

I buck up off the couch and his free hand falls to my pelvis to keep me grounded. His teasing eyes meet mine once more and although I can't see his lips, his eyes say he's smiling.

"Ethan," I sigh. His tongue continues a methodical, slow torture around the lips of my pussy. He blows a long stream of warm air on the damp skin and I feel like a million little fireflies lit up around us. My eyes fall shut and I lay my head back onto the arm of the couch. "You're way too talented," I murmur, as all thought processes fall to the wayside.

He gives me nothing but a small groan when I open my legs farther, wanting him right where he is. His tongue explores me like uncharted territory he's claiming as his. It feels so good, almost too good. I'm in sensory overload.

Then his finger circles my opening and my insides clench, wanting him there inside me. A low groan sounds from him while he slowly pushes his finger inside of me. My ass rises off the couch, wanting more of his mouth, more of his fingers, just more of him.

"Watch me," he says. I peek through one slanted eyelid to see his gaze on me. "Watch me devour you. Watch me make you come."

I try to open my eyes and when I do, I have a good view as he pushes another finger inside of me. My orgasm is so close and part of me just wants him to give it to me and the other wants to draw this out forever. He pumps his fingers in and out of me while sucking my clit into his mouth. My hand clings to the edge of the couch, my knuckles whitening under the tension.

I squirm and he pulls back for a moment, allowing me to buck into his hand. Then he buries his face between my legs, his tongue on my clit moving faster, his fingers arching and that's when all my cells explode, releasing all the tension thrumming through my body. Blackness surrounds me as I scream his name.

When I finally open my eyes, Ethan's licking his fingers and crawling up my body. "You're even more gorgeous when you come." His lips land on mine and I pull his pajama pants down. He shows how in shape he is because he holds himself up with one arm to get them off. Taking the back collar of his T-shirt, he throws it over his head and tosses it onto the floor.

"We need a bed," he says. "I can't do what I want to do to you here on this cramped couch." He stands and I immediately miss his weight, but he picks me up in his arms, carrying me to his bedroom.

Seconds later, I'm on my back on his bed and he's crawling over me. Co-workers or not, this is happening.

CHAPTER SEVENTEEN

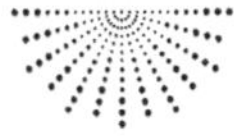

Ethan

Sunday morning, I head down to Andrews Bagel Co. to grab Blanca's bagel, leaving the woman herself in my bed.

"Man, I'm jealous." Seth comes out of the back wearing his apron.

"Of what?"

"Well, let's take inventory... basketball shorts, T-shirt, hair in every direction, sandals, and a smile that says I got some." He grabs my usual bagel and starts putting cream cheese on it. "Is this the girl you were carrying on about the other night?"

I run a hand through my hair. Usually the Andrews hire outside workers on Sunday. It's the one day they take for themselves. It was naive of me to think I could sneak in and out without anyone knowing.

"Guilty as charged. So I need a sesame with chive cream cheese too."

Seth laughs. "She spent the night."

"Maybe."

"You're taking this into relationship territory. Feels like it might be too soon." He busies himself cutting the bagel and spreading the chive cream cheese, continuing to let anyone in the bagel shop know my business since he has the ability of a two-year-old to keep a secret.

"I broke up with Sierra six months ago."

"Hey, I'm just looking out for you."

"I'm good."

"Clearly." He bags the bagels. "Here you go, Romeo."

"Don't be jealous." I take the bag and the two cups of coffee to fill. "Why are you here anyway?"

"An employee bailed. Probably got some like you and didn't wanna get out of bed."

"Whatever."

"When do we get to meet the lucky lady?" He waves off my money, but I slip it in the tip jar.

"In a bit. I want to see where this is going to go before I bombard her with friend introductions. You figure I didn't have that with Sierra and it's like her life became mine and vice versa. I want to take this slow."

Seth nods like he understands. Although, I've never seen Seth in an actual relationship. We call it the curse of three dates. So far no one has made it to a fourth date with him since I've known him. I've heard rumors that there is one girl who made an impression on him, but it was a long time ago and Seth never confirms or denies. I don't pry because it's none of my business. If he wants to tell me, he will.

"Have a happy Sunday." I raise the bag in thanks.

"It won't be half as happy as yours unless she's taken the

walk of shame before you get back." He laughs and calls over the next customer.

As I exit the bagel shop, I wonder why that thought never occurred to me. Why did I not even think she might wake up after I left and think I abandoned her? I didn't even leave a note. It's like we went from strangers to co-workers to lovers to boyfriend and girlfriend in a flash. Because that's how calm I am about us. Like the security of a relationship has already anchored me to her. Which means I'm in deep shit.

I unlock my door and step inside. The apartment is quiet. Scanning the living room and kitchen area, I spot her purse and shoes by the couch. The relief that rushes through me shouldn't surprise me because I was never this invested in Sierra or any other girlfriend this early in the game. It was clear when I met Blanca on the train that she was different, but I never thought she was *my* different. My walls are slowly lowering.

"Hey you." The bathroom door opens, and she stands in the doorway, wearing my T-shirt once again. She's practically lived in that thing for the last two days and I love it.

"I got us bagels."

"Awesome." She walks up to me, raises to her tiptoes, and kisses me like I'm hers.

So no awkwardness even though we'll be leaving each other today. That's good.

"What time do you have to go?"

She searches my small apartment for a clock, finding one on the microwave. "Well, I should get the scent of sex off me, so, I'll head home in a little bit. I have to catch the eleven train."

We sit on the couch and she lifts the lid off her coffee and blows on the steaming liquid which only spurs memories of her mouth on me last night. "Want to ride into the city together?"

A smile starts slowly at the corner of her lips but turns full watt. "Sure."

And just like that, after two days locked in my apartment having sex and eating only for sustenance, we're riding the train together.

Seth is right. This is starting to feel like a relationship already.

HOURS LATER, I'm on the train platform when Blanca walks up. Without missing a beat, her arms wrap around my stomach and our lips find each other's like magnets. I slide my tongue into her waiting mouth, and she steps closer, making our bodies flush to one another.

When the train barrels into the station, I tear my lips off hers and brush her hair back with my pinkie finger. "That's quite the hello."

"What can I say? I missed you after only two hours." She smiles and walks up the stairs to the train, stepping into our usual car and heading to the back.

It's crowded because it's Sunday and a lot of families are heading to the city, so we end up in in the middle of everyone, eyes all around us. She's wearing shorts, so I guess there's no way to hide if my fingers disappeared between her legs.

She slides her arm through mine and leans her head on my shoulder, her mouth close to my ear. "I think we had the same idea."

Her other hand skims over the bulge in my shorts and I shift, looking around to make sure no kid is peeking at us from somewhere.

"I think I wanna go back to my place."

She giggles and her fingers tease me, grazing over my

dick and then disappearing. Finally, I grab her hand. "Okay, we need to do something to get my mind off the fact that I can't have you right now."

She slides away from me, but I stop her with my palm on her thigh. Digging through her purse, she pulls out her phone. "Let's find out more about one another then."

"How?"

"Twenty questions."

I groan and roll my eyes. She hits me in the shoulder. "Come on. It'll be fun and you'll find out all those little facts you've been so curious about."

"Fine. Shoot."

"Give me a minute."

She reads on her phone for a few minutes while I scan the train car watching all the families. The kid next to us is climbing over the seat and the dad grabs him, apologizing to the couple in front of them. I'm not sure I'll ever be ready for that.

"Okay. If you had one day to live, what would you do?" she asks.

I lean forward and lean close to her ear, lowering my voice. "I'd fuck you all day." I draw back and smile when I see her flushed cheeks. I love that look on her.

She clears her throat. "Question number two."

"Whoa." I hold out my hand. "You don't get to ask all the questions."

She smiles in a way that says she got caught and hands over her phone.

"Okay." I scan the list of questions. "Surprisingly, I already know some answers."

She sits up and leans over my shoulder, her cheek practically touching mine.

"You sing in the shower. My guess is you'd rather ride a hot air balloon than bungee jump, you have a love of emojis and shorten words from your texts and emails." My thumb slides the page down, but she grabs the phone out of my hand before I can read anymore.

"Why would I rather ride a hot air balloon?"

"Don't be insulted. You just don't scream adrenaline." I slide closer to her and my hand cradles her cheek. "I like that about you."

"You think I'm so easy to predict, but you are too."

I wrinkle my forehead. "I am not."

"Sure you are. Like..." She glances at her phone. "You would not be cool with me making more money if we were married and I doubt you'd stay home with the kids while I worked."

My head rears back. "Why would you say that?"

She shrugs her shoulder. "A hunch. Am I wrong?"

The truth is, she's not. I want the opportunity to reach my dreams. I *want* to support my family and earn money. "Half right."

"Which half?"

"I wouldn't be cool if you made more money than me. If that makes me an asshole then so be it. But my mom made more than my dad most of my life and he didn't give a shit. The reason I want to make more is because I'd never want the household to rest solely on your shoulders. I'd want you to be able to do what you want without having to worry about how much money you can make doing it."

She holds up her hand. "So, you're saying that if you don't make as much or more than I do, you're not doing your job as a husband?"

I nod. "Exactly."

"And staying at home?"

"I'd love for one of us to be able to stay home, but if my wife has dreams as big as me, that's cool, we'll figure it out."

Her back relaxes a bit from how it was ramrod straight a few seconds ago. "And what are your dreams, Ethan Ryland?"

I lean my head on the back of the train car. "Not to work at Mars And Venus writing articles about sleeping with co-workers."

"Not sophisticated enough for you?"

I run my hand down her smooth leg and at some point her hand finds mine and we lock fingers. "No. I want to write something that matters. Something that will help people, even if it's just one person."

"Me too."

"Really?"

She nods. "I have this blog I started a while back. It helped me get the job at Mars And Venus. It kind of spurred me into leaving finance. It's all about surviving between college and adulthood. Finding your way in life. I wish I could write more stuff like that, but Mars And Venus is the first maga-zine to give me a chance, so I'm not gonna blow it."

I sit up straighter and pull out my phone. "What's the blog called?"

She chews her lip and grimaces.

"Come on." I tickle her ribcage.

"It's embarrassing. You went to school for journalism. I didn't and the early articles... ugh. They're terrible."

I lean into her, caging her to the side of the train and kiss her neck, whispering. "It's me, I'm your number one fan."

She sighs. "Fine. 'Post College. What Do I Do Now?'"

I type the name into my phone and the page pulls up. It's cute and as I read the topics of articles, I see that they're all good for recent graduates. I tell her so.

"The sad part is I'm not a recent grad."

I continue to read some articles and scan the pictures. "It's great. If you want more followers, I can help you be more searchable on the web."

"Really? I kind of suck at that end of things."

"Yeah. This could be your job, you know." I read the topic of another article, copy the link and send it over to my sister. "My sister is gonna love this."

Blanca gasps looking over at me with wide eyes. "Did you just send that to your sister?"

I kiss her again because her lips are too tempting and now that I can kiss her whenever I want, I want to kiss her all the damn time. "She'll love it. Relax."

"Thanks. So what *is* your end game?"

I blow out a breath, afraid to admit to anyone what I really want. I like to keep my dreams to myself so that if I don't reach them, there's no one to pity me.

"Honestly? I want to write somewhere where there are comments that say, you made me realize X. Where people change their lives because of what you wrote."

She cuddles up to me, laying her head on my shoulder and threading her arm through mine. "That's admirable."

Admirable and unreachable, I think to myself.

CHAPTER EIGHTEEN

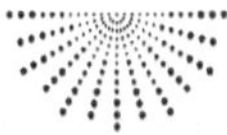

Blanca

By midweek, Ethan has hand delivered two lunches so I figure we should head out for lunch today. I grab my jacket and purse and head over to the cubicle next door.

He has his AirPods on and he's typing away. Glancing from side-to-side, I don't spot anyone, so I step in, sliding my hands down the front of his chest and kissing the start of a five o'clock shadow on his jawline.

He stops me right before I get to the middle of his thighs and he spins his chair around, his free hand moving to my neck and pulling me down for a quick kiss. This is by far the boldest we've been this week at work. Besides some footsie during the Monday morning meeting and a quick peck in the break room, we've behaved ourselves.

Ethan stokes this appetite in me that never seems to be quenched. It makes me feel like the new hot Victoria Secret model with angel wings on her back. His tongue slides into my mouth and he pulls me closer to him.

Knowing better, we don't get too carried away but Ethan sports a nice sized chub when he stands up.

"I figure we could go out for lunch today."

He grabs his jacket and his phone off his desk. "I'm game. Where to?"

"Truthfully, I'm done with Mexican food. I was thinking we'd grab some sandwiches and head toward the river."

"I thought you'd suggest my apartment," he says in a low voice that sounds like temptation.

We walk out of the office, past Mandy to the elevator keeping a good distance between each other. "We'll be back in an hour," I tell Mandy who's busy on the phone. She waves and as luck would have it, we end up on the elevator alone.

The doors aren't even closed, and Ethan's lips are on mine. His hands rush up my back, pulling me as close as I can get to him.

Then the elevator bounces to a stop and the doors part. Once again, our secret kisses are cut short and Ethan releases me, leaving me to grab the thin metal bar to hold myself up. He stands up and smiles at the man who steps onto the elevator.

"Good afternoon," Ethan greets him like the Boy Scout he is not.

I nod and by the time we reach ground level, I'm ready for some time alone. Truth is, as much as I would love to have Ethan again, it's all we seem to do. It's like we're hiding from the world, content in our little bubble of new coupledom.

We reach a small sandwich shop that reminds me of my Zia and Zio's deli in Chicago.

"Do you mind ordering for me? I have to go to the bathroom."

"Sure."

"Italian cold cut. Twelve-inch one."

"Italian, huh?" I smile like his sandwich choice has anything to do with me.

He glances around the small shop and takes me in his arms, locking them on my back. "I'm kind of partial to Italian lately."

"Is that a fact?"

"Especially, cute Italian brunettes."

I probably look like a lovesick thirteen-year-old with the way my blissful gaze floats up to meet his.

"NEXT!" a mean voice says. "HEY, are you going to order or suck face?"

"I think she's talking to us," Ethan whispers and he kisses me on my cheek, releasing me.

Sure enough, I turn around and there's an older woman behind the counter with no smile or friendliness at all in her demeanor. Definitely *not* like my Zia.

"Sorry." I rush over to her. "We'll have a twelve-inch Italian and—"

"Don't sell her anything," Dylan's voice distracts me from ordering my sandwich. "She's a bad girl, Hilda." He comes up to my side.

The woman, who I now know as Hilda, smiles at Dylan. Of course, she does. He's one of those people that you can't not smile at. He's permanently happy all the time.

"What are you doing here?" I ask.

He rears back. "I didn't know this was Blanca territory."

I chuckle and roll my eyes. "I just mean it's on the other side of town from your tattoo shop."

"Hilda and I go way back." He winks at her and she blushes. I bet if I got a dollar for every woman Dylan gets to blush in a day, I wouldn't have to work. "What about you?"

"Just out to lunch."

Hilda disappears and I huff. I have a feeling she's off to prepare his order because I didn't even get to finish mine.

"With *the* guy?"

And I guess I'm number two for blushing but it's not Dylan, it's the thought of Ethan that brings color to my cheeks.

I nod.

"When do we get to meet this guy who's holding you captive in his apartment all the time?"

I shrug. "It's still early. I'm not ready for him to meet my friends yet."

He rubs his hands together. "So I'm the lucky one?" He looks over my shoulder around the shop.

"NO." I push him in the chest.

Hilda returns with a box and hands it over to Dylan. He hands her cash and tells her to keep the change. "I might be eating in, Hilda. That's not a problem, right?" He's laughing so hard he can barely get it out.

"No." I glance behind me. No sign of Ethan.

"Okay. I'm not one to push, but I promise whenever we can meet Mr. Wonderful, I'll be on my best behavior." He winks and walks toward the door. "Until next week, Hilda."

Just as I'm about to release a breath, Dylan stops and walks back. "On second thought I think someone asked for a cookie."

"Dylan!"

He laughs and walks out of the sandwich shop.

My heart rate finally slows when he disappears. It's not that I don't want to introduce Ethan to my new friends, but we're a new couple and I think Ethan would take it as a sign of getting really serious. I don't want to scare him off this early.

"Hey," he whispers into my ear, arms around my waist. "Did you order?"

My head whips away from the door. "I was just about to."

I smile at Hilda who has lost her smile now that Dylan's gone. I look to the door one more time just to double check Dylan is really gone and then I relax into Ethan's arms.

WE FIND a bench by the river and sit down to eat our sandwiches.

"I never come down here." Ethan bites into his sandwich.

"This is my first time."

"I keep forgetting you're new to the area. And here I haven't shown you around at all."

I shrug with a sly smile. "I haven't minded what we've been doing lately."

"Me either. But this weekend I'm taking you on a real date."

"No complaints from me." I take a sip of my drink and bite my sandwich.

We sit and eat, neither of us saying much, but enjoying a sunny day by the river while a few moms and kids feed the ducks nearby.

"I forgot to tell you. I talked to my sister on Sunday about your blog. She loved it and has already told her friends about it. But she noticed that you haven't posted for a while?"

I turn on the bench to face him. "I was going to abandon it."

"Why?" His alarm feels complimentary. "It's great. You can't just let that go."

"I'm a ways past college and though I still don't have my shit together, I don't feel like I'm qualified to speak on the topic anymore."

He nods and licks his lips, swallowing down his bite of his sandwich. He places it next to him and pats the spot on the bench between us. When I don't slide over, he pats it again.

"What?"

"First of all who says you don't have your shit together?" He swings his arm around my shoulders, his fingers mindlessly running along my bare neck.

"My brothers are all either married or on their way. They have killer careers making money I'll never see in my lifetime. My best friend has a great career she loves. I just ... I haven't found my place."

He doesn't say much so I continue to nibble on my sandwich.

"You changed course, that's okay. If you were in finance would you be happy?"

"At least I'd be more established."

"I asked if you'd be happy?" He touches my nose.

"No, that's why I left."

He lowers his chin so he's staring into my eyes and takes my sandwich, placing it down next to me. "Exactly. You're happy right now. You have a budding career. Mars And Venus isn't the end all but believe me there are a lot worse jobs you could have in journalism. I should know. Plus, you moved to this great city and have an amazing boyfriend."

I smile at the warm feeling in my chest. "Are you?"

"What?"

"My boyfriend?"

His eyes stray for a moment, but he returns them to me. "Yes."

"But we've only been..."

"I'm not a casual kind of guy. Never have been. I knew when you came home with me that first night that we wouldn't be a one-time thing. So yes, I'm your boyfriend. That is if you'll have me?"

"Well." I shrug and hem and haw for a moment. He raises his eyebrows. "Of course I'll have you."

"Then it's official. Should we hold hands down the hallway at work to signify we're a couple?"

I laugh and my head falls into his chest.

"Now, I have some ideas for your blog. Come over tonight and let's get it updated."

"Are you sure?"

"Hey, you're my priority now." He gives me a PG kiss, acknowledging the families nearby, but I swoon just the same.

Having him as a boyfriend feels great, but the fact that he believes in me and my blog means more.

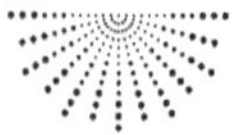

CHAPTER NINETEEN

Blanca

"He's not even picking you up?" Sierra asks from her spot on the couch, her iPad open and reading another article about Prince Adrian Marx.

"No. I'm meeting him."

"Blanca, this isn't like you." She shakes her head.

Rian pulls banana bread out of the oven. "What isn't like her?"

"That smells amazing. Save me a slice?" I say to Rian.

She huffs. "Come home and you'd have ample opportunity to have some, unlike last weekend."

"Yes, Mom."

She throws the hot pad at me.

"Blanca is a 'pick me up on the doorstep holding flowers and give me a goodnight kiss on the front porch' kind of a girl. She's not a 'let's bang the weekend away with no strings girl.'"

"I never said there weren't strings. Things are progressing but I'm not sure he's ready for friend introductions."

She rolls her eyes and then squeals.

"Guess she's forgot me already."

Rian laughs, as the loaf of bread slides perfectly out of the pan onto the cooling rack.

"Prince Adrian Marx is planning a trip to New York!" She stands up and Rian and I exchange a look to say she's nuts. "I have to find him. I have to at least get an interview."

"I think you're hoping for more than an interview," I say.

Rian giggles and nods in agreement.

"Hell yes. I'm not the 'goodnight kiss on the front porch girl.' I'm the 'bang me every which way you want in your hotel room for however long you want.'"

"Nice, Sierra." Rian shakes her head at her with a frown.

"It will be nice. As soon as I figure out a way to cross paths with him."

Knowing her, she will. Not much is an obstacle for Sierra Sanders.

The apartment door opens and Dylan takes a sniff. "What's that I smell?"

"You're like a drug dog," I say and shake my head.

He stops in front of me. "Well, thank you. That's a huge compliment. Drug dogs are highly intelligent."

Rian giggles because that's pretty much all she does when it comes to Dylan? He reaches out for the loaf and she slaps his hand. "It has to cool."

He takes a chair and flips it around so he's straddling the back. "Okay. How long?"

I grab my purse and put it crossways over my chest. "I have no idea how you're not fifty pounds overweight."

Dylan leans back and pats his trim stomach. "Want to feel my abs, Blanca?"

"Um… no."

He stands up and lifts his shirt. "Are you sure?" He runs his own hand down his six-pack. I'll admit they are a nice set of abs which makes me wonder when he puts in the time to achieve them. "I bet they're better than Mr. Wonderful's."

"Nope."

"Oh." He whirls around, his shirt dropping before Rian can catch a glimpse and she frowns. "I saw Mr. Wonderful."

I narrow my eyes at him. "No, you didn't."

"Wednesday. She was at Hilda's with him."

Sierra isn't paying attention, her head buried in her iPad. "What's he look like?"

"Not as handsome as me." Dylan winks and there goes Rian's blush. The difference between her and other women is that hers covers her entire neck too.

"You did not meet him."

"Almost." Dylan reaches for the banana bread and Rian smacks his hand again. "Come on. You always let me have the first taste."

Rian picks up the hot pad off the floor from when she threw it at me.

Dylan glances back to Sierra and then leans forward. "We have a bigger problem," he says in a low voice.

Rian and I lean in close where the banana bread smell makes it almost unbearable not to tear a piece off.

"Seth says Sigmund is dating someone."

"So?" I ask, not sure what the big deal is. They're broken up.

"Sierra will go ballistic," Rian explains.

"No. The Sierra I know has the motto that once it's over, it's over. She never dwells." Then I think about it for a second longer and remember Pauly Milano. In junior year she had us put three buckets of dead fish in his locker after she saw him holding hands with Samantha Lindor. Maybe I'm wrong.

"Let's face it. Cliffton Heights isn't that big. She's bound to run into him," Rian says.

"I'm not sure how we're supposed to stop that?" Against my better judgment I take a deep inhale and my stomach growls.

"Oh I'm going to pick out my outfit." Sierra leaves the room, still oblivious that we're all huddled around the banana bread talking about her.

"I think one of us should be with her at all times," Dylan says.

"That's stupid. Let's just tell her," I say.

Rian's face looks like I told her to hop the fence of the Lions exhibit at the zoo.

"I'll do it," I say.

"I have a sumo wrestler costume you can wear," Dylan says, and I swear he's serious.

I shake my head. "Where? Why?" I shake my head a second time. "Never mind. I don't need a sumo wrestler costume. I'm just going to tell her."

Dylan looks to Rian. "Okay, but I warned you." Then he gives puppy dog eyes to Rian and her shoulders deflate. She grabs a knife from the drawer and cuts him a slice. "Butter?"

Now I roll my eyes. "You guys are ridiculous. I'm leaving."

"Don't forget you volunteered," Dylan says.

"What? To tell her that her ex is dating someone. He could be broken up with her tomorrow. It is not a huge deal."

Dylan's gaze land on Rian. "She spends the night."

"Really?" she says, wide-eyed.

"Yep."

Obviously this is some huge monumental step for this Sigmund guy.

"Ohh." I wave my hands in the air. "If it's such a big deal that a girl spent the night at his place, then I think she's better off without him. I feel sorry for the girl."

"If you knew him like we did, you'd understand." Rian sits down at the table with Dylan.

"He doesn't do casual flings. And he doesn't allow just anyone to spend the night at his place. It means something to him, so whoever she is, it's serious."

"Good. Maybe he grew up after being with her. I gotta go." I glance at my phone. "I'm going to be late."

"Have fun," Rian says in a sing-song voice.

"You two have fun too." I waggle my finger between the two of them, Dylan not even noticing because he's grabbing the knife to cut another piece off.

On my way to meet Ethan at the Cliffton Heights gazebo I consider how I'll tell Sierra tomorrow morning though I'm not really that worried about it. It's over between them. There's no reason she should be upset that he's found someone else.

By the time I reach the gazebo, the sun is setting and the twinkle lights hanging across the inside are sparkling, casting a romantic glow over the entire scene. Ethan is sitting on the steps, staring down at his phone. He's wearing jeans and a T-shirt that stretches across his broad shoulders.

He happens to glance up from his phone and the smile that lights up his face when he sees me is warmer than the sun in the middle of July. My heart thumps inside my chest and I too can feel my smile growing wider.

"Hi."

He stands up, pocketing his phone and stepping closer to me. "Hi. You look beautiful."

I want to tell him he looks mouthwatering. "You look good too."

He picks up the backpack at his feet, swings it over his

shoulder and takes my hand, entwining our fingers and walking down the cobblestone path leading away from the gazebo.

"So, we're getting on the train to Peekskil."

"Are we going to visit Gil?"

He laughs and leads me toward the train station. "Nope."

"Are we visiting Blair, Jo, Natalie, and Tootie?" His eyes scrunch up and I slap him in the stomach. "You don't know *The Facts of Life*?"

"What's that?"

"That's it. Next date we're watching *The Facts of Life*."

"Whatever you want." We step up on the train platform.

"What's in the backpack?"

He circles to keep me from unzipping it. "None of your business." We stand outside to wait for the train. The air is a cooler when the sun descends all the way down beyond the horizon, but having Ethan close as a shelter feels safe.

The train comes to a stop and it's less crowded than Sunday during the day but more so than Sunday night. We find a seat together and our hands remain locked as I snuggle as close as I can to him. He bends down and kisses the top of my head.

I might as well use this opportunity to get an idea about how he feels regarding the whole introducing friends thing.

"Hey."

"Yeah?"

"Do you think maybe next weekend you'd like to come by and I'll introduce you to my friends?"

He doesn't say anything, so I sit up to gauge the reaction on his face. He doesn't look pale like he's minutes from throwing up, but he's not smiling either.

"Or not. We could wait a bit."

He stares deep into my eyes and his hand slides along my neck until his fingers swim in the strands of my hair. "I'd like that." And then he kisses me and since there aren't any kids around it's more R-rated this time.

It only takes a few stops before we're off at Peekskill and I spot what he might have planned.

"A movie in the park?" I bite my lip, denying a smile until I know for sure.

"Movie in the park." He nods and I wrap my arms around his neck, kissing his cheek.

"I've always wanted to go to a movie in the park. Thank you."

"I will say it's a Matthew McConaughey and Kate Hudson double feature."

"Alright. Alright. Alright." I imitate my best version of Matthew McConaughey's character from *Dazed and Confused.*

"You're adorable." He kisses my forehead.

"*How to Lose a Guy in 10 Days* and *Fools Gold.*"

I clap my hands and jump up and down. "YAY!"

"If I'd known sitting in the grass on a blanket, hardly being able to hear a movie would get this much excitement from you, I wouldn't have been worried you might be scared of sitting on the group because of bugs and stuff."

I slide my arm through his as we descend the hill to find our spot.

"No worries there. Three brothers." I point to myself. "Remember?"

Ethan finds us a spot that's a little more secluded and pulls a blanket out of the backpack.

I sneak a peek inside to find Tupperware containers. "You cooked too?"

He smiles at me as he arranges everything, and I slip off my shoes to get comfortable. The fact that he was thoughtful enough to plan ahead causes excitement to build inside me.

"Thank you," I say, my voice raw with more emotion than I'd prefer after only dating for so short a time.

He looks up from the container he's arranging, and his own feelings are there in his caramel-colored eyes. "You're welcome."

Then a kid runs through our blanket and breaks the moment. His mom apologizing as she runs after him.

"So feel free to say it sucks, but I made some Italian food."

I sit up. "You did?"

"It might suck, so I also made double desserts just in case."

I get up on my knees and kiss him some more. If there weren't people around here tonight, I might just act out a porno with him in the middle of this field to show my appreciation of everything he'd done for me tonight.

We part and Ethan inhales a deep breath. "Okay, movie in the park every week."

I laugh and fork a noodle.

"My attempt at Rigatoni ala Vodka."

I refrain from telling him my mom rarely makes this which means I've only really had it in restaurants. But one thing is for sure, he knows how to cook. "It's delicious."

"Thanks." He has a sort of sheepish grin on his face and it's adorable in a way that makes me want to straddle him. Preferably naked.

We both lay down on the blanket, eating bites and nibbles between kisses. By the time the movie starts, my head is on Ethan's chest, his arm secured around me as he props his head on his backpack. He kisses the top of my head and I squeeze my arm around his waist. There are a million stars overhead and I want to wish on them all that this will never end.

CHAPTER TWENTY

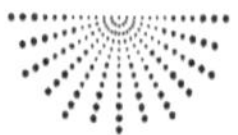

Blanca

*E*than's hand is secured in mine as we walk the dark streets of Cliffton Heights and somehow it feels like he's been a part of my life forever.

"Did you enjoy the movies?"

I laugh and my head falls to his shoulder. "Do you really have to ask?"

He stares down at me, the dim light from the streetlight allowing me to see his eyes. Eyes that are more transparent than he'd like to admit. He's made it clear that he wants to be with me, but I can still see that he's fighting something when it comes to me. I just don't know what haunts him. Who made him build these walls so high around himself.

"I wish you'd spend the night." He stops us on the corner until the walk symbol comes on. I'd like to think he's purposely delaying getting me home.

"I slept with you before ever committing, remember there is actually a good Catholic Italian girl inside me."

He chuckles and releases my hand, both of his palms coming to my cheeks and pressing his lips to mine in a gentle kiss. It's the one thing I've noticed with Ethan these past few days. He likes the fact he can kiss me whenever he wants. He's always leaning over and taking my lips in a series of kisses that are worth dreaming of. And then there're his hands that know no boundaries. Not that I'm complaining.

"Go out with me tomorrow? We'll keep it low key. Let me pick you up and we can end up having Sunday morning breakfast together?"

A giggle falls out of my lips. "A second weekend in bed?" My hand falls on his chest. "You're switching gears fast again."

His lips land on mine again. "I saw the light."

I study his eyes for a moment. The gold flecks alive and flickering. I desperately want to believe him, and for the time being, I will but my guard needs to stay up for a little while.

"Okay then. Pick me up at five. You can meet my roommates, maybe."

"Done."

His fingers brush down my arm, goose bumps quickly following his path until his hand is secure in mine again. "Let's get you home before I take you over my shoulder and tie you to my bed for the night."

It's hard not to go to his house. The temptation is almost overwhelming since Ethan has figured out all the places on my body that make me purr with want. But my roommates are giving me shit about being gone all last weekend and I'm here to rekindle this friendship with Sierra too.

"I'm right there." I point to the apartment, stepping off the curb. The strength of his grip loosens for a second.

"The Rooftop Apartments?" His voice cracks and he comes to a standstill in front of the lobby entrance, staring up at the building.

"Yeah, you know it? The rooftop is amazing. I get the name now."

"What…" He clears his throat. "What apartment do you live in?" He glances over to Ink Envy across the street. Dylan's at the front desk with Seth and Knox.

"You don't have to walk me up. Here is good." I motion toward the alcove of my apartment building.

"What button will I press tomorrow?" He looks like he's sweating now.

I giggle. "Oh yeah, duh. I live in four D. It has my best friend's name on it. Press Sanders."

Ethan's face pales but I don't get to ask why because his lips crash into mine with such force, my back presses to the glass door. His tongue slides through my parted lips and he kisses me with such passion and such fierceness I try to process where this desperation is coming from. It's not a 'I have to take you now kiss' or a 'come back to my apartment' kiss. It's a branding, he's claiming me. Like he's saying I'm his and only his. He slows the kiss, his knuckles brushing along my cheek in a tender moment as his eyes find mine. "I should have known. You were too good to be true."

"What?" I can feel my forehead wrinkle.

"You live in four D and I used to…"

"Blanca?" Dylan calls out from across the street.

I turn my head to see the three guys standing there.

Ethan's eyes close and his forehead rests on my temple. "I swear I didn't know," he says softly.

"Sigmund?" Seth says.

I glance between Ethan and the guys on the other side of the street.

"Fuck." Dylan shoves his hands into his pockets, staring at both of us.

"What? Sigmund?" I ask, desperate for any of the three guys to explain.

Seth nods and all three guys walk across the street to join us.

"I didn't know. Did you?" Ethan asks Dylan as he approaches.

Dylan shakes his head. "If I did, I wouldn't have told you to bang her."

"You're…" I point to Ethan. "Sierra's?"

"Ex. I'm her ex," he says emphatically.

Dylan, Seth, and Knox all stare wide-eyed between us. We all know what this means.

"The thought crossed my mind for a second, but I figured, what are the chances, you know? I mean, I thought Sig was just doing some freelancing gigs at a bunch of different places."

I want to strangle him for never saying anything, even if it was only a passing thought. I mean sure, I never mentioned Ethan's name and he writes under a pseudonym, but still.

"It wasn't like I knew the co-worker you wanted to bang was Blanca."

"Bang?" I raise both my eyebrows and cross my arms.

"No." Ethan takes my hands in his. "That's not what this is. I swear you're more than just some girl to me. But damn, you're Sierra's best friend? How come I never met you?"

"We were separated for a while. I was in New York and she was here." I rub my chest because my heart hurts like it's splitting in two. I have to figure something out.

"Wait, why does everyone call you Sigmund and not Ethan?"

He blows out a long stream of air and rolls his eyes.

"According to them I always overanalyze everything... aka Sigmund Freud."

I can't believe this.

"It changes nothing." He looks to the guys for confirmation. "Nothing has to change. Sierra and I are over. We've been over for some time."

"Man, you know..." Seth starts. "She's not going to take this as good news."

"It's none of her business," Ethan says.

"I have to go." I open up the building door.

"Blanca," Ethan says, and I turn toward him.

"Just give me a little bit. I have to tell her and figure this out."

"Seriously, we were over ages ago. Don't allow her to end this thing between us."

I place my hand on his strong chest and feel how fast his heart is beating. "Just... I'll call you, okay?"

He steps back and my hand falls off his strong chest.

The door shuts behind me and it's only once I'm by the mailboxes that I allow the reality of what this means to actually sink in.

He'll never be mine.

I haven't even reached the elevator before a big shadow looms over me. I slowly turn hoping it's Ethan, telling me we had it all wrong. He's not Sierra's ex. The one who still spurs on fights between her and Dylan. The one she isn't over yet.

But it's not Ethan.

It's Dylan and the expression on his face says I wasn't sleepwalking just now. He's not waking me up from a nightmare.

"Let's go up to the rooftop," he says.

We enter the elevator and he presses the button for the top floor where we can access the stairs up to the roof.

Silence spreads between us. I'm still processing what this will mean. Sierra should be who I choose. Forget Ethan, he was wishy-washy to begin with anyway and I'm not going to destroy a twenty-year friendship for a guy. That's not who I am.

But I'll still have to tell Sierra and I know that's going to hurt her.

Once we reach the rooftop, Dylan pulls out a chair for me and I sit down, pulling my legs up to my chest, staring up at the sky. The twinkle of the stars on the dark canvas behind them are a sight I didn't get to see in the city very often. These are the same stars I was wishing under hours ago which was a pointless venture.

"Sorry. I feel like I should've warned one of you."

"So you knew?"

He shrugs. "No, I swear. Though hindsight is twenty-twenty. The other night after we celebrated here and went out with him, everything he was saying… how he was describing you and the way you looked. He was pretty vague, but I can see now that it all perfectly described you."

"He talked about me?"

Dylan smiles. "Yeah. He likes you. I know he's a complicated guy, but he does like you."

"Too bad he's Sierra's ex-boyfriend."

Dylan blows out a breath. "It doesn't mean you guys can't date. It's been a while since they dated, and I know you're a better fit for him than her. They were like oil and water. They fought all the time. Over the stupidest things. It messed both of them up. But Sig is a good guy. He's a loyal friend and if he's open to me about how much he likes you than his feelings must be strong."

"How can you be friends with both of them?"

He props his feet up on the wrought-iron table, crossing

his ankles and leaning back. "Sigmund was my friend first. We met in college. I became close with Sierra and Rian and we'd all hang out on the rooftop sometimes, like we do now. That's how they first met. I'm not saying it's going to be easy, but if you like him, I'd just be straight with Sierra. It's not like you knew beforehand. You fell for him before you knew who he was."

"But I know who he is *now*. Sierra and I have had our differences what with us being best friends and then not talking for a few years. I finally feel like I fit in somewhere. I love living here with her and Rian and you guys across the hall, but with Ethan..."

Dylan's wide smile says he's happy for his friend. Happy that Ethan's crush likes him too. "Stop looking so googly-eyed. This isn't some sitcom where everything will be cleared up in thirty minutes. I know Sierra, and she's not going to take this lightly. She's going to hate me and she's definitely going to expect me to break up with him."

"But what do *you* want?"

"I want her not to be Ethan's ex!" I throw my head in my hands. Peeking my head up, I look at him through the slits in my fingers. "I wanted to explore what this was with Ethan because it feels..."

"Right."

"Why do you say that?"

He chuckles. "Because it's the same thing he said. That there's just something different between you two."

Damn it. This is not helping.

"This is the worst. Where did he go?"

"Him and Seth and Knox went to the bar. I'm gonna head there too. Do you want to join us?"

I shake my head. "You go. You're his friend."

He stands up and meets me at the edge of the rooftop, placing his hand on my shoulders. "You're my friend now too. I'll leave you with one last piece of advice. Sometimes you have to be selfish." He squeezes my shoulder and a few seconds later, I hear the rooftop door shut behind him.

That's when the first tear falls from my eye. Maybe coming to Cliffton Heights was my worst idea ever.

CHAPTER TWENTY-ONE

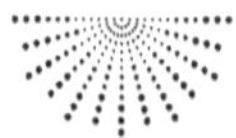

Blanca

*E*arly the next morning, I throw on a pair of yoga pants and a T-shirt. Shoot a text to my sister-in-law Val and tiptoe out of my room to find Rian up and already baking muffins.

"How early do you wake up to impress him?" I whisper because keeping Sierra asleep is my mission right now.

"These are for my parents, okay?"

"But some might miss the container and end up outside Dylan's door?" I raise both my eyebrows and she narrows her eyes. We both know I'm right.

"Where are you disappearing to this early? Mystery guy?"

I glance at Sierra's door and for a moment I debate telling Rian everything I learned last night. But I decide that conversation might take longer than I have before Sierra wakes so I'm better to get out of here.

"I'm heading to my brother's place in the city."

"Oh nice. Have a good time."

She places the muffin tray in the oven, and I head to the door. With my hand on the doorknob, I turn around. Rian is picking up her Kindle and she looks at me with a sweet smile on her face. Surely, she won't hate me. I had no idea.

"Hey, Rian." I step back into the apartment. Maybe it would be a good idea to get her take on all this.

She lays her Kindle down to give me her full attention. That's the great thing about Rian, she's always one hundred percent present. "What's up?"

Sierra's door opens and she runs her hand through her crimson-colored hair that's sticking up in all directions. Her boxer shorts are shifted around her waist and her tight tank top is about to expose one of her breasts. Getting herself together takes no longer than a minute and she only makes it to the couch. "Why are we up so early?"

"I'm making muffins."

"Let me guess. Chocolate chip?" She eyes me over the edge of the couch with a sarcastic smile. It's like a knife to my heart. If she only knew I've fallen for her ex-boyfriend.

"No, funny girl. Blueberry. My mom's favorite."

"And Dylan's second." Sierra falls back onto the couch groaning like she's in pain.

"I'm out," I say.

Rian perks up. "I thought you had—"

"Nope. Gotta get to the city to see my brother and it's a long train ride."

"Oh, let me get dressed. Who are we seeing? Carm?" Sierra sits up and acts like she's going to sprint to get ready. She's so not a morning person, but she has always had a thing for Carm.

"Dom. You know the one with the wife and baby?"

She rolls her eyes and falls down to the couch cushions in defeat. "Give them my best."

"Will do. See you two later."

I walk out before I can be stopped again and asked more questions. Talking to Sierra and withholding the information I discovered last night feels all kinds of wrong. It's why I hoped to sneak out before she woke up. Then I wouldn't feel more guilty than I do.

Heading out to Cliffton Heights on a Saturday at seven in the morning is like walking onto a set of a Hallmark movie. Everyone is all smiles. People walking their dogs, grabbing newspapers, holding trays of coffees they're bringing home for their significant others. Even the train station guy was friendly as I paid for my ticket. Who wants to work on Saturday morning.

I purposely pick the first car because Ethan appears to be a creature of habit and ours is always the last car on Sunday nights. I situate myself and stare out the window at the rolling green landscape with the hopes that somebody can give me the advice I need.

Dom opens the door to their high-rise condo, and I instantly wrap my arms around myself. I heard the rumors about Val and her hot flashes while pregnant, but it's like the damn arctic in here.

"It's freezing in here. You have icicles on your eyebrows." I point at my brother, and he actually touches them to make sure he doesn't. I hit him in the stomach as I pass him for the person I'm really here for this morning. "I'm kidding. You and Ryder need to stop giving her hell."

I curl up beside Val, pulling a blanket over her. The baby might be under layers of skin, but even he or she has to be freezing.

"I love you, Blanc, but you gotta get away from me with

that blanket. You and your brother, I swear," Val says, squirming away from me.

"Be careful, she punched me when I tried to cuddle last night." Dom sits in the chair across from them, propping his feet up on the table.

Val narrows her eyes at him, but he challenges her right back until they both laugh. I slide over to the other end of the couch. I have no idea what it's like to grow a human being inside you.

"How's the job?" Dom asks because he's business most of the time now. At least he let me walk in and sit before hitting me with the questions.

"It's good. I'm enjoying it."

"Any cute boys work there?" Val asks with a smile.

"Well…"

"Oh, spill." Val turns on the couch to face me. "I'm over Netflix. I've watched everything. I want some real gossip." The pleading expression on her face has me opening up in front of my brother. Which wasn't really my plan. I figured I'd talk a while and Dom would get bored and maybe head to the bedroom to watch a game or something.

"It's just this guy I work with."

"And?" Val prods.

I look to Dom and he rolls his eyes. "Office romance isn't a good way to start, Blanc. Tell me he isn't your boss?"

"No, it's not that cliché."

"But it's a little cliché?" Val asks, and the smile on her face says she hopes I'm about to fill her gossip meter full.

I shrug. "Kind of."

"An office romance! Are you guys pinned against one another?" Val asks, more hope and excitement in her tone.

I laugh. "No."

"Oh! Oh! Are you *his* boss?" Val raises her hand as if we're in a game show.

Dom groans and rolls his eyes again.

"Nope." I shake my head.

"What about… is he an ex?" Val asks.

My smile falls. "Sort of?"

"Is he an ex of one of your friends?" Dom asks.

I feel my face drain of color, and I nod.

"Dom! You can't opt out of playing and then steal the winning answer. I was playing!" Val crosses her arms over her tummy.

"Sorry," he mumbles and raises his shoulders up and down, looking at me.

And then I bury my head in a pillow and the tears from last night start all over again.

Val slides closer to me and wraps her arm around my shoulders. "Like how close of a friend?"

"My best friend. One of my roommates," I mumble into the pillow hoping they didn't hear. I'm so ashamed.

"Your roommate?" I hear Dom's feet fall to the floor.

"Relax," Val says.

"Wait." I look up to find Dom pacing the floor in front of us. "You work with him and he's your roommate's ex. How small is this Cliffton Heights place? Is there not enough dick to go around that you have to dip into your friend's ex?"

"Dominic! That's harsh." Val's hands run up and down my arms and although she tears the blanket off my lap, she does allow me to cuddle into her side like the awesome mom she already is.

"I just don't get it. I've told you, Blanca. You never mess around with people at the office."

"Well that's the pot calling the kettle black," Val says.

Dom narrows his eyes at her for a second and then relaxes. Obviously my brother was messing around with someone at his work before he got back together with Val.

"Tell that to Enzo," I say out of spite.

"He's lucky it turned out how it did. Plus, he was her boss. He could've been sued. He was a moron."

"Well." I square my shoulders at my oldest brother. "The moron is marrying the love of his life. Everyone is and the one guy I fall for ends up being Sierra's ex-boyfriend."

"Sierra Sanders?" Val whispers from next to me.

I nod. I'm fairly sure she and Dom are having a conversation over my head because Val's body gets rigid.

"You haven't talked to her in years. The office issue is the bigger problem. This is your first job in that industry. Rumors are probably already being spread about you."

I look up again and my brother's face is red. He's got his cell phone in his hands, probably ready to call the Mancini brother cartel to come over and keep me in line.

"There're no rumors."

"I think the friend issue takes precedence over the workplace." I love Val for speaking up. She's exactly right.

"And why is that?" Dom asks.

"Because it's where she lives for one. Plus friendships are more important than guys. Imagine if Lulu would've slept with you while we were broken up?"

Dom stares blankly at her for a moment. "I would never sleep with her."

"She's very persuasive," Val says.

"Babe, I can't stand the woman for more than five-minute increments. Why on Earth would you think I'd actually sleep with her? Plus, she's your friend." Dom leans forward in my direction. "So I never would have done it."

"I didn't know. Okay?" I throw my hands up in the air. "They dated when I wasn't in her life." I stick my tongue out at his judgmental self.

"Then what's the problem? Call it off. She can't be upset." Dom sits back down. "You'd think with the journalism thing and everything, you'd know which information to start with.

This isn't the end of the world. End the relationship and Sierra never even has to know." Val and I both stare at my brother long and hard until he finally says, "What?"

"God help us if we have a daughter," Val murmurs and I laugh.

"That's rude." Dom's obviously offended, his jaw is hanging open.

"She's here crying because she more than likes him. He's obviously someone important to her, so it's not as easy as her calling it quits." Val points at me like Dom doesn't realize I'm even here.

"So stop yourself from caring." He shrugs.

I groan and Val's arms tighten on my shoulders. "Jesus, Dom. Get out of your head for a moment. Your sister is hurting here. She loves the boy."

"Love? You're too young." He grabs the remote and changes the channel.

Val stands up, it takes her a minute with her belly, and grabs the remote from his hand, turning off the television. "She's twenty-eight."

"She can wait until she's in her thirties."

Val grabs my arm and yanks me up to my feet then puts her hands on my shoulders and turns me toward my brother. "Dominic Mancini, meet your younger sister, Blanca Mancini. She's not nine anymore. She's twenty-eight. A grown woman. Treat her as such."

Dom huffs, but he blows out a breath. I swear only Val has the power to get through to him. "You really like him?"

I nod.

Val sits down on the couch.

"You want to date him in a serious way? Don't go through all this bullshit just for a fuck."

I bite my lip to stop myself from telling Dom that I

already had sex with Ethan, and it was fantastic, more than I could've imagined.

"You go to your friend and ask permission."

My eyes widen and I look over at Val. She smiles at her husband and turns to me, nodding in agreement. "You need to tell your friend what's going on and how you feel."

"And if she doesn't want me to date him?"

They look at one another and then back at me. Val allows my brother to be the bearer of bad news. "Then the ball is in your court. Which is more important, friendship or the douche?"

"He's not a douche."

Dom leans forward and his hand falls on my knee. "Blanc, I'm your big brother, they're all douches to me. It's just the way it is."

Val laughs but smiles proudly at my brother. If she could tolerate the heat of body contact, I think they'd sneak off to the bedroom to have sex.

I sit back down on the couch and pull a pillow to my chest. When we were kids, Sierra couldn't share her popcorn at the movie theater. We always had to have our own. I'm not sure much has changed on that front. But my brother and Val are right, I have to tell her how I feel.

Just then my phone dings.

Ethan: *We need to talk.*

Yeah, we do.

Me: *I'm in the city. Be back this afternoon. Your place?*

Ethan: *I'll be here.*

CHAPTER TWENTY-TWO

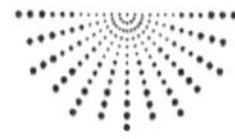

Ethan

I pocket my cell phone and prop my feet back up on the coffee table.

"She just got off the train," I tell Dylan, who's been here all day.

Lucky me, he brought Rian's blueberry muffins. One thing I missed about being with Sierra was Rian's baking.

"What's the plan?" Dylan asks for the millionth time.

"I told you. I'm leaving it up to Blanca. I have no ties to Sierra anymore."

Dylan stares at me with a bored expression like he knows me better than that.

Sierra's gonna have a conniption, think I planned this from the get-go and possibly come after me with a machete to the balls.

"It's true. It affects Blanca more than me." I pick up a pillow and throw it at him. "I'm still pissed you had the thought that it sounded like Blanca, and you didn't say anything."

"Man, I told you, I didn't know. Besides, I don't know if I would've told you. You'd just throw something away that seems pretty great for you."

"How do you know?"

He puts down the controller to my Xbox. "Your face gave it away. When you talked about kissing her in the elevator, I knew you were done. Off the market. Something was different. Plus, the minute I met Blanca I thought about fixing her up with you. You two just kind of fit."

"Really?"

He raises his eyebrows at me. "You having doubts?"

I shake my head. "If we didn't work together, I'd be fine. But you know I like to keep that shit separate."

"But you still nailed her."

I shrug, picking up the remote to play a game to try and push this shit situation out of my mind. "How could I not?"

"Because she's different, so stop being a pussy and just lay your heart down on the table for Blanca to claim."

"Who knew Romeo had so many tattoos?"

He laughs and grabs another blueberry muffin, chomping the top of it off. "I'm not Romeo, that'd be Seth. The Andrews versus the Ericksons. Which bagel place will stand after the bloodbath of bagels across Cliffton Heights?"

"Are you suggesting Seth has a thing for The Bagel Place girl?"

He looks at me like I'm an idiot for not figuring it out myself. "No one hates someone that much without their being real feelings under all that hate."

I nod because Dylan's always been good at seeing things like that. Except with it comes to him and Rian. Every one of us knows how she feels except him. One day I'll have to pull him out of the darkness but right now I have my own problems to deal with.

"What if it ends badly?" I ask Dylan.

"Then it ends badly. But you obviously like her. You've crossed the line a lot farther than you ever have before." He picks up the other remote, presses restart, and the game starts over with two players.

"I do."

"Then stop dissecting everything that could go wrong and enjoy the ride. Maybe nothing bad will happen and in twenty years, the two of you will be writing opposing articles in Mars And Venus."

"God, I hope not. I mean, if I'm still working at Mars And Venus in twenty-years than I haven't gone anywhere in my career."

"It's not a bad job." I see him shrug in my peripheral vision.

"It's not the New Yorker either."

He shakes his head and the buzzer rings, telling me that Blanca is downstairs.

"That's my cue. Want me to scale the balcony?" Dylan asks, setting the gaming controller down.

"She knows we're friends," I remind him.

I buzz Blanca in and open my apartment door. I could still smell her on my sheets last night and had wished we'd stayed at my apartment. Then all this shit with Sierra would've been pushed to another day—like never.

Blanca knocks lightly on the door and pushes it open. She looks like she got about as much sleep as I did last night. Dark circles ring her eyes and her hair is thrown into a messy ponytail. She's wearing yoga pants and a short shirt that reveals all her curves. Though she looks less put together than her normal self, she still looks good.

"Hey," I say, wrapping my arms around her waist and picking her up to kiss her.

"Hi." Her body doesn't relax into mine, it's tense and unsure.

"What's up, Blanca?" Dylan says, getting up off the couch.

I place her back on her feet and she tosses her purse on my small table by the front door, heading into the living room. "Does everyone know?"

Dylan shakes his head. "No. Seth and Knox are all waiting to take their cue from you."

She buries her head in her hands. "I'm a horrible friend. I should've told her this morning."

"I didn't get to ask last night. How good of friends are you? Because I dated her for over a year and I never heard your name." I walk over to take a seat beside her on the couch.

The hurt on Blanca's face says she wishes something was different between her and Sierra. "We lost touch for a few years, she's the one who brought me to Cliffton Heights. She gave me a new start and a fresh start for our friendship was born in that moment as well. We're childhood friends, we grew up together."

Well fuck. I'd hoped they were roommates in college who didn't get along all that well. Childhood friends means so much more. Not that I have any friends from childhood. Dylan's my oldest friend and technically I met him when I was an adult.

"We didn't know. I'm sure she'll understand."

"I have to talk to her." She pulls her phone out of her back pocket and cradles it in her hands.

It's then I realize they're shaking. "Blanca," I say.

"I should go." Dylan stands. "Let me know if you need anything."

"Thanks," Blanca says.

I shoot him a nod of appreciation before he leaves the apartment.

"Blueberry muffins?" Blanca raises her eyebrows at me.

"So you know Rian's in love with him too?" I ask.

She smiles. Crazy world. We now have so much more to talk about since I lived with the same people she does now.

"Want one?" I ask.

"Had one this morning. Fresh from the oven."

I laugh and pull her into my lap. She comes easily and I take the opportunity to kiss her jaw. "Sierra isn't unreasonable. The two of us didn't work out. That has nothing to do with you and me."

"About that. Can you tell me more about why you guys broke up?"

I stop kissing her and my hand falls off her hip. I blow out a breath because why would anyone want to tell their new girlfriend about their ex and why they didn't work out? I don't want to tell her I was selfish at times. That it wasn't only Sierra, it was me too, but that I learned from that relationship and I won't make those mistakes with her.

"We just didn't get along. We fought all the time."

"I've heard that, but what about? Were you jealous? Did someone cheat? I need more information." She stares down at her fingers as she picks at her nails.

"I don't really want to rehash my relationship with Sierra, and I don't see why it matters. What happened with her has nothing to do with my relationship with you."

She slides off my lap to sit next to me on the couch.

Her face is makeup-free and I love that she's just as beautiful without it. Another thing I love about Blanca is that she's transparent. She'll never tell me one thing and mean another.

"I like you, Blanca, a lot and I know I've been a dick about the work thing. It's hard for me not to worry that I'll lose my job or vice versa because of being involved with each other, but it's too late. I'm one hundred percent in this."

She inhales a deep breath. "And it has nothing to do with getting back at Sierra for whatever you broke up over?"

"Seriously?" I jolt to my feet, needing space. I'd never do that even if I hated Sierra, which I don't. "How could you think that of me?" I stalk toward the kitchen.

"I don't know because I'm in the dark when it comes to you two. She hates you. I have no idea how you feel about her. I'm flying with no radar here."

She follows me into the kitchen.

"I don't hate her. We had our problems. Our fights were pretty out of control which usually resulted in me shutting down and disappearing for a few days. We just weren't a match. No one cheated. No one lied. No one did anything terrible. It was just a relationship that didn't work out. That's all."

"Okay." She weaves a design on my counter with the tip of her finger and it's clear she wants to ask another question, but she's scared.

"What is it?" I ask, exasperated at having to rehash things about Sierra.

She looks up at me, square in the eye which tells me this is important to her. I slap my mental armor on to prepare myself. "Did you love her?"

I close my eyes for a second and when I open them she takes a step back. I try to grab her hand, but she backs up.

"That was a stupid question," she says in an almost whisper. "You don't stay with someone for a year if you don't love them. Of course you loved her. She's great. How could anyone not fall head over heels in love with her?" I can see her withdrawing from me the more she convinces herself I had some undying love for her best friend.

"I thought I loved her. I told her I loved her. But by the

time it ended, I'm not sure what I felt. Love wasn't it then, I can tell you that. It's complicated. Haven't you ever had a relationship that was a large part of your life that left you empty?"

"I haven't had a lot of relationships. None where I loved the other person."

I want to scream out Bingo! We have our answer as to where all this insecurity I never knew she possessed is coming from—she's inexperienced to long-term relation-ships. "Blanca," I say, finally grabbing her and pulling her to my chest. "I'll tell you this, I've never felt this thing between us with anyone else."

"What do you mean?"

"You know what I mean. It's the same thing you've been talking about these past weeks. There's something here between us and I've never felt this way before. Something that told me to screw the work situation and just go with it. That what we could be would be worth it." Her forehead falls to my chest and she balls my T-shirt with her fists.

"She won't let me have you," she mumbles.

I kiss the top of her head. How did I not realize how much I want her until I feel her pulling away? "Who says she gets to be the one to give us permission."

She tilts her head up and rests her chin on my chest, staring up at me. "I can't date you if she tells me no. It's not right. She's my friend."

Anger rushes through my veins. "She's your best friend from years ago. You said yourself that you two were estranged for years. You're gonna throw this away because Sierra throws a temper tantrum over the fact that I want you and not her?"

Her hands tighten pulling my T-shirt tighter as if she's afraid I'm about to leave her. "I live with her. I…"

"Let's go together. We talk to her together." I place my

hands on her cheeks so she can't stray from looking at me. "I'll be right there with you."

"We can't. That'd be like an ambush. But before we continue this, I need to talk to her."

I stare into her gorgeous brown eyes. Eyes that have transfixed me from our first meeting on the train, so honest and pure. "But—"

She puts her finger to my lips and shakes her head. "Me alone." Rising on her tiptoes, she replaces her finger with her lips.

Her lips press to mine and my hand falls to the back of her head not allowing her to move away from me. Our tongues glide along one another's with a kiss we've perfected over our short time together. A kiss I'd hoped of having numerous times with her, but now it feels like a goodbye kiss. The kind someone gives someone as a parting gift.

She ends the kiss and falls back to her heels, her hand running along the stubble on my cheek. "I'll call you."

"Blanca, let me come with you."

She squeezes my hand. "Bye Ethan."

I've never hated those two words more than I do watching her open my apartment door and disappearing through it.

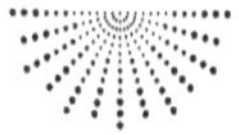

CHAPTER TWENTY-THREE

Blanca

I take the long way home, stopping at Scrumptuals for a few pick-me-up brownies and cakes that will hopefully make Sierra take the news better than I expect. Everything that's ever come out of her mouth about Ethan has been negative.

Opening up the door to the apartment, I hear shouting. Dylan has one foot on the edge of the couch and one on the coffee table. Seth stands by the window with one foot on each arm of the chair. Sierra's standing on the kitchen table with no chairs in sight while Rian has one foot on a kitchen chair across the room and the other on a cushion on the ground.

"Lava!" Sierra yells and points to the ground.

I drop my purse on the entry table and walk across the room. "How old are we all?"

"Come on. It's fun," Sierra says.

"Are you playing Piranha?" I ask, sitting down on the couch.

Dylan shoots me a sympathetic look.

"No, we're playing Volcano and Lava and you, my friend, have died from the burning lava," Seth says.

I shrug my shoulders and put my feet up on the table.

"Time out. Blanca went to Scrumptuals," Dylan says. He and Seth each climb off their spots.

"We were at a standstill anyway. You need to play with an odd amount."

I pay no attention to Rian because they're playing a childish game I used to get yelled at for when I was younger for throwing beautiful hand stitched pillows onto the dirty floor.

"I gotta get to work anyway." Dylan jumps off the couch. "Seth, didn't you say you were looking at a new piece?"

"Yeah, I'll join you," he says.

Sierra falls onto the couch next to me and grabs the box of sweets from me.

"Rian, I bet Seth could use your input," Dylan says to her.

"Really?" Her face beams and she grabs her purse, following them to the door.

"See you guys later." Dylan shuts the door and it leaves Sierra and me alone.

My stomach knots and clenches so bad my hands fall to it.

"Aren't these brownies the best? Don't tell Rian, but I think they're better than hers." She cringes and I don't say anything. "How is Dom?" She pops another mini brownie into her mouth.

"Good. Val is six months pregnant, can you believe it?"

"I can't believe they actually got married. I mean, they

were the couple who were fated to be together from such a young age that it was like a horror story when she got pregnant with Ryder. The fact that they found their way back to each other all those years later is really something."

I half listen to her. I wasn't really surprised. Val and Dom were made for one another, it was just my pig-headed brother who probably kept them apart.

"Maybe I should've gone with you so I could visit my dad." Her head falls back against the cushion. "Last time I talked to him he said he had a woman he wanted me to meet."

My head falls onto her shoulder. I know how hard that must be for her.

At ten, Sierra's mom went to war for our country and gave her life in return. I'm not sure her or her father ever fully got over it. They were both in the military and deployed at different times. It was a devastating loss and Sierra rebelled hard after that. So much so that Mama told me I couldn't hang out with her for a while. She was never quite the same after that. Still awesome, but not as soft or smooth as she used to be. She had more jagged edges after losing her mom.

"Maybe this person will make him happy."

She nods. "I don't really want to find out."

I find her hand between us and clench it because what people don't understand about Sierra is how vulnerable she is when it comes to her family. I have to think that might have been a problem with her and Ethan since he goes to see his family every Sunday.

"I'll go with you if you'd like."

She turns to me and smiles. "I'd like that. Thanks."

I nod. Taking a deep breath, I figure it's now or never.

"I need to talk to you about something." I sit up straighter but don't let go of her hand. I turn to face her, and concern runs deep in her eyes.

"What is it?"

"You know last night how I went out with that guy from work?"

"Yes, and I was very upset you came home." She winks and smiles.

I'm about to crush her.

"When he walked me home, we ran into Dylan, Seth, and Knox."

Her shoulders fall. "Shut up. They met the mystery guy before me?" Her lips tip down and she almost pouts. "I'm your bestie! It's supposed to be me who judges whether he's good enough. I should tell you, as long as the guy drinks beer, watches sports and likes tattoos, the guys will love him. Their standards are very low."

An awkward chuckle is the best I can do in response.

"This can be fixed. Invite him over tonight." She stands up and heads into the kitchen, opening up the fridge. "We'll go up on the roof and then we can all go out. He can spend the night here if you'd rather not spend the night there. Does he live alone? Or does he have roommates? Is that why you didn't spend the night?"

"Man, you really are a reporter, Sierra." She looks at me over her shoulder.

"Score! So if this goes well, we won't see you around very often, huh? Remember hoes before Joes." She laughs, cracking open a can of Diet Coke and sits down at the table, picking up a blueberry muffin. "Can you believe Rian lied to us? She never even went to her parents. These were totally for Dylan."

I just stare at her, working up the nerve to say what I have to.

"Why are you looking at me like you're about to give me bad news?"

I round the back of the couch to take a seat at the table. "The guy from work. You already know him."

She tilts her head. "I do? How do you know?"

"Because Dylan, Seth, and Knox knew him when they saw us together."

She purses her lips and surprise as well as intrigue falls over her face. "Who is it?"

"I just want you to know, I had no idea."

Her face pales. She's smart, investigative smart. It doesn't take a lot because she pushes the Diet Coke aside and grabs a muffin, taking a chomp out of it. "Sig?"

"I only know him as Ethan Ryland."

There. It's out and there's a rush of relief that encompasses my body. Sierra will react however she will, but at least I'm no longer withholding a secret.

"The guy from the train?"

I nod.

"The guy from the office? The bagel? The taco date?" She mumbles that last one to herself as if she thought he hated Mexican food.

"I'm so sorry. I had no idea until the guys found us outside the apartment last night."

"You guys have slept together." She seems to say this more to herself than me, but I nod anyway.

"I didn't know, Sierra." I reach for her hand, but she tucks her hands under the table.

"You like him?" I say nothing because I want her to absorb this information before we have that conversation. "You do, right? I mean I know that just from the way you talk about him." I open my mouth to speak but she beats me to it. "I could tell you a thing or two about him. He's not Mr. Nice guy. I should've figured it out because of the train ride on

Sunday night. He always went home on Sundays. I was never invited on those trips. His family life was always so hush-hush. I told you about how he punched my brother in the nose on Thanksgiving, right? Who does that? He was always so competitive." She stops talking and looks at me. "But if you like him, go ahead, I'm not gonna stand between the two of you. Maybe it's true love with you guys."

A five-year-old could see the passive aggressiveness she's throwing out there. She doesn't want me to date him, which I already knew would be the case the minute they told me who Ethan was. In some layer deep down, Sierra still likes him or has some soft spot for him. Otherwise she wouldn't hate him as much as she does.

"No. I'll break it off." The words escape in a rush and are painful to say, but it feels like the right thing to do.

She stands up and pushes her chair in. "Not on my account. I'm fine. Totally over him. You should invite him over tonight. I'd love to see the two of you together." Now she's just being completely fake.

"Sierra, can we please talk about this?"

"There's nothing to talk about. I forgot I have a kickboxing class today." She looks at the microwave clock. "I'm going to be late."

"Sierra?"

"It's fine, Blanca. The boys always loved you more than me. I'm not surprised Ethan does too."

"That's not fair. Neither one of us knew who the other were."

She turns around at her bedroom door. "I said it's fine. Go ahead and date him, but just so you know, he really is an asshole and not mature enough to have an actual relationship. Don't say I didn't warn you. But I wish you both the best." She disappears behind her door and I slide down the chair, resting the back of my head on the top.

Her immature reaction to the news doesn't surprise me. I've always given her a pass because of her mom dying young but I want to shake her right now and tell her to be real with me. Regardless, one thing is clear, she is *not* okay with me dating her ex-boyfriend.

CHAPTER TWENTY-FOUR

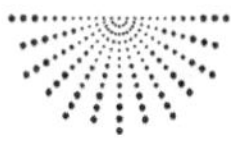

Ethan

I half hoped when I got on the train this morning, that I'd run into Blanca. She left me a cryptic message last night about how she was staying in but didn't mention anything about Sierra. I would have gone over there too if not for Dylan keeping me at Ink Envy for the night.

Now that I head to the bus to get to my mom's, I realize how blinded I've become since she entered my life. Everything I do revolves around me thinking of her and it's only been weeks. How did I think I'd be able to not be with her?

With a two hour commute between the train and bus, I have way too much time to think. She's become an obsession. I really hope I see Blanca on the train tonight. Sierra might have poisoned me in her head.

I stop at the grocery store on the corner, picking up a few items to make for dinner. My cell phone rings while I'm weighing the grapes, but I take the call anyway in case it's Blanca.

"Hey Mom," I answer.

"You've left already?"

Her depressed tone puts me on alert.

"I'm already at Berwins."

"Oh, I'm sorry. Your dad isn't doing well today, so they said visitors might not be welcome."

"I'm still here to see you."

We refrain from communicating that she's the only reason I come home every Sunday. To leave enough food in her fridge for the week. To go through the mail and water her plants.

"Do you want me to meet you?"

I glance at my mostly empty cart. "Nah, I'm almost done. Is Kori there yet?"

"No. She said she'll be a little late."

"Okay. Well I shouldn't be more than a half hour."

"I should come down. Pay for the groceries at least."

"It's fine Mom, relax. I'll be there shortly."

"Thanks."

Her gratitude has much more of a deep meaning because the last thing she wants to do is come down to the grocery store and we both know she barely has enough money to survive. On her only day off from work, she shouldn't have to spend it on her feet.

I grab enough groceries for her to last the week and the ingredients to make hamburgers and a pasta salad. I even stop at the bakery and buy the Polish cookies my mom loves with the dried cherry in the middle.

By the time I'm finished I'm thankful I didn't run into anyone I know because with people from the neighborhood come questions. And I'm not up for answering any questions about where my dad is and how come I moved so far away from home. I don't need that guilt today.

I use my key to get into my mom's apartment building and walk up the three flights of stairs. As the door creaks open I find her on the couch with the television on and I already know what today will bring.

"Mom?"

She glances over her shoulder, sniffles and tries to hide the fact she's crying. It shouldn't piss me off that my dad has made her cry almost every day since I was twelve. It's not entirely his fault.

"Let me help you." She stands and tries to move all the papers off the small two-person kitchen table by the window that looks out onto the fire escape.

Helping me unpack the groceries, she smiles at the cookies like I made her year. It's the reason I'm here every Sunday. For that look.

"How's work?" I ask, putting away all the items that belong in the fridge.

"It's okay. The hours were cut at the deli for a few part-timers. Thankfully, not me though."

"Truth is, I wouldn't mind if your hours were cut. You're on your feet too much." I shut the fridge door.

"Come and tell me about this girl at work." She pats a spot on the couch beside her.

"I told you it's new."

She smiles over at me. "I know mi Tesoro and she's someone special."

Little does she know and I'm not about to bring my drama into her life. She already lives what feels like an episode of a sixty-minute drama on TV. Who else is stuck in their own personal hell every day?

"At least tell me her astrological sign? You know Sagittarius is your best bet."

Her phone rings and the smile she had lights up even more as she hurries up to answer it. I'm just happy for the reprieve.

"Hello." She pauses. Her smile dims slightly but then beams again. "Oh great. My son was disappointed. He comes all the way from Cliffton Heights every Sunday to see his dad. Thank you for calling." She hangs up and stands, grabbing the cookies and tucking the container in the bag she fills for him every week. "Come on. Your dad can have visitors."

"What about Kori?"

My mom pauses for a second. "Text her and tell her to meet us there."

I desperately want to tell her that I'll stay here to prepare dinner. That after everything with Blanca, I don't have it in me to deal with my family issues at the moment. When I woke up this morning, I thought I'd call with a sick voice in the hopes Blanca would come over, but I couldn't do that to my mom.

Like the good son, I stand, pull out my phone, and text my sister to meet us at Willows Court Assisted Living. Her thumbs up emoji says she's about as excited as I am to travel down memory lane.

"Hurry. You know how badly he misses us." My mom opens up her apartment door, shooing me out with her hand.

Walking past her it's hard not to smile at her excitement but I wonder sometimes if it's fake. Regardless, I'm not the one who's gonna call mercy on our happy family.

BEING poor just extends to your medical care as you get older. Willow Court Assisted Living doesn't greet you with a majestic building and a beautiful water fountain in the middle of a courtyard. There isn't a long drive up past iron gates and white pillars bookmarking the front door. White Court Assisted Living is a fifteen-story building in the middle of the Bronx with graffiti sprayed on the brick exterior.

It's a mixture of regular people growing old and people who have no idea they're growing old. Sadly, my dad is the latter of that group. But every Sunday, my mother drags us through the sliding glass doors, past the array of wheelchairs and the noxious smell of a lack of hope to the double-paned windows where we each get a sticker labeled visitor.

We head up to the thirteenth floor where the memory care department is. I guess the belief is it takes longer for an Alzheimer's patient to make it down the remaining floors which makes it harder to lose track of a patient.

"Oh, he's going to be so happy to see you." My mom beams at me as the elevator rises. I bet Kori bails.

The elevator doors open and there sit five older men and one older woman in wheelchairs in front of the nurse's station. The scent of antibacterial wipes and sterilization accosts my nostrils and I choke on the vomit rising up my throat.

"Beth!" My mom waves to my dad's favorite nurse. A nurse that half the time he doesn't even recognize.

"He's all dressed and ready for you guys in the living quarters."

My mom gives me the shocked expression she does every time he's not in his room. You'd think he got his memory back from how excited she is.

We navigate the path to the living quarters which is a small space for family to spend time with their loved one. We find dad where he usually is—at the chessboard playing another patient. Amazing how he can't remember to go to the bathroom or feed himself, but the man can still check-mate you in three moves.

"Xavier!" my mom practically screams, and I swear every other male in the room besides my dad looks up to her. "Xavier," she says again, lower this time, weaving through the tables and chairs to my dad's table.

He's in jeans and a T-shirt that says, "I'm kind of a big dill" it's green and the pickle has a top hat while thrusting. He wears it every day unless the nurse says it's lost which just means they need to wash it. I'm not even sure he understands the meaning. At first my mom fought with him about wearing a different shirt but as with everything she grew tired and now compliments him on it.

He moves his queen and the opponent, who I'm not even sure knows he's playing chess, accepts defeat easily.

"Xavier," my mom says again like she just ran ten miles and is out of breath.

He stares at her for a moment with a blank look. She takes out the photo when they went to the prom and then their wedding. He stares at the picture she puts in front of him. They're both labeled with marker. She points to herself, "Maya." Then she points to the picture. "Xavier." She points to him and then to herself again. "And Maya." She holds out her hand with the ring and takes my father's hand to lay along hers.

There was a point in my life when that hand scared the crap out of me.

My dad smiles but I'm not sure he understands she's his wife. His vision shifts around the room, landing on me sitting in the chair across from him and he starts positioning the chess pieces on the table. I glance at my mom. There's no way I'm playing chess with the man. My mom's pleading eyes says different and I already know before I straighten in my chair that I'll be playing chess.

"Call Kori," I tell my mom.

She ignores me and puts a picture of me at age ten in front of my dad. "Ethan. Tu Bebe," she says.

He looks at the picture and there's the smile. The wide smile like he's so proud to have a son. "Mio?" he asks and my mom's eyes well up. I swear she gets off on this every time. Wait until Kori shows up.

My mom nods, wiping a tear. My dad reaches over and touches my hand with his. It's cold and not calloused like it used to be. He moves his pawn and my mom stands to call Kori.

"Did I tell you that I'm in line for a big promotion," my dad says after my mom walks away. "Maybe vice president. That's where hard work will get you, Ethan. A vice presidency."

I nod and don't say anything.

"What about Little League this year? With your arm, you should play. I was telling Dick Heddle just yesterday how my hand stung when we were playing catch after dinner the other night."

I move my pawn and say nothing because I'm no longer the eight-year-old boy he thinks I am and I'm not going to play along. The worst part about having a parent with Alzheimer's isn't the fact that he doesn't remember you most of the time, the worst part is he doesn't remember all the shitty things he did to his family. All he remembers is the king he thought he was before he got fired and forgot the hard work mentality he once preached to me.

"Kori can't come. She said she'll meet us at home."

"That's nonsense, Maya, tell your mom to bring her here."

My mom stares at me for a moment. "You're right, Xavier, I'll call her now."

I roll my eyes and continue playing chess without recognizing I could've already checkmated him. Because no matter how much I resent him, I'm not going to rob him of being the chess champion.

What could be worse than this?

My cell phone vibrates in my pocket, but I silence it, trying to be the dutiful son. When the voicemail notification sounds, I pick it up to listen.

"Hey, Ethan, it's Blanca. I'd hoped to talk to you. I told Sierra and I'm sorry, but I just can't see you anymore. I'm with her now and thought I could call you while she talks with her dad. I'll talk to you tomorrow at work. We can still be co-worker BFFs though. I'm sorry."

She's got to be kidding me. She ended us with a voicemail?

I pocket my phone and move my knight. Rage is quick to overtake me. I want to stand from this table and call her and demand for her to see me. Tell her I'll deal with Sierra myself.

"Chess is a lot like life, Ethan. It's all about strategy," my dad says.

I huff. Who would've guessed my dad could still give me great advice just when I need it. Winning Blanca Mancini over will be just a like a game of chess. Good thing I've been playing since I was six.

CHAPTER TWENTY-FIVE

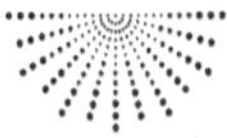

Blanca

Walking into Mars And Venus on Monday morning sucks. No one knows about my short-lived affair with Ethan, because the guy has no idea how much his co-workers don't care for him. His cold shoulder toward everyone who shares the same company name on their paychecks pays off for me today because as I smile at Mandy and head down the hall to my cubicle, I don't have to worry about knowing looks.

I reach my cubicle and he's there. Not at his desk, at mine, in my chair, tossing a stress ball in the shape of a money bag from hand to hand.

"Ethan," I say, and he spins around.

I do a quick scan of what he's wearing and wonder if he upped his outfit today just to tempt me. He's in a pair of jeans and a button-down with the sleeves rolled up, his hair perfect, his smile on point. The disappointment that I only got to sleep with him a handful of times weighs heavy in my ovaries.

"Did you not go home to your parents' last night?" he asks.

I open up my drawer and drop my purse inside then set my bagel and coffee on the desk. "I went to Sierra's dad's place instead. We took a different train home."

"To dodge me?"

I blow out a breath. "Of course to dodge you." I look around and duck my head, lowering my voice. "I told you in the message. We can't be together."

"Did she just flat out say no?"

I grab his arm to pull him out of my chair. He only ends up taking residence on my filing cabinet. "She said I could date you, but it just doesn't feel right. She didn't mean it."

A hollow laugh falls from his mouth. "Let me guess. She told you I was an asshole but that you should do what you want."

I sigh. "I saw how hurt she was, okay?"

"She's so passive-aggressive it's ridiculous. So that's it then? We're just over before we really even began?"

"What do you want? If I recall correctly, you never wanted this to start in the first place. So here you go, you're off the hook."

"That's not true." His voice raises and I stand up, covering his mouth with my hand.

"There are people here."

He nods and I release his mouth. He purposely slides his tongue out and licks his bottom lip. All I remember for a moment is the way his teeth would bite down on my lower lip. "I had my reservations, but that all ended the minute I brought you to my apartment. I told you I was all in."

"Listen."

Just as we're about to get to the point, Mr. Copeland

comes by, standing idle in the cubicle opening for a moment observing us. My heart beats like a bass drum in my chest. If he senses we're in a relationship, it could be the end of our jobs. Finally he smiles. "I need to know what you guys are writing about this week. You two were supposed to turn something in already."

"Sorry, do you mind if we take the conference room this morning to talk it out?" Ethan asks.

I narrow my eyes a little at him. The two of us in a conference room with closed doors and no windows is not a good idea.

Mr. Copeland's smile grows. "Sure. And I have you two booked for a photo shoot Wednesday in the downtown area. They want to do an outside vibe by the river."

"Perfect." Ethan smiles.

My lips turn down at the corners. Since when is he so agreeable?

Mr. Copeland fixates on Ethan for a moment before knocking on the cubicle wall and heading down the hall.

Ethan jumps down from the filing cabinet. "Time to go to the conference room I guess." He leans forward and I rear back. "Now, now, I do hope you can keep your hands to yourself since we're just co-workers and all."

He disappears and I hear him gather his stuff before he returns to the opening of my cubicle with his notebook, coffee, and bagel. "Ready?"

I turn around with a huff and grab my things.

He waves his hand out in some grand gesture. "After you, work BFF."

My shoulders slump but I go first. Halfway down the hall, he passes me. "Sorry, I can't look at your ass anymore," he whispers as he passes. He opens up the conference room door and it dawns on me how secluded we really are in here. He closes the door after I sit down.

"I think we can leave the door open," I say.

"No, we have top secret stuff to talk about."

Taking what would usually be Mr. Copeland's chair, Ethan's leg touches mine and I retract from the contact. "What are you doing?"

"Nothing. Sorry." He peeks under the table. "Thought it was the table leg."

"Ethan."

"Blanca."

"She was my friend."

"Was?" He raises both his eyebrows.

"We were close and yes we parted ways, but she brought me here. Gave me a place to live. A place to start over. We're just getting our friendship back on track and I missed it, okay? I don't have a ton of girlfriends and I can't go against girl code the first month of a friendship. It's wrong. Especially since…"

It doesn't matter what he thinks. He doesn't have to know all the reasons I made my decision.

"Especially?" He leans back, crossing his arms. Cocky and arrogant like usual.

"You weren't exactly doing cartwheels to get me to go out with you. I'm not going to throw away a friendship for what could be a few more dates and then you're sick of me."

"Huh," he says and sits up straighter in the chair, grabbing his coffee and sipping it.

"What?" I ask with a whine in my voice.

"It's just that a few nights ago, we agreed we shared something special. Something neither of us has felt with someone else, but now you're so quick to give it up."

My hands land on the table with a thud. "She's my *friend*."

"Okay." He shrugs.

"Okay as in you'll stop all this ridiculous behavior?"

"I was acting ridiculous? I was just being what you wanted me to be. Your work BFF, right?"

"We *can* be friends."

"Okay. We'll be friends. Let's talk about the articles then."

"Perfect." I smile. Maybe we can overcome what's happened between us, as difficult as that seems.

"I say we pick Are Bestie's Ex's Off The Table?" I slam my pen down and Ethan laughs. "I'm kidding."

I doubt he was.

"We can do how to be a good friend. I'm sure you have a lot of tips for that." He winks at me.

I stare at him until he holds up his hands laughing. "You're so serious now. Is that the work BFF side of Blanca Mancini? She's all serious and I'm her funny sidekick?"

"You know what, let's just go to Mr. Copeland and tell him we can't do this opposing article thing anymore because you're acting like an immature jerk." I stand up and gather my stuff but his hand lands on my wrist.

"I'm kidding. I mean I'm mad and I'm not in agreement about this new classification of our relationship, but we're not going to risk our jobs over this. This opposing articles thing has the capacity to give us some credit and hopefully boost us to where we want to be."

"Are you telling me you're going to play nice?" I really wish his hand on my wrist wasn't making my skin burn with want.

"Yes, Mom, I'll play nice."

I sit back down. "I did come up with some topics."

Ethan claps his hands and runs them along one another. "Let's hear 'em."

"Can men and women just be friends?"

He quirks his eyebrow.

"Yeah, that's stupid." I cross it off my list. "Are flowers cliché?"

He shrugs.

"Great first dates?"

"I think Copeland wants us to pick points we can each argue. Go back to the first one. I know it might not be the wisest what with the current state of our relationship, but do you believe women and men can be friends?"

I lean back in my chair. "Yeah. I mean, I've had guy friends."

"Perfect. I don't see it. The physical attraction will always be there."

"Maybe they aren't physically attracted to one another. Take Dylan. He's attractive, but I don't want him."

"But Rian does. And imagine one night, just you and Dylan up on the rooftop. Heavy conversation about childhood traumas and you start crying. He puts his arm around you and soothes your worries. The two of you grow closer and bam, you kiss."

"That's absurd. You're setting the whole thing up."

"I'm giving you a real example of what it could be." He links his fingers and rests his forearms on the arms of the chair.

"No. He could hug me and it would mean nothing."

"Okay, what about us?"

"That's different."

"We're here late one night. Everyone is gone and it's just us. I find you in the break room getting a drink of water. My intent is to talk about the articles, but when I find you, you're drying a wet spot off your blouse. Your white blouse that is now transparent and gives me a great glimpse of your very erect nipple. Our eyes meet and bam, we end up screwing on the table."

I don't say anything but stare at him. He laughs. "I think men have sexual fantasies about their female friends, but it's not the same for women."

"Great. That's why I take the male perspective and you take the female. I'll tell Copeland we've decided on the article."

"I'm not so sure."

"What's not to be sure of? We're friends. You have no intention of sleeping with me again, so you should have no problem proving your point."

I tap my pen on my notebook. There's a hidden agenda for him, I'm sure of it, but I'm going to prove him wrong. No way am I losing to him again.

CHAPTER TWENTY-SIX

Ethan

"She's more evil than I thought." I pick up my coffee and shake my head, staring out the window.

"Are you really surprised?" Seth asks, sitting down at our corner table in his parent's bagel shop.

"That she's purposely telling someone not to date me. I am."

"Technically, she's not telling Blanca not to. She actually told her she could date you," Dylan chimes in, eating his second bagel. How does this man stay so in shape?

"It's clearly passive-aggressive," I remind them.

Knox says nothing because he rarely talks about anyone. Gets too much confrontation with his job as a cop, I suppose.

"Give it time," Dylan says.

"Fuck time."

They all stare at me and slowly put their bagels or coffees down like they're ready to give me an intervention.

"I know you like Blanca. She's cool and all, but do you really want to have to deal with Sierra for the rest of your life if the two of you work out? I mean she's constantly going to be saying things," Seth says.

It probably doesn't come across, but I do have a soft spot for Sierra. They probably don't realize it, but I think I know why she's doing this to Blanca and me. She harbors a lot of 'not good enough for anyone issues' with the death of her mom. Her dad lives in a fantasy world where he thinks his daughter has it all together. Half the reason we'd fight was because she thought I didn't like her enough or that I was already half out the door. Although I had no clue that Blanca was her friend, I'm sure she sees this as direct proof that she's not good enough.

"I really like Blanca and I don't care for someone telling me whether or not I can date a certain person or not."

They all sit there silent like there's nothing I can do to stop this.

"How are my boys doing?" Mrs. Andrews wipes down the table next to me.

"We're good," Dylan says.

"Hey Mom, have you met Blanca yet?" Seth asks.

"No. I heard you mention Sierra and Rian's new room-mate, but you haven't brought her around." She stops wiping and gives her full attention to her son.

I refrain from mentioning that Blanca goes to their competitor.

"Ethan and Blanca work together," Seth says.

His mom's blue eyes light up. "Oh? You found a place to land, did you? Where are you now? Bring her by. I have some great topics. You know there isn't enough about menopause and how that affects the bedroom."

We all laugh while Seth pounds his forehead on the table. "Mom, no one wants to hear about your sex life with Dad."

She rolls her eyes like her son is being dramatic.

"It's nothing these boys haven't heard before." Her hand runs along Knox's shoulder. "Right boys?"

We all agree just to piss Seth off. Then his narrowed eyes set on me and I shake my head.

"Blanca and Ethan are more than co-workers. They were dating and now Sierra is mad. What do you think they should do?"

Just like that Seth throws me under the double-decker bus.

"Just so you know, next time your mom wants to talk about sex toys, I'm setting it up where you bump into her at a sex shop," I whisper.

Dylan chokes on his coffee and Knox shakes his head, telling Seth that was uncool.

Mrs. Andrews sits down at the table next to us. "You like her?"

I'm polite so of course I answer. "I do."

"And what does Blanca think?" she asks.

"She thinks her friendship with Sierra is more permanent than us. That she doesn't want to mess that up because we could be over after one more date."

Mrs. Andrews nods. "You know, there was this time when me and Mr. Andrews—"

"Shit, nothing good comes from that start to a story." Seth stands up and disappears into the kitchen.

She shoos him away with her hand. "All I was going to say was there was a time I thought Mr. Andrews' intentions weren't pure. That he only wanted to get me up to Lover's Point in the backseat of his Trans Am to do the deed. He started seeing Gwen Bakersfield too and she had no problem hopping in the back seat. She was loose."

I nod, not sure how this relates to my situation.

"Where's Gwen now?" Dylan asks.

"She's in New York. Married some man twenty-years older than her. I'm sure she's making use of those toys, so her husband doesn't break his hip."

I bite my lip with the hope that we can get through this conversation without any specifics of how great of a hip Mr. Andrews has.

"I told him I was done. That if he wanted Gwen then fine, but all she was, was a pair of tits and ass. That if he wanted a real woman, one who would love him for his faults, one who would be a partner by his side, then he had to prove it to me."

I scrunch my eyebrows at Dylan and Knox. Both are on the same page as me. This has nothing to do with my situation.

"I know it's different. But you and Sierra weren't meant to be together. She was your Gwen and if it's bothering you this much that Sierra has put down her iron fist than maybe Blanca is me."

I tilt my head trying to figure out the puzzle she's talking about.

Dylan laughs but covers it up by spilling his coffee. He tries to stand but Mrs. Andrews uses the rag in her hands.

"All I'm saying is if Blanca is so important, shouldn't you be fighting for her instead of complaining in a bagel shop with your friends? Mr. Andrews fought and look at us."

Seth walks out of the back and Mrs. Andrews' smile shines as bright as a full moon. "I'd change nothing. Gwen had to be in our life for us to get here. Otherwise he'd take me for granted." She pats me on the back. "If you really want her, why would you allow her to just walk away from you?"

Mrs. Andrews moves to another table asking how their orders were and I just stare after her.

"So?" Dylan asks.

"She's right. I already want to fight for her, but I have no idea how."

"Seriously? That's easy. Everywhere she goes, you go," Dylan says, balling his paper from the bagel and tossing it into the bag.

"Please don't make me file a restraining order against you," Knox adds.

"Nah. But we have a photo shoot tomorrow and I plan on using our close proximity to my advantage." Ideas float around in my head.

"Jesus, don't get arrested. I can't stand it when you dipshits do stupid shit." Knox stands up and throws a ten on the table. "I'm off break." He squawks into his radio that he's back in service and with a wave he's out of the bagel store and back in his squad car.

"I have one place I can help you. For my birthday we're doing a scavenger hunt in the city," Dylan says.

"Awesome, but you know Sierra is gonna have a problem with that."

He nods. "She has to get used to it. You were my friend first and I should've stuck up for you sooner. I'm on your side with this."

"Thanks, man."

"No problem. Now you better get to work too." I eye my phone and stand, leaving a nice tip for Mrs. Andrews.

"See you Seth!" We wave to him and he tries to wave back but Mrs. Andrews is currently pinching his cheeks and telling him what a great son he is.

I try not to be envious.

WALKING to the river's edge, I spot Blanca sitting on a park bench. She's wearing one of those jumpsuit kind of outfits. It has spaghetti straps and gives me a glimpse of her shoulders and tan arms.

I opted for a pair of linen shorts and a button-down to remain casual because that's what Mars And Venus is. We're not the stuffy suits. We're the young graduates who write about hooking up with co-workers and the best happy hour spots in Cliffton Heights.

"Hey," I say and sit down next to her.

She looks up and I realize she's wearing a lot more make-up than usual. "Hi. The truck is right there." She points to a trailer that must be where she was.

"I have to get done up?"

"They said they want powder on your face and some eyeliner at least."

I roll my eyes and stand, heading in the direction of the trailer.

Twenty minutes later, I'm out with what feels like five pounds of crud on my face.

"Is this really necessary?" I stand in front of Blanca and she laughs.

"You look very beautiful," she says.

I shake my head. "This is why I'm in print journalism and not television."

She laughs and I take it in, absorb it into my bones. I love that sound. I haven't heard it often enough since everything went down. It's clear she's bothered by this, but she's the one who has to tell Sierra to stand down.

"Are you two ready?" A guy holding a camera comes up to us.

Blanca stands and I have to backstep in order not to touch her. She lowers her head and follows the photographer's assistant over to where they want us.

"Phil said he wants this to be casual and to capture the two of you having fun. So this is a little unorthodox but can the two of you walk down the path and just talk?"

Blanca looks at me over her shoulder. "What do you want us to talk about?"

The photographer looks to me and then back to Blanca. "Phil said you guys were good friends. That you have fun in the office, and he didn't think it would be a problem to get some candid shots. Is that not the case?"

I squeeze through the small opening of the assistant and the photographer. "No, it is. It's just the pressure of the camera following us. How about you give us a few minutes to warm up?"

"This isn't a porno," Blanca says behind me. "I don't need to be fluffed."

I raise my eyebrows at her, and she throws her hands up in the air and walks away.

I hold up my finger to the photographer who sucks at keeping a straight face. "Give us one minute."

"Sure thing."

I run after her and we end up at the river's edge. "So, that was interesting."

She whips around and shoots me a death glare. I've never been on this side of Blanca's ire before. "I don't care. I'm done caring. They're not happy. Oh well, I'm not very happy either."

"Hey, I'm all for running away. Want to disappear for a while? My car is parked in the public parking lot and I can drive us up to Vermont and spend a few days in a cabin. Just you and me. But I will warn you, there are no clothes allowed."

Her lips uptick a little because she knows I'm joking. Not that I wouldn't do it if she said yes.

She knocks her shoulder into my chest, and I put my arm around her, kissing the top of her head. God, how can you miss someone you only had for such a short time? But my heart aches having her, knowing she can't fully be mine.

"Let's get this over with. A few hours with me isn't going to be so bad, is it? I showered and put on deodorant this morning." I pretend to sniff my armpits and her hand swats my stomach. "There's the violent Blanca Mancini I've missed."

She laughs and we both stop when the shutter of a camera sounds behind us.

"Come on. It's just us. Nothing to stress about."

For the rest of the afternoon, I'm gifted with a smiling Blanca. We sit on park benches with ice cream cones, kids walking around with balloons down the pier. A million seagulls flock around us as I stand like a statue in their midst and Blanca runs away. We ride bikes and laugh. We laugh about everything, mostly at the photographer's assistant because the guy was put through torture having to round up two bicycles and props for our "candid" photoshoot.

Spending an afternoon with Blanca only solidifies how perfect we are together and that I need to figure out how I'm going to checkmate her.

CHAPTER TWENTY-SEVEN

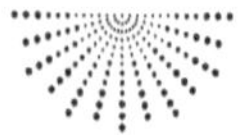

Blanca

Two weeks into this friendship with Ethan and I have to admit, he's made it bearable. Sure, his flirtatious glances and sexual remarks make it tempting to cross that line, but Sierra and I are in a good place again.

"Ready?" Ethan knocks on my cubicle wall. He's dressed like he's going to the city.

"Come on, you two." Cassie rushes over, a lollipop in her mouth. "Uncle Phil is so worried the two of you are going to screw this up."

I stand and grab my jacket since the evenings have been cooler lately. "We won't screw this up." I look to Ethan. "We're not going clubbing after so what's with the getup? No one can see you, it's radio."

He straightens his jacket. "When's the last time I saw you wearing a dress?"

Cassie laughs.

I slide between the two of them and head to the elevator.

Ethan is still trying to stifle his laughter as he joins me. We stand in silence for a moment before he leans closer. "You look beautiful," he whispers.

My chest shouldn't warm but it does. After two weeks, I figured he'd moved on.

"Thank you."

We step into the elevator and all I can recollect is the feel of his lips on mine. The way our bodies fit together like a puzzle as he pressed my back to the elevator wall.

"How's Sierra? Still pissed?"

Talk about a douse of cold water. He just pummeled me with a tsunami.

"No. We're good."

He nods and my eyes follow the yellow buttons as they descend one story then another. I don't remember this elevator being so slow.

"That's good. Back to pillow fights in your underwear?"

I glance over at him and his smirk turns full force, dimples and all. "Truthfully, I'd rather not talk about Sierra right now."

What I won't tell Ethan and what I haven't told anyone is —I'm annoyed with her. Not once has she asked me how I am when it's clear I broke things off with Ethan. She's never been concerned with how I might feel about the situation. I didn't know I was crossing a line because I had no idea who Ethan was. But I'm not completely surprised. I'm not sure if she would've been like this whether her mom passed away or not but the fact that both sets of grandparents bought her anything she wanted when she was growing up probably didn't help. Anything she wanted to do was done, anywhere she wanted to go, she went. Anything to make up for the fact that her mom had died.

"Fine with me. I was just simply wondering if her friendship is worth giving up those kisses in the elevator for."

My head snaps to his. Was he thinking the same thing when we stepped in here? My gaze falls to his lips and as though he wants to torture me, his tongue slides out and licks his bottom lip from one side to the other. My ovaries scream to forget about Sierra.

"It's the right thing to do," I say in a low voice.

He rolls his eyes and turns to face the doors just in time for them to open. "Come on, we have a train to catch."

I walk by him fully aware that he's probably checking out my ass. I want to sway it a little, but I don't. Will this ever get easier?

WE REACH the city and the rush of people and constant noise around us makes it feel like home. This is what I need. Somewhere my thoughts can be drowned out by the world.

"I think it's two blocks down. Walk?" Ethan asks and I nod, following him.

"Miss it ever?" I ask. Ethan said he had to work on his story for the majority of the train ride, so it left me to pretend to work when I was really watching him from where he sat across from me. His strong fingers typing and pausing when he needed a moment of reflection. The way he'd glance out the window for a second before his fingers would explode into typing again. Words flow out of him so easily. Is it because he trained at school for it?

"Nah. I really like the smaller town feel of Cliffton Heights. You?"

The minute I got off the train I felt like I could breathe, but I can't say it's New York City that gives me the feeling.

"Sometimes I miss being close to my brothers and my parents."

"You're close. I thought you secretly planned their demise so you could be your parents' favorite?"

I smack him in the stomach and he cowers down.

"I forgot about that violent streak of yours for a second." He grabs my hand and links it with his. "Just so you can't hit me again."

I stare at our adjoined hands. I need to stop. I should pull away, but I don't. We continue walking down the Manhattan streets like a couple. What's the harm if I indulge in the fantasy for a minute?

If only his hand wasn't so warm. So welcoming. And didn't feel so right.

Ethan is quiet the rest of the walk, never taking his hand out of mine until we reach the rotating doors in front of the radio station building, then he places his hand on the small of my back ushering me to go first.

When we're inside the building, I wait to see if he'll take my hand again, but he doesn't. He walks in front of me to the security desk, telling the guard who we are and who we're here to see. We hand over our IDs and when the security guy slides them back, Ethan snags mine.

"Blanca Anna Mancini," he says. "Of course. You're a Sagittarius?" he mumbles.

I grab his out of his hands. "Ethan Santiago Ryland?"

"My mom's last name."

"It reminds me of that game *Where in the World is Carmen Santiago?*" I laugh, and he plucks the plastic from my hands.

"That was *Where in the World is Carmen Sandiego?*"

"Oh." I cover my mouth. "Whoops."

After going through the rest of the security steps and riding a jam-packed elevator, we wait in the small reception area to be called in.

"I didn't mean to offend you." I knock his knee and lean in. He's been quiet since the Santiago thing.

"You didn't."

"Are you sure? I wasn't stereotyping or anything."

He finally puts down the magazine and looks at me. "Relax. I'm not offended."

"Okay."

"Okay." He picks the magazine back up.

"So, you know astrology?" I ask.

He chuckles and the other man in the reception area peeks at us from over his magazine.

"Not exactly. My mom is a big believer in it."

"What sign are you?"

"Aries. As my mom says, the classic Aries."

"I used to read about it when I was younger to see if I was compatible with the guy I was into. I'm a Sagittarius so what does that mean?"

He glances like 'are you serious' and I nod. Again, he closes the magazine and puts it down on the table. "Of course Aries and Sagittarius are compatible."

"We're compatible?" My giggly schoolgirl voice needs to disappear before I start writing Blanca Ryland or Mrs. Ethan Ryland on my folders at work.

"Did you really question that?" he asks, a bit sardonically.

Our eyes lock. I love the gold flecks in his eyes that light up when he's flirting with me. "I suppose not."

"The problem with you being a Sagittarius is that you always get bored. You need a lot of adventure. But I come with some faults too."

"I don't think wanting adventure is a bad thing."

His eyes lock with mine for a moment. "Except when you don't accept the adventure. When you push the adventure away."

"Mr. Ryland. Miss Mancini. We're ready for you."

Ethan winks and stands, grabbing his messenger bag from the floor. The other man tips back the corner of his magazine and smiles at me because he was eavesdropping.

"Blanca?" Ethan calls out and I scramble to my feet, grabbing my own bag and purse.

I meet them at the door, but my mind is anywhere but on what's going to happen when we're inside. I don't even catch the guy's name we're following down the hall.

By the time I'm across the table from Ethan with a pair of headphones and a man and woman's voice in my ears, I'm reminded that we're apart because of me.

"It's great to have you both here today. Thanks for coming in," the male host says.

Ethan nudges my foot and I look up to see the interview is starting.

I smack on a smile. "Yeah. Hi."

The young DJ laughs at me but says nothing. "It was Katie over here that first read the article about five things a male or female wants in the bedroom that their partner probably isn't delivering. Now tell me, do you guys try these things out together?" Everyone in the room laughs and brings his magnetic personality up a notch.

"No. We actually make it a point not to read each other's articles until they release."

"So you two aren't a couple or anything?" The guy waves his finger between us.

"No. Right, Blanca?" Ethan asks, testing me with those intense eyes.

"No. We're not."

"I have to say the hatred in the articles for the other one seems so genuine, I figured it was a love-hate thing. Like you're screwing in the copy room once it's over."

Everyone seems to think it's a joke and laughs. Little do they all know.

"Strictly professional." Ethan winks at me. "In fact, I'm her best friend's ex."

"WHOA!" the woman chimes in. "So, you're off-limits."

He can't be serious that we're going to talk about this. Why would he bring that up?

"Why is that? I mean, I think if I wanted to date my best friend's ex-girlfriend, it wouldn't be a huge deal," the male DJ says, and the woman laughs.

"You're crazy. Yes, it would be a problem," the woman says.

"What do you say, Ethan? I mean are guys just more chill about things like that?"

Ethan glances over to me and I wish I had any idea what he would say.

"Maybe others put their friendships in a higher regard than you do," the woman co-host jokes.

Everyone laughs again, but I sit in silence waiting for Ethan to respond.

What would he have done if Sierra wanted to date Dylan? Would that have been okay?

"What's the saying, bros before hoes?" Ethan says.

"Whoa now, Ethan, I was liking you before that statement." The woman shakes her head at me, but I'm smiling because whether he agrees with my decision or not, he's sticking up for me. On public radio.

Just as we're about to share a moment, his head snaps forward to the DJ's booth. "But that doesn't pertain to us because there's nothing between us except that we like to argue."

"Well, watch out you two, all that aggression can turn up the heat and lead to the bedroom. Just ask Cara."

Cara, as I now know her, throws a ball of paper at him and the room cracks up in laughter once more.

My phone chimes and I pull it out from under my thigh to sneak a peek.

Carm: *You better get your little celebrity ass down to the Trading Post and bring your sidekick too.*

Shit. My brothers must have been listening. Why did I mention it to them at all? How do you bring your crush to meet your overprotective brothers when they're sure to give him the fifth degree? Then again, maybe this will scare Ethan off for good.

Somehow that doesn't make me happy.

CHAPTER TWENTY-EIGHT

Blanca

"We're going to lunch with your brothers?"

Ethan was even less excited as I was to hear about my brother's text. He's asked me that question twice now as though the answer would change three blocks down from the radio station.

"Yeah. Just think of them as my brothers, nothing more."

"What does that mean?"

"You know. We're not a thing so it shouldn't matter what they think of you."

"We're not a thing only because you pushed me out of the picture."

I stop at the streetlight and laser my eyes to his as people sigh and shuffle by us to get to their destination. "What does that mean? So you didn't mean what you said in there?"

He shrugs. "I get the nobility of what you did, but I don't agree with it. I did in that newsroom because I didn't want him to pry anymore. I didn't want us to lose face and lose our jobs when Phil finds out we've slept together. But if you want my honest opinion, I wouldn't have thrown you to the curb if roles were reversed."

I open my mouth for a second and then shut it, turning on my heels to cross the street. I step off the curb and a taxi whizzes by honking its horn.

Ethan grabs my arm, pulling me back and I fall into his chest. More like into his arms, like he's dipping me in a romantic dance.

Our gazes lock for a brief moment. Then we're kissing before I even know what's happening. His hand molds to my hip and my hands get lost in his hair. His messenger bag hits my side, but I lose myself in the softness of his lips.

He's everything and more.

It isn't until the sound of whistling makes it into my consciousness that I'm aware we're in the middle of the New York financial district making out like two people having an affair. Strike that. People having an affair would be more discreet.

I tear my mouth off of his, my hands rushing to my swollen lips. "Why did you do that? You can't do that."

I step out into the street and luckily the hand signal says I have eight more seconds before I'm a pancake in a pothole.

"Blanca," Ethan calls out to me, but I hold up my hand.

"I told you we couldn't."

He takes my arm and guides me into the opening of a parking structure. "You kissed me."

"No, I didn't."

If only I could remember who initiated the kiss. I don't fully, but I'm not telling him that.

"Admit it."

I tear my arm out of his grasp. "Admit what?"

"You like me. I like you. Sierra is keeping us apart because she's selfish. You should be mad at her. I know how she is. You can talk to me."

"Sierra shouldn't expect her best friend not to date the man she's clearly still in love with?"

"What?" He throws his hands up in the air. "She doesn't love me. She hates me."

"Hate and love are opposite sides of the coin, but they still meet in the middle. You probably still love her."

He steps back, his eyes boring into mine. "Do you hear yourself?"

I cross my arms. "What?"

"You're convincing yourself that we don't work. We were at the start of something awesome. Something not everyone gets in life and you're here saying I love my ex-girlfriend?"

"We have no idea what could've been. You didn't even want to date me because we work together."

He runs his hand over his forehead, shaking his head. "Was I really not clear about what I wanted?"

"Come on. We have to go eat with my brothers."

He stays in his spot. "You know what? You go. I'm going to head to the train. I'll catch you tomorrow."

"They're expecting you," I whine because I do not want twenty questions when I show up without him.

"They need to learn to live with disappointment."

"Ethan."

He shakes his head and steps back from me again.

Enzo turns the corner, spots me and a huge smile morphs his stern face. "Blanca!"

Ethan picks up his head and a pleading look crosses his face.

"Hey… Enzo." I hug him and when he sets me down he stares at Ethan.

"You're the one?" When Ethan doesn't say anything, he looks down at me. "He's the one?"

"If by the one you mean my co-worker, then yes. This is Ethan Ryland."

Enzo leaves my side putting his hand out to Ethan. "Nice to meet you. I'm Blanca's older brother."

Ethan shakes my brother's hand and then Enzo points across the street. "We're almost there. Come on. Dom's treat and you have no idea how tempting it is for me not to order steak and lobster. The man is cheap."

Ethan stays idle in the middle of the sidewalk and Enzo realizes he's not joining us. We stop and Enzo looks to me as if to say, 'what is wrong with him? Does he speak another language?'

"You're not coming?" Enzo asks.

Ethan looks to me and I say nothing, letting him make the decision on his own.

"Am I missing something?" Enzo asks. "Are you two in a fight… like a dating fight?" Enzo steps away from my side and looks between us like he's ready to lecture us on how not to sleep with someone you work with. I'd like to bring up how he met his fiancée Annie then.

"Of course he is." Carm walks out of the parking garage, one arm already cocked out in preparation. Before I can warn Ethan, Carm's big arm is around Ethan's neck and they're walking toward us. "I've heard about you." Carm studies Ethan for a second.

Enzo laughs and all the pieces together fit. They set this entire thing up.

"Where's Dom?" I ask.

"At the table of course. You know he beats us there. Probably staring at his watch because we're late." Enzo walks across the street.

"So tell me about yourself, Ethan. You always been a fan of office romances?" Carm continues to push Ethan along, practically in a headlock.

I mouth I'm sorry to Ethan even if I was annoyed with him a minute ago.

We walk into Trading Post and Enzo weaves through the group of stockbrokers like a bouncer in an overcrowded nightclub until we reach a big table where Dom sits with the three women who recently joined our family.

Now I know for sure this was a setup.

"Hello everyone," I say in greeting.

I glance back to Ethan who looks like he wants to throw up, but before he has a chance to escape, Carm squeezes the back of his neck and has him slide in next to Dom.

"This is our oldest brother, Dom," Carm says.

Dom takes his hand off his wife's leg to hold it out for Ethan. Once the two say their hellos, the girls all rush by me to welcome Ethan. Val's eyes are all dreamy as they shift from Ethan to me.

"Blanca, we've missed you," Annie coos and I narrow my eyes.

"You just saw me Sunday."

"You know how hard it is to talk with Mama there. Come sit." She pats the seat on the other side of her so she can still be next to Enzo.

"We're splitting the table up, boys and girls?" I roll my eyes and slide into the seat because I need to be far away from Ethan at the moment anyway.

"The boys want... Ouch!" Bella grabs her leg and stares at Val.

"It's a muscle spasm. The baby is stripping me of my minerals." Val smiles sweetly like 'feel sorry for me having to carry this bowling ball around all day.'

"They do know we're not together?" I ask my question more to Val.

"I thought when you came over..."

"Turns out Sierra isn't cool with it, so I broke things off."

None of them say anything, but instead, exchange looks with one another. "Girl code?" Annie asks.

"We just reconnected after all these years. She wasn't cool about it and who knows how long it would last with him anyway," I grumble.

They all nod their heads but don't offer any advice. My vision shifts down to the end of the table where Ethan is already in heavy conversation with Carm. "I knew I'd heard Mancini before. You're the billboard guy."

"Oh great, someone else to boost Carm's ego." Bella laughs. "He tried to convince me to do a billboard with us in bed."

"I told you a cute morning in bed with the newspaper, coffee and breakfast might work," Annie adds.

"Annie, I hate to break your naive heart but that's not what Carm had in mind." Bella grins.

"Ew." I stop the waitress and order myself a drink. She scans the table and then heads over to my three brothers and Ethan.

"So, how serious were he and Sierra?" Val whispers.

The guys' attention is all on the television by the bar, their conversation shifting to football, talking fantasy leagues and how much their leagues cost.

"Over a year." I raise my eyebrows.

"That's a long time." Bella bites the inside of her mouth. "But," she reaches over and touches my hands, "you're sacrificing your own happiness."

I squeeze Bella's hands for her concern. "Who knows where it would've gone with us. We were in the early stages."

"I think it's admirable." Annie puts her arm next to us. "But he is adorable."

"You want in?" Carm asks and my attention shifts to the other side of the table. "I think we need another to make it even and Val won't let Ryder play."

"I'd rather him not gamble yet," she chimes in with a roll of her eyes.

"It's not really gambling," Carm says.

Dom gives Carm a look to say, 'shut the fuck up.' Knowing Dom, he's already said as much as he could to try to get his stepson to play in the Fantasy Football League.

"We'll spot him," Carm eggs him on.

"I said no, and my word is final," Val says.

Carm holds up his hands. "Whoa, Mommy Dearest. Chill."

Val's icy glare hits Carm and he cowers like he always does. I stifle a smile.

"You really need to teach me that look," Bella says.

"Well, we've got Ethan to join our pool now." Carm recovers quickly. "And no you don't need to learn that, babe." He blows her a kiss and she blushes.

"I don't know," Ethan says.

"Come on. You said you were in a league before. If your buddies want in, we just have to make sure we have equal numbers. We have a killer draft night in a private room. It's a great group of guys. You won't regret it."

Leave it to Carm, the convincer.

I lean forward on the table to see past Annie and Enzo. "Carm. He's my co-worker."

"Relax Blanc. I like him." His attention turns back to Ethan. "What do you say?"

Ethan looks down at the table at me. There's no way he'll agree to this. But he puts out his hand and shakes Carm's. "I'm in."

"UGH… why?"

Everyone's gaze shifts to me. The girls understand that he's weaseling into my life when we're not anything. How will Sierra take this?

"Should we rock, paper, scissors it?" Carm asks and I want to take my napkin and shove it into his mouth.

"No. You know I don't do that immature act to see who wins," I snip.

Annie squeezes my leg under the table, silently saying to keep my shit together.

"You should come to a Sunday dinner," Carm continues and my mouth hangs open.

"Carm. We're not dating," I say between clenched teeth.

"They're not dating," Enzo repeats and then his head flies to mine again. "You're not?"

"No. He's Sierra Sander's ex."

Enzo waves me off. "We heard."

Carm turns to Ethan. "She must've been a hard one to handle."

Ethan laughs. "Demanding as hell."

"She used to come into our bedrooms when she'd be over to play with Blanca."

He cannot be serious. "There are so many problems with what you just said."

"What?" Carm asks.

"She wasn't over to play." I put play in quotations. "And she had a crush on you guys. Try growing up with these three as your older brothers. It was not easy."

"Sorry man, Blanca's girl code all the way," Carm says with what sounds like disappointment.

Ethan's gaze finds mine and I wiggle in my seat.

The waitress returns and takes our orders and the conversations switch back to football for the guys and work for me. We talk about the baby coming, Annie and Enzo's upcoming wedding, Bella and Carm's vacation next week.

Halfway through lunch, my eyes linger and I find Ethan in a game of rock, paper, scissors with my brothers. They're all laughing and having a great time. You'd never think Ethan only just met them.

Annie leans over to whisper in my ear. "He's like the fourth Mancini brother."

I say nothing but my heart is screaming, *he's mine.*

CHAPTER TWENTY-NINE

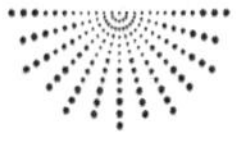

Ethan

To say I was terrified when Blanca said we were having lunch with her brothers is like saying I'm cool coming face-to-face with a black bear. But they were all cool and seemed to know a little about what transpired between us.

Carm was the most outspoken and joining their Football Fantasy League is probably a bad decision, but it's a way to keep me in Blanca's life.

Once lunch is finished, I eye Blanca to see if she's ready to head back to Cliffton Heights, but she's laughing with the girls. I try to be discreet while watching her because there's nothing better than Blanca's smile. It has the ability to light up an entire room.

"What's your plan?" Carm's forearms rest on the table and he leans forward.

My vision quickly falls away from his sister. "What do you mean?"

"You look at her like I look at my hottie at the end of the table. Sierra cockblocked you. What's your plan?"

"Stay out of it, Carm," Enzo says.

"This lunch ambush wasn't my idea." Carm looks offended.

All their eyes land on Val, who's too busy talking about indigestion and swollen ankles to notice.

"She's a romantic," Dom says like that's just the way it is.

"As is Blanca." Enzo tips his water glass at me before taking a sip.

"Which makes me ask… what is your plan? Bounce some ideas off us." Carm leans back in his seat.

My vision shifts once again because Blanca laughs so hard she almost spits out her drink. Bella continues to tell whatever story it is that's entertaining all the women.

"Look at my girl down there. Probably telling some story that doesn't paint me in the best light, but she loves me regardless of the stupid shit I do."

"See that look?" Enzo points to Carm. "That's you right now in case you were wondering. That's why he wants to know what your plan is because if you don't come up with one, he will. And trust me, you do not want to go with whatever Carm's plan is."

"Trust us on that one," Dom says, and the three brothers laugh like it's an inside joke. "Besides, if you don't figure something out soon, you're gonna lose your shit. I know I would."

"I fear I already did right before we ran into you."

Enzo and Carm share a glance.

"You heard?" I ask.

Enzo's smile slides on easily and Carm outright laughs. "We heard. In all truth, we were going to surprise the two of you when we saw you crossing the street, but then you guys stopped, and we had to hide."

"Then you heard me."

"Yeah, and that's not the way to win Blanca," Enzo says.

They all shake their heads and I want to ask Dom what he's shaking his head about. He wasn't even there.

Enzo glances down the table and then back to me. "Think of the cheesiest romcom out there? Something you'd hear about from someone else and think 'what kind of idiot would do that?' You need to do that for Blanca."

"You gotta smack those feelings right on your chest and tell her what she's missing without you. Tell her about the man you are and how cut you are that you can't have her," Carm says.

It's true. I'm awake most nights thinking about her. Thinking about where we would be if she wasn't Sierra's best friend and I wasn't Sierra's ex. That if we met in the city before she reconnected with Sierra, would things be different.

Even worse is the constant hard-on. The beating off in the shower, at night and in the morning. Which only turns to sexual thoughts with her and since I've already had her, it's excruciating to know exactly what I'm missing. It's not like I can convince myself that she might not suck me off well or that she's probably too inexperienced or not a team player. I know all that isn't true. And I know what a rock star she is in bed.

I nod at her brothers, taking it all in.

"Hey, we've been there. With that big guy right there it was the like pulling twenty pounds of feelings out of a pinhole. He was the worst." Enzo points to Dom and he sighs but doesn't deny it.

"We had a lot of issues, but hey, I'm bringing the first Mancini grandchild to Mama, so guess who her favorite is now?" Dom winks and his hand falls to his wife's belly where she links her hand with his.

I'm not usually the jealous type but watching them happy makes me wonder what I'm missing with Blanca.

Carm's ordering another round of drinks when my phone vibrates in my pocket. Seeing my mom's name, I excuse myself from the table.

"Mom?"

"Oh good. Your dad needs you. He's acting up and they can't calm him down. They want one of us to go over there. I told them you're in Cliffton Heights. I can't get a hold of Kori and you know I can't take off. Carol is off on maternity leave and there's no one to cover for me."

I run a hand through my hair, stepping out of the way of a man who wants to go to the restroom. "I'm in the city."

"Oh heavens. Thank goodness. So I'll tell them you'll be there in?"

I estimate the train and bus ride from downtown to the Bronx in my head. "Probably an hour."

"That's better than if you were in Cliffton Heights. I'm so glad you're close."

The thick layer of guilt is clear in her tone. She's silently saying if you lived in the city, it'd be so much easier.

"I'll leave now and call you after."

"Thank you, Ethan. I love you."

"Love you." I pocket my phone and turn around only to find Blanca there.

"Everything okay? Was it Mr. Copeland?"

"Yeah, it's fine. No, it wasn't Phil. I have to go. Do you mind getting on the train by yourself? I'll be in the city a bit longer than we thought." I dig my wallet out and prepare to throw cash down on the table.

I head to where I was sitting.

"Where are you off to?" Carm asks.

"I've got something to do. It was great meeting you all." I shake all their hands and throw some cash on the table.

"Oh no, it's Dom's treat." Enzo winks at him and he sighs.

"You can't just go. We were in the middle of—"

I ignore Dom when Blanca comes by my side with her purse swung on her arm like she's coming too. "What are you doing?"

"For the record, that's certainly not the tone I'd use to win her over." Enzo's eyebrows raise.

"I'm coming with you."

I grab my messenger bag and swing it over my shoulder. "No, you're not."

"Strike two," Carm says. All the brothers' arms now crossed over their chests.

"Listen, Blanca. It's a family thing and…"

"You looked upset when you hung up the phone. We'll go and if you want me to stay in the taxi, I will. I won't interfere, but it's senseless for us to take separate trains."

"You can take our car. We're heading to the office after this." Carm pulls out his phone. "Hey babe, Travis is off lunch by now, right?"

Bella lifts her wrist to check the time, probably on a watch that could pay my rent for a year. "Yeah."

"Perfect." Carm presses a button on his phone. "Hey Trav. Change of plans, you're going to pick up my sister and her…" He looks at me and smirks. "Her platonic co-worker at the restaurant here and take them where they need to go and then to the train station. After you're done, you're done for the day."

He says a few other things and clicks. "It's a black Range Rover. He's around the corner, so give him a minute or so. My—"

"Our," Bella clarifies, and everyone laughs. Everyone but me and Blanca.

"Of course. *Our* company logo is on the side of it."

"Thanks." There's a relief that I'm not at the mercy of a taxi or public transportation. By taking Carm's driver, I'll get there earlier, which will hopefully make the orderly and nurses happy.

"No problem. We'll see you soon," Bella says.

"At Sunday dinner," Carm adds.

"Mama's next," Dom says, his eyes widening like I should be scared.

"Pops too. Let's remember, Blanca is his only daughter," Enzo says and they all grin at one another.

"You should stay with your family," I tell Blanca, ignoring them for the most part. They weren't that scary so hopefully it's the same for her parents should there ever come a time I meet them.

"No." She hugs and kisses everyone, telling them she'll see them Sunday.

Without waiting for me, she walks out of the restaurant before me.

"Thank you for everything." I wave to everyone.

"Remember, open up your chest and let your heart fall out. That's how you get Blanca," Carm calls out after me.

We file out of the restaurant and the Range Rover with Carm's half naked body plastered on it is already waiting for us. Blanca wastes no time in climbing into the backseat, saying her hellos. I get in next to her and both of them stare at me for the destination. I stare at Blanca because she's about to find out something about me I don't share with anyone.

"Willow Court Assisted Living in the Bronx."

Travis nods and pulls away from the curb.

"A grandparent?" Blanca asks.

"My father."

Her head rears back in surprise and her hand covers mine, squeezing.

I want more than anything to pull her closer to me. To allow her to comfort me, but we're not a couple. She's decided that her friendship with Sierra is more important, so I slide my hand out from hers and pull my phone out, checking my email.

She stares out the window as we go from one of the wealthiest parts of the city to the poorest. Whether I like it or not, Blanca Mancini is about to find out exactly where I come from.

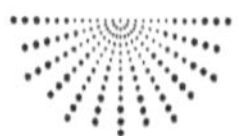

CHAPTER THIRTY

Blanca

I allow Ethan to keep his space from me on the way to his dad's assisted living facility. Hopefully, I was able to mask my surprise when he said that's where we're going, but from his reaction, I'm guessing I didn't do a good enough job.

We arrive outside a big building that reads Willow Court Assisted Living. The outward appearance is nice but dated. The letters of the name bear more rust than paint, the planters on either side of the door are unable to hide the years of use.

"Thank you, Travis." Ethan attempts to hand him money for a tip, but Travis puts up his hand.

"I was instructed not to take any money."

Ethan tucks the cash back into his wallet, grumbling something to himself as he exits the SUV.

"Thanks Travis," I say and follow Ethan.

My feet land on the cracked sidewalk and Ethan's eyes drill holes into my head.

He peeks his head back into the truck. "Hold up a sec, Travis."

My eyebrows crinkle.

"You should go." He places his hands on my shoulders and turns me back around toward the truck.

I dig my heels into the ground. "No. I'm coming." I swivel around but Ethan presses me closer to the car. "Why don't you want me to come?"

I flip back around. His shoulders deflate and he lets out an annoyed breath. "You don't want to see what's in there."

"Listen. Whatever is going on is affecting you. I see it in your face, in your demeanor. I know we're in this gray area right now in our friendship but I'm here for you." I grab his hand, linking our fingers.

He doesn't pull away which I take as a good sign, stepping forward to allow Travis to leave and us to visit his father.

"You can stay in the waiting room."

Progress although I have no plans of staying in the waiting room. "Okay."

We say goodbye to Travis and after he turns the corner, we walk into Willow Court.

"We have to sign in here. You can wait here, but I have to go up to the thirteenth floor."

"I'll go too." I dig in my wallet for my driver's license and hand it over to the woman like Ethan did.

He blows out a breath. "Blanca," he sighs and runs his hand down his face.

The woman behind the glass smiles at me, handing me back my ID and giving me a visitor pass like Ethan's. "See, I've been vetted." I put the sticker on my chest. "Elevators?"

He looks like he's trying to get me to vanish into thin air, but Ethan Ryland has kept this secret long enough. This is where his demons reside and I'm going to find out what they are.

I hear a ding and a man with a woman in a wheelchair come out to the hallway. "Let's go."

My investigation skills are on point because we come to the elevator.

"Listen, my dad…"

The elevator arrival interrupts and we step inside, but it's crowded and Ethan doesn't continue with whatever warning he was about to give me. I slide my hand in his, squeezing with the hope that he understands I'm here for him.

As the elevator climbs, the number of people thins and by the time we're on the thirteenth floor, there's one orderly left who's getting off at fifteen.

He nods politely as we step out and the first thing I notice are the line of wheelchairs in front of the nurse's station as if they're the welcoming crew. Some of the people are complaining and others are talking loudly to the others, but a sweet old lady with red tips on her gray hair smiles sweetly at me.

I'm so enamored with her, I don't notice Ethan talking to the nurse for a moment. He nods consistently and then holds up his hand and says something.

Ethan leads me to a bench on the other side of the wall. "Sit here. I'll be back."

"Are you sure?"

"Yes. You've come far enough. I'll be five minutes tops."

He says nothing else and I let him walk down the hall, but I follow him with my gaze, watching him turn into the room second from the end of the hallway. He's only in there a second before a man yells and a shoe comes flying out of the room.

Two orderlies jog down the hallway. Ethan chimes in on the yelling, but I can't make out exactly what's being said, so I slide to the end of the bench and lean as far as I can in that direction. Still nothing.

The yelling stops when the two orderlies go into the room. Ethan walks out, his hand in his hair, pacing back and forth. I try to conceal myself, my back straight to the back of the bench. He crouches down to the ground and puts his head in his hands.

My heart breaks for him and I want to strip him of the pain that's wrapping itself around him like a straitjacket. I rise off the bench, but one of the orderlies comes out of the room and Ethan stands. They talk for a minute and I lower back down to the bench. Maybe I'm overstepping.

Another shoe flies out of the room and a large crash echoes down the hall. A few of the wheelchair greeters turn toward the noise and then talk amongst themselves.

Ethan picks up both shoes and as the orderly tries to keep him out of the room, he strong-arms him and slides past. His yelling over his father's is disturbing the entire floor and the nurse who was talking to Ethan when we first stepped off the floor glances to me and then heads down the hall.

That's permission enough, I assume. I slowly rise off the bench again and take one step down the hall and then another until I'm past the nurse's station. Walking at a normal pace, the voices become clearer.

"It's a fucking pair of shoes. Just put them on," Ethan yells. "I'll fucking tie them."

"Who the hell are you?" A man's voice. "Get out! Where am I?"

"Xavier," a sweet voice who I assume is the nurse says. "This is your son, Ethan."

"My son is eight. Not a grown man."

My eyes close and I lean against the wall.

"I was eight twenty years ago."

"Ethan, stop antagonizing him. Take a walk. Maybe with

the friend you brought in. After you've cooled off, come back in."

"When I leave here, I'm leaving."

I cross the hallway and peek into the room. I can't see his dad, but Ethan is rummaging through a metal lockbox. He walks back over to his dad and slams a picture on the table. "Ethan." He points to himself.

"Who's playing a joke on me?"

"Go, Ethan. Please. Let us calm him," the nurse says and places her hand on his arm.

Ethan's chest rises and falls. Without a word, he turns to the door.

I scramble knowing there's no way I'll make my way to the bench without him seeing me. So, I stay on the opposite side of the wall.

Ethan's footsteps halt when he spots me, he rolls his eyes, shakes his head and walks down the hall without me.

"Ethan," I say, following him.

He presses the elevator button and this time there's no time to waste before it arrives.

"Talk to me," I say.

But he says nothing as the elevator stops at almost every floor before we reach the bottom. Instead of going out the front door, he turns the opposite way and we end up in a courtyard with old outdoor furniture and flowers that look like they could use some tending to.

Ethan sits down on a bench and I sit next to him, although there's an uncomfortable feeling between us.

"As you know with your eavesdropping, my dad has Alzheimer's."

"I'm sorry."

"Yeah."

I slide closer, hoping this means we can actually talk about it.

"He has these outbursts. Today he forgot how to tie a shoe and got mad. Another day he'll get into it with his best friend here over whether or not he likes bread pudding."

"I'm sorry," I say again. God, can't I think of anything else to say?

He turns his head in my direction and his eyes say it all before the words come out of his mouth. "I know. Everyone's sorry. Since I was eight years old, everyone's been sorry." He stands up. "The pity in your eyes right now? I've seen that my entire life and that's exactly why I don't tell people. Exactly why I wish you would've stayed in the waiting area like I told you to."

I stand and place my hand on his back. "You can talk to me. I want to be there for you."

He whirls around. "Be there for me? What are you gonna do, Blanca? Develop some miracle cure for my dad to get his memory back? Even if he did know what the hell was going on around him, nothing would change. My mom would still work six days a week struggling to survive. Out of all of us, he's actually the lucky one who doesn't remember our childhood. Lucky bastard."

He shakes his head at me and rolls his eyes. "Want another tidbit to feel sorry for me about? My dad got laid off when I was eight, tried to get a job for a few years. When that didn't work, he became a day laborer until he decided he'd rather sit down at the local bar all day and drink with his other unemployed buddies. Want to know why I can cook? Because I was the man of the house while my mom tried to work as many shifts as she could to keep food on the table and a roof over our heads. I took care of Kori, made sure she got into college, got her the school loans because I learned that all by myself first. But the man who caused us all to be in that position gets to sit up there" —he points up in the air— "and has no fucking clue that he was the world's worst father.

He's stuck in a time and place where he had a great job and our family was happy. How does the man who caused my nightmare of a childhood get to live with no memories, no regret while the rest of us still suffer the consequences?"

"I wish I could answer that." I wrap my arms around his middle and hug him tightly.

He doesn't hug me back, but he doesn't pull away.

"I think my mom prefers him not remembering because she loves him so much and knows it would cause him pain, but he didn't give a shit about us. What kind of man lets his wife work until she can't stand anymore? What kind of man deserts his family to spend it down at the bar and then comes home drunk and vengeful? Why does *that man* deserve to still have his family visit him every Sunday with smiles and hugs?"

I feel sick hearing everything he and his family have been through. My stomach churns and my chest feels like it's caving in on itself.

"Life is unfair. But you can't change any of this, Ethan. You can't give your dad his memory back. And you punishing him for things he doesn't remember ever doing is only going to affect you. You choose your life. You choose the way you want to live and this resentment that you hold for him isn't healthy."

He blows out a breath. "You think I don't know that. I do, but I can't stop. I hated him for so many years and now I'm supposed to just forget it and feel bad for him when he never felt bad for any of us."

I take his hand and lead him over to the bench. "You're never going to forget, but you need to heal, and all this anger isn't going to allow you to do that. Have you thought about group support or therapy?"

He shakes his head.

"That might be where to start, but you can't fix your dad.

You have no control to change anything except yourself and how you react to the circumstances."

"Ethan." A woman opens the door and her shoulder's sag in relief.

"Mom?" He stands and she steps into the courtyard, her eyes only on me. "I told you I'd handle it."

"I know, but you shouldn't have your day all messed up. I was able to leave a little early and thought I'd take over."

Ethan hugs his mom and kisses her cheek. "Mom, this is Blanca." He gestures in my direction.

She puts out her hand and I stand to shake it. "Nice to meet you."

She smiles at Ethan and he shakes his head but a slow smile forms on his lips.

"I've got to get up there. You two go. I'll call you later." She kisses his cheek. "Very nice to meet you. Come by someday."

"I'd love to," I say.

She pats her son's cheek. "Love you."

"Love you."

They share a moment I feel awkward witnessing, then his mom walks out of the courtyard.

"Come on. Let's get home."

"Don't you want to say goodbye?" I ask.

He opens up the courtyard door. "No. I don't."

CHAPTER THIRTY-ONE

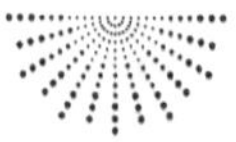

Ethan

Our hour and a half train ride leaves too much time to think. Especially when the woman I want to be with is sitting next to me—so close and yet so far away. Her small hand is tucked into mine, but I'm not naïve enough to assume it will remain there as we step off the train.

"You're right," I mumble.

She faces me. "I'm what?"

The first real smile I've had in the last few hours creases my lips. "You're right. I'm punishing him. I mean, I go every Sunday more for my mom than him. But I'm distant and half the time only engage with Kori. I keep everything festering inside me."

"I think a support group would help. There's a reason they exist. I'm sure no one knows how to deal with a family member losing their memory without some help."

I still have a hard time seeing the pity in her eyes.

"I tell no one. Talking to strangers..." A shiver runs through my body at the thought and I cringe.

I cannot even imagine. Plus, they all probably love their family members and there's a large amount of hatred for my dad that resides inside me.

"I'll go with you."

"Why?"

"We're friends. Nothing changes that."

"Not even Sierra?"

She removes her hand from mine, crosses her legs and shifts her body so that she's faced a little away from me. "Stop it."

"What?"

"I'm sorry but she's my friend."

"And how do you think being friends with me would work? What? You tell her you're meeting a friend and be vague so that we can go to a meeting? Sierra is not going to allow you to be either my friend or girlfriend."

I hate the fact the one woman who despises me has so much control over my happiness.

"It's not about allowing. We're co-workers already. She doesn't control my life."

"And yet here we are hiding our feelings from one another. Trying to be platonic."

She blows out a breath and a message comes over the speaker announcing Cliffton Heights as the next stop, so she heads to the doors.

I follow her and once we're each holding a pole waiting for the train to come to a stop, Carm's words blink in my head like a neon sign. He's right. I'm not going to win her over by arguing with her.

"I'm sorry, okay. I just... I want nothing more than to take you back to my apartment, bury myself deep inside of you and forget all this shit of today."

She swivels her head in my direction and her cheeks are pink because I know she wants it too. "That doesn't change the situation."

"I know, but I'd feel a hell of a lot better having the woman I want. The woman I can't stop thinking about. The woman who drives me crazy."

The train stops and she walks down the stairs with the rest of the commuters and turns to head to her apartment. This time I'm not saying goodbye, I'm walking her home.

"Where are you going?" she asks.

"I'm walking you home."

She stops and puts her hand on my chest. "You can't."

I put my hand on hers. "I can do whatever I want."

"Please Ethan, you're going to make this worse than it has to be."

Anger still rises up inside me, but I attempt to push it back down so that I can do what Carm suggested, open up my chest and let my heart fall out.

"Walk with me, please?" I hold out my hand.

She stares at it for a moment and then her eyes lock with mine. "Just one walk."

Her warm hand touches mine and I grip it in mine, leading her through downtown instead of directly to her apartment. We'll get there eventually.

We don't say much to one another. We pass both bagel shops, Scrumptuals, Las Tacos. We pass the gazebo and the barber shop where I get my haircut.

"There's so much I wanted to do with you."

She sighs but doesn't say anything in response.

"That's my barber shop." I point to the traditional looking shop with a red and white pole out front. "And that's the newspaper I turned in an article…" Then it hits me. Fuck. "I forgot."

"What?"

I pull her toward my apartment but when we get close, she tears her hand out of mine. "I can't go up there."

I insert my key. "It's not for anything other than your blog. I completely forget."

She stands there, not saying a word and for a moment I think she's going to say no, but she eventually walks through the building door and I follow.

When we reach my apartment, she sits down on the edge of the couch cushion.

Grabbing my computer from my bag, I pull out my laptop and boot up my computer.

"What about my blog?" she asks.

"I did some research and I found you a sponsor."

Her face drops and all the defensiveness she had to come up here disappears. "You what?"

"Well, your existing blog got you a sponsor. A messenger bag company is going to send you one to review. They want to gear it toward women in their twenties who have to commute."

"Ethan..."

I busy myself typing in my password and finding everything. "I did some research about blogs and although yours is great, you might be too broad. I'm not suggesting you change anything if you don't want to, but a lot of your posts are about money and exploration. I was wondering if you should concentrate on how to do things on the cheap. You could totally—"

She turns my computer her way. The new design I created for her is on the screen. She uses the mouse and clicks through the blog I designed. "You did all this?"

"Yeah."

"For me?"

Looking up from the computer, I see there's wetness building in her eyes. That's good, right?

"Why would you do that?"

"It seemed like your passion and I wanted it to be successful."

"But? I don't understand."

"What?" I brush the hair that's in front of her face and tuck it behind her ear.

"No one.." She shakes her head and that stray hair falls from behind her ear once again. This time I leave it. "I mean…"

"Blanca, I care about you. A lot. I know I suck at romantic gestures and gushing on about my feelings, but I want you to be happy."

"This must have taken you weeks."

I chuckle. "I've had some spare time."

"When you should've been concentrating on what *you* want.'

I shrug. "I'd rather spend it like this. You're talented and at first, I wanted to just get you sponsorships to be able to monetize the blog, but then I started doing some more digging and researching. That's where this new format came from. I totally understand if I overstepped."

She places her finger on my lips and leans forward. "You didn't overstep."

Our eyes lock and I see it there in her eyes. Clear, transparent and alive. This separation is killing her just as much as me.

"I have to go. Thank you." She grabs her bag and rushes out of my apartment.

I run down my stairs and catch up to her by the mailboxes. "Blanca!"

"No Ethan. Don't follow me. We can't."

I grab her arms and turn her around. Tears stream down her face and I pull her into my chest. "Stop this. Let's just go to her and talk. Make her understand what she's asking of us."

She draws back and wipes her tears. "I can't hurt her like that."

"But—"

Her hand splays on my cheek. "I'm sorry, Ethan. Maybe in time things will change. When more time has passed."

I grip her wrist. "Give us a chance."

"You have no idea how badly I wish our paths had crossed at a different time. Thank you for everything. I'll see you at work."

She eases up onto her tiptoes, kisses my cheek, and falls back down to her heels. "Forgive him, okay? You have a bigger heart than you realize. You need to open it up to him."

Tears well in her eyes again but before they fall, she walks out of the alcove of my apartment building and into the street.

She might be willing to admit defeat, but there's one thing I haven't done yet. Pulling out my phone, I scroll through six months' worth of missed calls until I find it.

Me: *We need to talk. Tonight at The Red Penguin. Nine.*

CHAPTER THIRTY-TWO

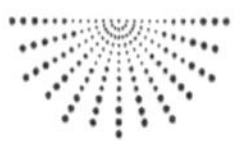

Blanca

Sierra and I walk through downtown Cliffton Heights after watching a John Hughes marathon at the movie theater. We pass Scrumptuals and all I think about is Ethan.

"Have you been there?" Sierra slides her arm through mine.

I could lie. I *should* lie. "I have."

She stares at me for a moment and then she realizes. "Oh that's right. I keep forgetting he was mystery man."

Lucky for her to be able to forget. I sure haven't.

"What was your favorite movie tonight?" I ask.

We pass Scrumptuals and head toward the coffee shop on the corner that I've only been to once since I usually buy my coffee with my bagel in the morning.

"Hands down *Ferris Bueller's Day Off*. I see why SJP nailed him down when they were young."

I laugh.

"What about you?" she asks.

"You know me. *The Breakfast Club.*" I shrug.

"How could I forget? You love that opposites attract thing."

I'm not sure that's why I love *The Breakfast Club,* but I don't argue because Sierra will argue to the death that she's right.

"I mean you and Ethan were opposites. I'm telling you, you did a good thing by not continuing that relationship. It would have ended badly."

I stop for a moment. This is our first time discussing Ethan since the night she told me to continue dating him but locked herself in her room.

"I'm not sure we were opposites."

She huffs. "Come on, he's so aggressive and you're so passive. He would've walked all over you in the end. Eventually you probably would've been miserable."

I open the door to the coffee house and Sierra walks in ahead of me. "I'm not sure I had enough time with him to see that, I guess."

She pats my shoulder. "See? I saved you."

I say nothing as my ire builds and we both order our coffees.

"I heard he's going to Dylan's birthday party next month. You okay with that?" I ask.

She rolls her eyes. "I can handle him, but are you going to be okay?"

"I see him every day at work. We have a lot of interaction there." With my coffee in hand, I lead us out of the coffee shop.

"How is your little magazine doing?"

I stop outside on the sidewalk. A couple has to unlink their hands to get by me. Whatever, happy couple.

"Seriously?"

She turns at the intersection. "What?"

"You know what, Sierra, I can't. I just can't anymore. I think we shouldn't talk about Ethan. You're clearly jealous." I walk past her and through the crosswalk.

"Jealous? Why would I be jealous?" She follows me.

I whip back around. "Because you want to know why he likes me. Because anytime you don't get something you want, you get jealous and spiteful and mean. I liked Ethan. A lot. But here I am trying to be a good friend to you."

Hurt flashes across her face and for the first time I can remember she looks vulnerable. But it's gone in a flash, replaced by anger. She raises her hands in the air. "Don't do me any favors."

"Fine, I won't."

"Fine."

I leave her on the corner and walk in the opposite direction of Ink Envy and everything I've grown to love since moving here.

Opening the door to the first bar I find, I slide onto a stool and order a shot of whiskey.

The bartender gives me a strange look but pulls out a shot glass and pours me a shot.

I take a second to study the bar and see that almost every surface seems to be covered in red velvet fabric—the bar stools, the bench seats, even the walls look like the wallpaper is red velvet with some type of paisley decoration printed into it.

"Why is everything red velvet?"

The man next to me clears his throat. "Because red velvet is sexy."

I turn to the right and sure enough Ethan's nursing a beer. "You."

He eyes my shot. "Rough night?"

I slide off the stool and approach him, nudging my way between his thighs. "Yes. Let's go back to your place. I'm done being a good girl." I smack my lips on his, but he pulls back with both of his hands on my shoulders.

"Good girl?"

"Yes. I don't have to do everything right. I can be bad."

"I'm sure you can," another man nearby says.

Ethan glares in his direction. "Fuck off."

My forehead falls to his chest and I mumble. His finger lands under my chin and he urges me up. "Mind telling me what's going on?"

I take a sip of his beer because let's face it, I'm not a whiskey drinker. It sounded good and I get the appeal in the dark moment of a movie when the hero asks for one, but I'm already throwing up thinking about swallowing it. "Sierra and I fought."

He nods.

"I have good news for you." I run my finger down his chest. "She gave me permission to date you."

He stops my finger and holds my hand to his chest. "There we go with the permission thing again."

"You know what I mean. I got the green light."

"In the heat of a fight?" he asks as I try to get my hand free.

"Does it really matter?"

He takes his beer from my hand and downs the rest of it, stands up and puts some money on the bar. "This is for hers too."

"Great. Are we going back to your place?" I turn around and head for the door.

Outside, my eyes have to adjust to the streetlights after being in such a dark bar. I circle on my heels to head to Ethan's apartment, but he takes my hand and turns me around the other way.

"Where are we going?"

"We're getting this cleared up right now. I've allowed this to be in everyone else's hands for long enough." He tugs and I fight at first but eventually realize he's stronger than me.

"This isn't a good idea."

"Sorry babe, I'm in charge now."

I laugh. "Can we use that in the bedroom? Like now. You take me home. I'll move in with you. Forget Sierra and her rules."

"You know very well that would never work."

"Yes, it would."

He stops me and backs me up to a light post, caging me in with his body. "Not long term. Maybe tonight but not long term and I don't plan on things between us being short term, Blanca Mancini."

My heartbeat races and my stomach flips. "Okay."

Five minutes later, we walk into Ink Envy.

"Fuck," Seth says, his propped up foot falling from the table.

Dylan stops the tattoo he's working on, takes his gloves off, and heads into the waiting area. "Sig, this is not a good idea."

Ethan doesn't move, instead his eyes are on Sierra who's pretending she has no clue what's going on. "Sierra, we need to talk."

"Hi Ethan," Rian says, but you can tell she's uncomfortable with the confrontation.

"I'm not talking to either one of you. I told her to date you. So go off and be merry." She waves her hand, dismissing us but never once looking us in the eye.

Ethan releases my hand and weaves his way through the coffee table and chairs. Rian practically climbs the chairs to get out of his way. "Now Sierra. I'm not taking no for an answer. You ignored my text earlier, but I'm not letting this go. You've fucked with my life long enough. It's over. Let's clear the air."

Dylan eyes me. "Where's Knox when we need him?"

"Oh, the police will be called tonight," Seth murmurs.

"No one is calling the police. This is ridiculous. Ethan, I will handle Sierra." I step forward.

Ethan holds up his hands. "Nah, we're going to talk." He holds out his hand for Sierra.

She rolls her eyes and pretends like she's not going to go, but she stands up without accepting his hand and leaves the shop.

Ethan follows her after squeezing my hand to tell me it will be fine.

Seth places his hand on Dylan's shoulder. "At least they won't destroy your place."

I watch them walk across the street and disappear into our apartment and a nauseous feeling overtakes me.

Rian puts her arm around my shoulders. "Don't worry about it. This will end well. I have a good feeling about it."

I smile for her benefit because I know the two of them and this could end up making things worse.

CHAPTER THIRTY-THREE

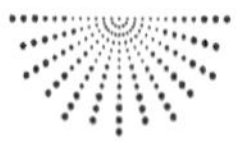

Ethan

Walking into my old apartment warps me back to a more difficult time in my life. A time where I didn't feel like myself, what with the way we always fought.

Sierra sits down in the chair, so I take the couch.

"Listen, we need to clear the air. You obviously hate me—"

"You hate me too." She pulls her legs up and crosses her legs.

"I don't hate you, Sierra. Our relationship ended and you made it clear you wanted me out of your life. So I got out of your life."

"Until you started dating my best friend."

I sigh. "First of all, it's not like I went and dated Rian. I had no idea who Blanca was when I met her. Nor did she know who I was. If we did, maybe nothing would've happened." I'm lying because the pull between Blanca and me was there immediately, but Sierra doesn't have to know that. "She's trying to do the admirable thing here."

"I'm saving her from you. You'll hurt her just like you hurt me."

And there's never been a more true statement from Sierra Sanders than that. "You think you didn't hurt me?"

She looks away. "But I know how you close off when it comes to your family. You met my dad, but I never met your parents. The only reason I met Kori was because you got your days mixed up and she showed up here before you could shoo me away. You were always so secretive and would never let me in. Why would I sign my best friend up for that kind of treatment? Blanca is all about family. It's one of the things in her life she values most."

"I get it."

"And your constant competitive nature. How do I know you're not pursuing her just because you want to stick it to me or something?"

"Really?"

She shrugs. "You could be."

"I'm not."

"I don't know and honestly…" She clams up, standing up and heading toward the window. She stares down at what I know is a great view of Ink Envy. "I just got her back. With you in the picture, I'll lose her again."

I meet her by the window and follow her line of sight. Sure enough, there's Ink Envy but there's no commotion. I'd wondered if Blanca would be standing outside.

"If we can handle being around each other, you don't lose her."

She looks to me and exhales a deep breath. "I'd have to hear all the icky details of your sex life. If you're the man she's with, we can't bond the way girlfriends do."

"Sierra, I don't want to upset you, but she's different."

She wraps her arms around her chest, her eyes never leaving the window. "I know." Then she turns to me. "Don't you think I know that?"

"She met my mom today."

Sierra guffaws. I hold up my hands. "Completely by accident but I *wanted* to introduce them. I *wanted* my mom to know the woman I..."

"You love her?" She heads to the chair and I follow suit and sit down on the couch again.

"I can't tell you that because she deserves to hear it first, but I care deeply for her. And I think she feels the same for me. I get that this puts you in a shit position, but I'm asking you to please try and overcome this. Not for me, but for her."

Her gaze strays anywhere but me. "You have no idea what you're asking."

"I do and I promise, I won't hurt her. If I do, I give you permission to cut my balls off."

"Seriously?" Sure, now she looks intrigued. Damn redheads and their tempers.

"Yes."

"With a rusty pair of scissors?"

"Sure."

She giggles but stops abruptly. "You really do care about her that much, huh?"

"I do."

"I want to know the answer to one question." She sits up straighter and looks me in the eye.

"Anything."

"Why her and not me? It's not like I'm still in love with you, but I can't help but wonder what's the difference?"

I lean my forearms on my thighs and stare down at my intertwined fingers. "I can't answer that. I have no idea. It could be because we're Aries and Sagittarius, or maybe our stars align, it could be that we're not as similar as you and I are. Truth is, I wish I could give you a reason why we didn't work out. Hell, I tried to figure that out for months after we broke up. But I can't give you that answer, Sierra. I'm sorry."

She nods. "I swear to God, I better not find you in your boxers slurping a bowl of Captain Crunch on my couch every morning."

I stand up and open my arms. "I swear you won't. So do we have a truce?"

"I'm not hugging you."

I wave my hands. "Come on, I know you still find me hot, but try to control yourself." She stands up and lightly places her arms around my waist. "Thank you, Sierra. Anytime you need anything, let me know."

She nods. "Now go get her and you better be good to her. I'm going to leave a pair of scissors out on the balcony, so they get nice and rusty as a warning."

I laugh and hug her one more time. "I've kind of missed you in a weird Stockholm syndrome kind of way."

She hits me in the stomach.

"Ouch, you're just like Blanca."

"Except I'll hit lower."

I retract a step and cover my privates. "Do you mind if I call her up?"

She appears deflated and falls back into the chair. "No, come on, let's go downstairs. I need to talk to her too."

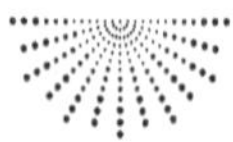

CHAPTER THIRTY-FOUR

Blanca

I sit in Ink Envy anxiously counting each second that goes by, waiting for either Sierra or Ethan to appear. Just when I feel like I can't take it anymore and wonder if I should go make sure they're both alive they walk through the door together. All our friends' eyes are on us. Knox is there now standing guard in his police uniform.

"Did you really call Knox?" Sierra asks.

"You bet we did," Dylan says from his table as he tattoos a customer. "You two cannot be trusted."

I stand up and wait for one of them to say something.

"Can we chat for a minute outside?" Sierra asks.

"Yeah, of course."

I can't tell from the expression on either of their faces whether it went good or bad but I say a silent prayer as I step out onto the sidewalk that this is something Sierra is willing to try and get past.

"I need to apologize for the way I've been acting. I should've just come out and said how I was really feeling rather than being a passive aggressive bitch." She's staring down at her fidgeting hands in front of her.

"And how are you feeling?" I ask and hold my breath, waiting for her response.

Her chin lifts and her watery gaze meets mine. "I can tell that he really cares about you. More than he ever cared for me."

I open my mouth to say something but she holds her hand up.

"It's true. And that's good. That's great actually. It means you have a much better chance of making it than we did. When you first told me I was shocked. I mean, I didn't see it coming and I wasn't really sure how I felt. And the more I thought about it the more it made me feel like I did when I was a kid." She swipes at her eyes and I take a step forward, reaching for her hands.

"When your mom died?" I ask.

She nods, her lips pressed together like she needs a minute to gain her composure. "I've never told anyone this but before my mom re-enlisted, I asked her not to. I saw the scared faces of the other children of soldiers who got deployed. I was old enough to realize how much she'd be gone, and I begged her." A tear slips from her eye and lands on linked hands. "I'd cry myself to sleep in her arms night after night asking her why she couldn't just be one of those moms who stays home with her child, like your mom."

I drop her hands and wrap my arms around her, pulling her in for a hug.

"She didn't choose me," she whispers. "She didn't choose me and then she died."

I squeeze her tight until she pulls away, sniffling and wiping the tears from her cheeks. "I guess when it felt like Ethan chose you over me—even though I know that's not how it went down—it brought up some old wounds."

"I'm sorry, Sierra. I had no idea."

"I'm not exactly an open book." We both chuckle and meet one another's gaze "I never should have taken it out on you or kept you away from Ethan. I'm sorry."

"I'm here for you whenever you need to talk. I hope you know that." I reach for her hand again and squeeze it.

"I do." She squeezes my hand back. "I want you to be with Ethan. It might be weird for me at first but I'll deal."

"Are you sure?" I ask as hope unfurls in my chest like a blooming flower.

She nods. "But I'll be on him if he doesn't treat you right."

I hug her tightly and sway back and forth. "Thank you, Sierra. I totally owe you. I know how huge this is. Do you want me to go to Sandsal and kidnap Prince Adrian Marx? I'll totally do it for you."

Sierra pulls away, rolling her eyes. "Not yet, but I'll keep you posted. Now let's go tell everyone so they can let Knox get back to work."

We step back into Ink Envy and everyone stares between the two of us.

"Blanca and Ethan are going to date. I'll deal." Sierra shrugs like it's no big deal, but I know how much it took for her to confess what she did out on the sidewalk.

"Thank God," I hear Dylan mumble.

Ethan opens his arms to me but I stay where I am. I nod to Sierra at my side and give him a look. When he's still looking at me expectantly I say, "No PDA."

"Blanca?" Sierra calls out. "Just hug your boyfriend."

"Are you sure?"

"DO IT!" Sierra yells and we all jump.

I step over to Ethan and he pulls me in, kissing my temple.

"Now let's talk about how I win dinner with Prince Adrian Marx. The two of you owe me some big favors."

Sierra makes her way over to the couch and takes a seat, now looking completely unaffected like she didn't just pour her heart out to me.

We sit down on the chairs and link hands. Ethan's arm hangs around the back of my seat as I talk to Rian and Sierra about the infamous prince she's trying to snag a date with. Ethan talks with Seth about Fantasy Football and how my brothers offered him an in.

"I'm in." Sierra raises her hand, obviously half listening to the guys.

"You don't even watch football," Seth says.

"Plus, remember all my brothers are taken and they aren't princes." I chuckle.

Sierra smiles and leans back. "Yeah, the Mancini men don't have anything on Prince Adrian Marx." She waves herself in a dramatic southern bell fashion.

Ethan's hands slide along my back when I lean forward to grab a piece of pizza and I turn to find him staring at me.

For a moment, I let my mind wander about whether it would've been this way from the start had he not been my bestie's ex. I guess it doesn't matter because we're here now and here is a great place.

When I lean back, he leans forward and takes a huge bite of my pizza. I screech and take it away from him which spurs a tickling episode and the piece of pizza falls to the floor.

"Hey! This isn't the Ritz, but you're buying me a new rug," Dylan says from behind the front counter as he checks his latest customer out.

I pick up the pizza and wipe up the sauce with a napkin.

"Please, how many women have you slept with on it?" Ethan asks.

My eyes instantly glance at Rian but she has her act perfected. She's laughing with everyone else, but I do notice that her fingernails are digging into the arms of the chair.

"I have a strict no fucking rule except in my office." Dylan smiles and hands a card to the guy leaving.

"So, we're all good?" Dylan asks.

My gaze falls to Sierra. We both smile. "Yeah. Things are awesome." She winks and that boulder that took up residence in my stomach finally lifts.

THE NEXT SUNDAY…

I WOKE up in Ethan's arms this morning with gratitude rather than the guilt I'd grown accustomed to.

"Morning." He rests a tray with bagels from Andrews Bagel Co. on the bed. "FYI, Mrs. Andrews demands you come in on Monday."

"But I like seeing Evan."

"Evan?" He tilts his head in an unapproved glare.

"Evan is a woman and she prepares my bagel for me. She's cute."

"Not as cute as you." He leans forward and captures my lips in a kiss.

"Didn't you wake up on the sweet side of the bed this morning." I chuckle.

"Actually, I woke up in the sweet spot of my amazing girlfriend this morning."

I throw a napkin at him and he stands up, removing his shirt.

"What are you doing? We have family to see."

He takes away my bagel, but I snag half of it, continuing to eat as he lowers me down to my back. "Not for a few hours." His lips cast kisses along my neck, as I bite off a piece of the bagel. "Babe?"

"Uh huh?" I mumble over chewing.

"Can the bagel wait?" He picks up his head, taking the bagel from my hands and placing it on the table next to the bed.

"But I'm hungry." I pout.

"Don't worry, this won't take that long."

I frown. "That is not what a girl likes to hear. If you think just because we're girlfriend and boyfriend now you can lack effort in that department, you have another think coming."

He shuts me up with a kiss and his body weight lands on top of me. I wrap my arms around him ready to get lost in Ethanland again. Just as we're getting comfortable, he pops his head back up.

"What?" I inhale a deep breath.

"One more thing. Can we stop by my family first and then go to yours today instead of splitting up?"

His request takes me by surprise and my lack of response reveals that.

"I just don't want to separate from you. That's if you're cool with me meeting your parents?"

It takes me a moment to process, but I nod. "Yeah. I'm good, but Ethan, are you sure you want me to…"

"Positive." He brushes my hair off my forehead. "I want my dad to meet the woman I love."

I swallow down the lump in my throat. "Love?"

He kisses me briefly. "I love you, Blanca, and I don't care who knows it."

"Boy, where is that man who doesn't date his co-workers?"

He laughs. "You killed him."

"Nah." I shake my head. "I just loved him."

EPILOGUE

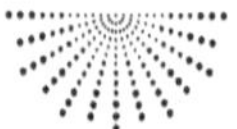

Blanca

Two months later…

"**U**se some muscle," Rian directs Seth as he tries to get my suitcase of books out of the apartment.

"This really sucks, Blanca. You just moved in." Rian frowns.

"She's two doors down." Ethan raises his hands for the millionth time today, annoyed by all the I miss yous and the delay in getting us into our new apartment.

He and the guys already did his whole apartment this morning.

"Shouldn't it be a plus to have three strong brothers? Where are they?" Seth asks.

"Right here." Dom walks in with Carm and Enzo behind him. "Who's the moron?"

"That would be Seth." I grin and give each of my brothers a hug. I'm not naive enough to think they're only here to help me move a few things. They didn't even help Ethan this morning move all the big furniture.

"Where are the girls?" I ask.

"They stopped at some bakery place."

"And Val?" I eye my oldest brother because Val is in her last month of pregnancy.

"I tell you this, if she goes into labor while I'm in butt fuck nowhere, I'm going to lose my shit. I mean, is there even modern medicine out here?"

Seth laughs and slaps him on the back. "I like this one."

"Again, who is this?" Dom thumbs in his direction.

"Let's go, Seth," Ethan says, but Enzo helps him with the other side of my bookcase instead.

"Do you need help?" Carm asks Seth. "Looks like you're struggling there."

Seth mocks offense even though he was just complaining. "I'm fine, thank you."

"Suit yourself." Carm falls onto the couch and presses power on the television. Football blares in my ear seconds later.

"Carm, this isn't social time. I'm moving."

"And Mama said you better not be pregnant." He points to me but waits until I actually confirm I'm not.

"You guys all live in sin," I say.

"We're guys. It's different." I pick up a magazine and throw it at him. It opens in his lap to the spot Sierra has re-read a million times. "The Prince. I'm so sick of hearing about the Prince." He rolls his eyes.

"He's in town. Sierra won a dinner with him." I'm just as excited as my friend.

Carm apparently is not. "Don't tell Bella. I mean, look at me. Why am I competing with this guy." He flips over the magazine and points to the Prince.

"He's heir to an entire country," Rian chimes in, sitting down in the chair.

I guess this is break time.

"Who are you?" Carm asks.

"Rian." She holds out her hand.

He leans forward, shakes it. "I'm Carmelo Mancini, multi-million dollar realtor. I don't have to compete for my girl-friend's attention."

Rian looks him up and down and shrugs.

"What was that?" Carm asks, forehead creased.

"What?" she asks.

"You shrugged."

"No, I didn't."

"You did."

I allow them to argue and walk Dom down the hall to my new apartment. We have an alley view, but we're closer to the stairs leading to the rooftop which sold it for us. That and being close to our friends.

Dylan is setting up the television when we walk in, the same football game Carm is watching blares from mine. Ethan's living room has just shifted from his apartment to ours, but we'll need to purchase a bigger kitchen table.

"Ethan." Dom holds out his hand.

"Hey Dom." They shake and then Ethan opens up our fridge where all the beer he bought yesterday is and starts passing them around.

"Oh no." I walk around taking them out of their hands.

"Who invited buzzkill?" Dylan asks and then winks at me.

"We have a few more boxes and then it's beer and game time."

Just as we step into the hallway, the three women in my brothers' lives are getting off the elevator.

"I love this town. Let's move," Annie says to Enzo, her

small box from Scrumptuals open in her hands. "They have the cutest little gazebo here."

Enzo stares at me like he's blaming me for her falling in love with Cliffton Heights.

"It'd be a great place to raise the baby. I mean, Ryder barely learned how to ride a bike without getting hit by a taxi. Maybe we need to move," Val says.

Dom puts his arm around his wife's shoulder and looks into her box from the bakery. "What did you get?"

"He's like a pro at changing the topic," Seth remarks. "I think I want to be your brother when I grow up. So intimidating and he makes his presence known." He puffs out his chest and walks with his arms out from his sides.

Ethan laughs, his hand falling down and squeezing my ass.

"We'll be right there. I have to show Blanca something." Ethan shuts our door and locks it.

"Hey. My brothers like you, but that can change."

His hand molds to my hip and he presses his body to mine. "I just want you to know, today is the happiest day of my life so far and I'm so excited to see your bedhead, smell your stinky morning breath, and feel you drool on my chest."

I hit him in the stomach. "Hey!"

"Believe it or not, it's a good thing. Because I also can't wait for morning showers together, breakfast in bed, and making love until dawn."

I sigh and my head falls back to the door. "I love the sound of that."

"I love you." He kisses me and as his tongue slides into my mouth, it's Sierra's voice I hear on the other side of the door, her fist pounding, demanding entry.

"What, Sierra?" I ask.

Ethan's still not willing to accept defeat on our private moment.

"You're not taking your bed, right? Mind leaving it for Adrian? Maybe your dresser too?"

Ethan groans and steps back.

I swing open the door. "What?"

Sierra stands in the hallway with her hair all askew wearing sweat pants and an I heart New York t-shirt which seems… odd to say the least.

"Oh, my God." She rushes into my apartment and shuts the door. "He wants to live with us!" she whispers.

"I'm sorry. Who does?" I whisper back.

"Adrian!" Her smile is gigantic and although whatever is making her this happy is awesome, I'm still not following.

"HOLY SHIT! CARM, grab your camera. It's PRINCE ADRIAN MARX!" I hear Bella yell in the hallway.

"I'm not getting shit. He's not that great, you know. Running a country isn't any harder than selling an over-priced penthouse in Manhattan."

I run back down the hall, Sierra and Ethan following and when I reach my old apartment, sure enough, there he is.

Bella's mouth is hanging open.

Val is searching the pantry, uncaring.

Annie is sitting down, watching everything go down with rapt attention.

All the guys are on the couch watching the football game.

Rian raises her eyebrows at me.

The broad shoulder guy wearing a pair of sweatpants and an I heart New York t-shirt that matches Sierra's, turns around and yeah, maybe his teeth do gleam a little like in those princess movies. But what's with the matching outfits?

"Hello, I'm Adrian Marx." He has a slight accent, though I'm not sure what it is. French, maybe?

Bella leans forward. "Prince. Adrian. Marx."

He chuckles at her and puts out his hand. "Where do I sleep? In your bed?" he asks, looking at me.

Ethan's arm quickly hangs over my shoulder. "Not happening."

"Sierra mentioned I could borrow a bed while I stay here. Temporarily, of course. Would you like compensation?"

"That accent." Bella sighs.

"I have an accent too. A New York accent," Carm yells.

"No, that's okay. So you're moving in here?" I clarify because I'm so confused right now.

"Yes. Sierra said yes."

I turn in her direction and she's giggling. "Can you believe it?"

I shake my head. "No. I can't."

The End

Let us start his ramble by asking you to please trust that we'll deliver a story that will explain and rectify Sierra's sometimes cold persona. When we wrote the scene where she finds out about Blanca and Ethan, we knew she might be unlikable to some readers. We thought about softening her but that wouldn't be her true character, as you'll see in A Royal Mistake. If you're a faithful Piper Rayne reader you might remember how a lot of readers were unsure about Dane, Jagger, Dax and all the other heroes who came off as crass playboys who would never change their ways. But you trusted us and look how that turned out! LOL All of those heroes had wounds that cut deep and Sierra has hers. Okay, we're jumping off that soapbox now.

We were on the fence about spinning Blanca's story out of White Collar Brothers. Not because we didn't want to tell her story, but we had thoughts about ending that world we started back with Modern Love. For a while she was going to go to Climax Cove and live among our Single Dads Club fellas. We wanted her to be close to her brothers so we could cameos out of them, but far enough away that the series had a different feel and she wouldn't be living in their shadows. Enter the fictional town of Cliffton Heights and a group of young people finding their way in their careers and love.

You might have gotten a bit of a *Friends* feel for the set-up in this book. It's true. We're both huge *Friends* fans and liked the idea of having a group of friends all living on the same floor of a building, so we lovingly borrowed the friends-with-nearby-apartments set-up from one of our favorite shows. Maybe we were trying to live vicariously through our characters. LOL

We know you didn't get a whole feel for every character in this book, mostly due to the fact that in order for Ethan and Blanca to be on the page together they couldn't be with The Rooftop Crew. We promise in book two you'll get more funny group scenes and get to know more of the characters. We have to leave *some* surprises to come, right?

Obviously, we're indebted to the following people because without them, this book never would see the light of day!

Wander Aguiar for an amazing photo
Florian and Laura for being our models and muses for Blanca and Ethan
Hang Le from By Hang Le for the gorgeous cover
Ellie from My Brother's Editor
Shawna from Behind the Writer
Dani Sanchez and the Wildfire Marketing gang
All the bloggers who carve out time to read and review our books.
All our early ARC readers
And of course, all our unicorns. <3

ABOUT THE AUTHOR

Piper Rayne, or Piper and Rayne, whichever you prefer because we're not one author, we're two. Yep, you get two USA Today Bestselling authors for the price of one. Our goal is to bring you romance stories that have "Heartwarming Humor With a Side of Sizzle" (okay...you caught us, that's our tagline). A little about us... We both have kindle's full of one-clickable books. We're both married to husbands who drive us to drink. We're both chauffeurs to our kids. Most of all, we love hot heroes and quirky heroines that make us laugh, and we hope you do, too.

www.piperrayne.com
Amazon
Goodreads
Facebook
Instagram
Pinterest
Bookbub

Mad about the Banker

The Single Dad's Club
Real Deal
Dirty Talker
Sexy Beast

Hollywood Hearts
Mister Mom
Animal Attraction
Domestic Bliss

Bedroom Games
Cold as Ice
On Thin Ice
Break the Ice
Box Set

Charity Case
Manic Monday
Afternoon Delight
Happy Hour

Blue Collar Brothers
Flirting with Fire
Crushing on the Cop
Engaged to the EMT